A COMPUTER PLAGUE

In the last few weeks he'd planted Bushi Nakamura's altered virus in the military systems of the nuclear powers. He'd been testing the results—all suprisingly satisfactory. With a few codewords and instructions, he easily controlled everything from telephone communications to bank deposits to the military computers themselves.

Iran would be the last country to be infected. The last country whose computers would become his. As an unstable nation, it could be particularly useful to him.

Then he would, quite simply, assume technological command of the world.

Other books in the TRIPLE THREAT *series*:

Code Sakura

TRIPLE THREAT

A COMMON ENEMY

THE SPECTACULAR SUPERTHRILLER BY
MARK SADLER
AND GAYLE STONE

A BYRON PREISS BOOK

LYNX OMEIGA BOOKS
NEW YORK

TRIPLE THREAT
Volume II: A Common Enemy

ISBN: 1-55802-013-6

First Printing/June 1989

Copyright © 1989 by Byron Preiss Visual Publications, Inc. Cover art copyright © 1989 by Byron Preiss Visual Publications, Inc. *Triple Threat* is a trademark of Byron Preiss Visual Publications, Inc.

This book is published by Lynx Books, a division of Lynx Communications, Inc., 41 Madison Avenue, New York, New York, 10010. The name "Lynx" and the logo consisting of a stylized head of a lynx are trademarks of Lynx Communications, Inc.

Cover artwork, logo and design by Alex Jay/Studio J

Printed in the United States of America

0 9 8 7 6 5 4 3 2 1

FOR PAUL STONE,

WITH LOVE AND ADMIRATION

PROLOGUE

On a cold morning in early May, Viktor Markov stood in the shadows of the cavernous lobby of the Kosmos Hotel. Cigarette smoke and excitement filled the lobby air. Armies of foreigners massed around their Intourist leaders' colorful banners for the day's assault on Moscow. The room reverberated with a lively babble of languages—Russian, French, English, Spanish, Japanese. *Glasnost* thrived.

Markov understood the questions and commentaries in each tongue, but he ignored them. He was a patient, portly figure waiting for an imaginary wife who'd returned to their room on the twentieth floor for a forgotten cosmetic. And everyone knew that Moscow elevators had minds of their own. Slow minds.

He shuffled his feet, just another face in the multifaceted throng.

Then a tourist, a large man, accidentally bumped into him.

"*Desculpe,*" the tourist said, startled. Excuse me. Sheltered by the man's body, Markov took the rolled documents and slid them inside his cashmere overcoat.

"*Nao faz mal,*" Markov replied politely in

Portuguese. It doesn't matter. He spoke with a slight emphasis on the "z" sound. It was characteristic for him to stress all sibilants.

Apparently disgusted with himself, the Portuguese tourist joined his group. He shook his head at his clumsiness.

Markov waited longer then strolled outside. The impatient expression on his face showed his weariness of the hotel's loud noise and excitement. No one seemed to follow.

The sky was brittle blue. The temperature was dropping. Moscow's spring was late this year. He lit another cigarette and stood on the steps, smoking and admiring the heroic Cosmonaut Memorial that soared 295 feet above the bustling Prospekt Mira. There was no sign he'd aroused anyone's curiosity.

He strolled past the long rows of Intourist buses lined up like troop carriers. Just beyond, his Volga sedan waited with the darkened windows. Despite the advances of *perestroika*, Soviet Volgas continued to look like overgrown Fiats assembled in unlighted closets. For a man of his impeccable taste and style, the Soviet Union was frustrating.

He climbed into the car and started the motor. To any observer he looked the epitome of the highly placed Soviet bureaucrat on his way to work. Seldom did anyone guess who he was, or his real occupation.

He drove the Volga into KGB headquarters off Dzerzhinsky Square and strode inside. In his office, he took off his cashmere coat and hung it neatly on a hangar. He was a fastidious man, impeccably organized. Brilliant. One must be to accomplish global goals.

He unrolled the documents on his desk and leaned over.

Slow, deep anger rose like bile in his throat. The documents were copies of control circuitry for a faster breeder reactor. The note said similar blueprints had been stolen over a year ago from a careless United States plant and delivered to General Akbar Salehi, commander-in-chief of Iran's armed forces.

This confirmed what Markov had suspected for weeks. Iran was developing nuclear capability, might already have it.

Iran! An insane country! Even after the death of the Ayatollah Ruhollah Khomeini and the ascension of the new religious leader, the Ayatollah Mohammed Masumian, Iran was an ammo dump waiting for a match. Markov didn't have time to deal with this. Not now when he was so close to consolidating his power. And if Iran had nuclear warheads and bombs . . .

Suddenly he sat down.

Slowly he smiled.

This could be turned to his advantage. He considered the problem for a while. Yes, he could do it. He would assume an old cover, go to Tehran, and manually input Bushi's virus into Iran's military computer system. No one in the KGB need know of these blueprints. He would help Iran keep its secret—until it was useful to *him* to let other nations know.

CHAPTER
1

White sand extended wide up from the sapphire Pacific. Jacob Bolt lay flat and sacrificial on the warm grains in a deserted, scimitar-shaped cove sheltered by fragrant frangipani and bougainvillea. His tired body soaked up the heat from the shimmering sand and sun. Near his feet the surf roiled and crashed. In the emerald foliage behind him birds sang and fluffed rainbow feathers. Above him the balmy May trade winds rustled through palm fronds.

"A white hibiscus," Tami said beside him. "*Kokio keokeo*, white-white. Sorry, I don't have a lily."

Bolt felt the hibiscus land on his naked chest, light and scratchy. She meant a death lily, and that he exuded the vitality of a corpse. He grinned. His eyes remained closed beneath his Rayban sunglasses. God, he was tired.

"Is that a hint?" he said dryly.

Bolt saw her in his mind. Midtwenties, tiny and slender, high tight breasts beneath the string bikini top. Her name was Tami Tanaka and she was Hawaiian-Japanese, maybe with a touch of Caucasian and Filipino. She was beautiful in that moist, allover golden glow that came from the right genes and a beach lifestyle that would make him envious, except he knew he'd be bored nuts after a while. With the life-style. And probably with her. Eventually.

"I thought you liked me," she pouted. Her fingernails ran down his chest and circled his navel. Kept moving down.

He grabbed the fingers, kissed the tips. All in the dark, eyes closed. Her image perfect in his mind.

"I adore you," he swore. "Am passionately in lust with you. Life was mere survival until you picked me up."

"You picked *me* up," she said indignantly.

"I did? What good taste I have."

He knew she was smiling. For a moment he thought that in the paradise of this time and place he could comprehend the universe. It should all make sense. How two days ago he and Hugh Willoughby could be fighting for their lives to wipe out a killer coke ring operating out of Tokyo, and today he could be alone with a beautiful woman, peacefully resting in a remote cove on a flower-scented isle inhabited by less than fifty thousand regular folks. Here on Kauai, Hawaii's fourth largest island, no foreign government kept a ministry, much less an intelligence station. This was a real vacation for him. At last. And if he looked as if he'd already been sacrificed to the ancient Hawaiian gods who protected this South Seas Shangri-la, well, he could think of far more unpleasant ways to go.

And there was lovely Tami. "Lovely Tami," he murmured. Tonight. After rest, play, a few drinks, dinner. No hassle. No rush. He would seduce her, rip off all her clothes, and . . .

"You have muscles, Jake," Tami said appraisingly. Bolt detected appreciation.

"A few," he admitted. "Here and there."

"Excellent contouring," she continued. "Long and lean." There went the fingers of the other hand. Over his chest, arms, thighs. "Are you a runner?" Up the inside of the right thigh. Rising.

"When I've got something worth chasing." He grabbed the fingers, kissed those tips, too. They tasted of salt and soap. He held both hands on top of the hibiscus on his chest. He sighed. His heart was starting to pound. Maybe he wasn't such a corpse.

"How did you get that darling little scar?" She kissed his left earlobe where there was a small ragged white line.

"A gypsy bit me. She had long canines. You know, eye teeth. She was very passionate."

Tami giggled. "What do you do, Jake? For a living, I mean?"

He felt her breath warm against his mouth. Fresh. Moist. Lips almost touching his. Teasing. Heat spread out from his groin.

Suddenly he opened his eyes, rolled her over roughly onto the soft sand. For a moment he saw fear in her face, saw her recoil as the power and heat of desire burned out of him as naked as she would be soon. She was almost as beautiful as the image in his mind.

"Dinner's a long way off," he told her, eyes locked on hers. She didn't move, captured prey. "After dinner's even longer."

He leaned down, slowly. Kissed her, slowly. She hesitated. Then her mouth rose into his, ravenous, and he swallowed the taste of her.

He pulled the strings of her bikini top and it fell open, revealing two small, sun-golden breasts. He touched the erect tips. She moaned. He licked the ocean salt from them. She moaned again and pulled at his Lycra trunks. In the haze of his own desire he watched her intent black eyes as she tugged and worked the trunks off, the only thing she could think of. The only thing in the world. Until her cool hands massaged his hot hard flesh.

"I want you," she said, pulling. "Now!"

Infected by her heat, it was all he could think of, too. And now his need was greater than hers.

Later they snorkeled in the crystal cove. Explored shadowy underwater lava caves. Followed shy luminous fish through waving ocean grasses. Hovered above ragged reefs layered with sea life. And at last returned to the sandy shore.

While Tami dressed, Jake took photos of her with Susan Sumono's gift Minolta. She primped and mugged. He laughed and shot. A record of a rarity—Jake Bolt on vacation. Susan had used the first couple of frames. Bolt shot the rest, the whole damn roll of film.

On the trail back to their rented Land Rover, Tami said, "You're a real athlete, Jake."

"Yeah, and I swim, too."

She laughed. "Do you come to the islands often? Next time, let's meet in Honolulu and fly over together. I live in Honolulu. I'd like to see you again. And not just because of the sex."

It *was* because of the sex, or at least she wanted him to think so. She looked him up and down in the bold way certain women had.

He found her amusing. "Wouldn't miss it," he told her. "Or you."

She walked on, glanced at him again. Then looked straight ahead. She wasn't quite sure what to make of him. "Where do you come from?"

"Baltimore, Chicago, Los Angeles," he said. "You name it, I've lived there."

"Oh." She was waiting for more.

"Sure, we'll meet in Honolulu."

She smiled. She was on firm sexual ground again.

The tropical vegetation that lined the trail was lush and varied. There were purple orchids, giant ferns, yellow ginger, and violets as tall as young trees. Kauai, the Garden Isle. Tranquil and serene. Bolt planned to lose himself here for seven days. Minimum. Maybe longer if he got lucky and Langley still hadn't tracked him down.

They threw their gear into the Land Rover's back seat.

"You play tennis?" he asked.

"Sort of."

"Good. Tennis tomorrow morning, and we'll take a boat up the Wailua River in the afternoon." Odd that a woman like her was vacationing here without a man.

"Love it!"

It was dark when they arrived back at the rambling, gingerbread Lei Kai Inn just south of the Wailua River. Stars appeared in the inky sky. As they parked in the gravel lot, a slow tribal drumbeat began. Tourists flocked onto the inn's wide front porch. Bolt and Tami strolled through the mild evening air toward the pulsating sounds.

Suddenly there was a loud shout, and young

Hawaiian men carrying burning torches dashed from the back of the white wedding-cake inn. Dressed only in blood-red *malo* loincloths, their bodies glistened as they ran light-streaked patterns through a grove of ghostly coconut palms. Each man paused a heartbeat to torch a giant firepot. Ruby flames exploded in the darkness. The tourists clapped. The melodic drumbeat grew louder, faster. The young men raced, lighted more firepots. And soon the night flickered and sparkled red and amber beneath a black dome of silver stars. A stunning visual drama.

The applause was thunderous.

"Maybe we've overestimated the value of electricity," Tami said, awed.

"We've lost a few things getting civilized," Jake agreed. As they strolled indoors, he considered modern man. Some primitive drives seemed destined to last forever. Both good and evil. For a much-needed change, he was concentrating on the good.

Beneath the thatched roof in the inn's foyer, the manager sat behind a front desk crafted from fake Polynesian drums. The entire inn was decorated in movieland South Seas decor. Even the sinks in the bathrooms were giant clam shells. Bolt admired the audacity of such heavy-handed taste.

Ordinarily a calm, dignified man, the manager shoved one hand after the other across his thin gray hair. His aloha shirt was askew. And his leathery face was disturbed, confused. He stared down at an IBM PC.

"Computers!" He threw up his hands. "You've come just in time. Now I can abandon this torture, I'll get your room keys!" He stood and reached toward the pigeonholes behind the desk.

"What's the trouble?" Bolt asked as he looked over at the PC. The screen showed a series of user errors.

"My wife will know," the manager said as he slid the keys across the desktop. "She's in Princeville tonight. Guess I'll have to wait till she gets back."

He sighed heavily, sat, and instantly popped up again to get keys for other guests. Bolt leaned farther over the desk to type on the keyboard.

"You shouldn't!" Tami said, alarmed.

"What are you doing?" the manager cried and rushed back.

"Is this what you wanted?" Bolt said.

The manager stared, sat slowly in his chair. "It's magic. How did you do it?"

The monitor's screen was filled with tomorrow's reservations.

"Simple," Bolt said. "It's your command. *Guestsl* You were typing in the lowercase letter *l* instead of the digit—the number—*1*. The computer doesn't recognize Guestsl with an 'el' at the end, so it kept announcing you'd made a mistake."

"Ah, Mr. Bolt." The manager came around the desk and pumped Bolt's hand. "I'm in your debt."

"Are you a computer scientist, Jake?" Tami asked curiously.

"What I am is starved." He looked down at her. "How about you?"

"Dinner in an hour," the manager promised as he walked them toward an iron-latticed elevator. "I'll have a table waiting."

In his room, Jake carried his backpack straight into the bathroom. He showered, dressed, clipped his nylon holster inside his belt, and took his P-230 SIG-Sauer 9mm pistol from the backpack. He hefted the pistol, savored its familiarity, an old friend.

The P-230 was designed by the Swiss firm of Schweizerische Industrie-Gesellschaft—SIG—and manufactured by the West German company J. P. Sauer und Sohn. By combining the two companies, SIG dodged tough Swiss regulations controlling military small arms exports, and Sauer reentered the military weapons business despite the restrictions that followed Germany's World War II defeat. The P-230 was a testament to determination and ingenuity, qualities Bolt admired greatly.

The P-230 was also the Swiss police's weapon of choice, and Bolt's. It weighed less than two pounds and was fairly compact, under seven inches long. Bolt prized its reliability, accuracy, lethal 9mm punch, and—as with an old glove or an old habit—its comfortable fit. He dropped the SIG-Sauer and silencer neatly into the holster. He was on vacation, but he was no fool.

He stood in front of the mirror and pulled on his linen sports jacket. Six foot two, one eighty. Tanned, brown-haired, brown-eyed. Midthirties. Not bad.

All dressed up to meet a wahine, lovely Tami. And bang her brains out later. Again. After all, what were vacations for?

In the King Kamehameha room, Bolt and Tami sat at a small table laid with silverplate and china. Casablanca fans turned lazily overhead. Introduced by the inn's manager, the obsequious waiter hovered so near that Bolt figured he was expecting either a big tip or a promotion if he took good care of the genius who fixed the computer. These days, a little information went a long way.

The food was fresh and superb: *a'u* swordfish, *ahi* yellowfin tuna, island-grown broccoli and rice, warm braided breads, pineapple, mangoes, and traditional *poi*, made from taro root.

"*Luau* is Hawaiian for taro leaves," Tami told Bolt, pausing between bites. They were almost finished. "Hawaii grows most of its taro right here on Kauai." She glanced over her shoulder to see how close the waiter was. He was evidently far enough away, because she leaned toward Bolt and whispered, "Are we going to sleep together tonight?" Her eyes flashed.

Sometimes vacations turned out the way they were supposed to. "That can be arranged," he said and poured wine into her glass. It was a Ballard Canyon chardonnay 1986, crisp and fruity, from the Santa Ynez Valley. One of California's best. Bolt expected this night to be long and gratifying.

She drank. "You know," she went on, whispering, "I don't ask just anybody to sleep with me." Her oval black eyes were big and solemn.

"I figured that," Bolt grinned. "Otherwise you'd have every guy in this restaurant over here. Panting."

She seemed to like that idea. She surveyed the tourists and locals, rotund to lean, acne-faced to silver-haired. Most of the men returned her appraising look. Some kept staring.

Bolt gestured for the check. It was like keeping a pet female panther who happened also to be chronically in heat, he decided. She shook her mane of glossy black hair.

"Some of them aren't so bad," she told him. "But they're not . . . *you*."

Again she gave him that up-and-down, stripped-to-the-genitals stare. The lady had simplified her priorities. And he was it. What more could he ask?

He leaned toward her, his lips inches from hers. "You're beautiful." Her tropical scent filled his head. "Lovely, lusty Tami." In an instant his mind was back on the beach this afternoon, staring down at the golden breasts, tasting the sea salt, moving hot and slick inside her. . . .

"Too bad we didn't meet earlier," she said, her words breathed into his mouth. "Like at the Honolulu airport when you arrived from Tokyo. I mean, we could've flown straight on together to Kauai and gotten just one room."

"Very convenient," Bolt agreed, smiled, inhaled her essence, but the alarm was ringing in his mind.

When had he told her he had come to Honolulu from Tokyo? Had he ever been that drunk when they were together? No, never. And he hadn't told her about Tokyo.

He still smiled, "Let's go."

She grabbed her handbag, and they hurried together toward the elevator. The old machine creaked upward.

Who was she and what did she want?

"Will you stay here long?" She pressed against him and looked up through her lashes.

"Think I should?"

Her innocent questions took on another dimension. She was not what she was supposed to be, but what was she? One of Vernon White's little tests? A Willoughby joke? An enemy? Or just a slip of the tongue he had forgotten? He felt the thrill through him. The risk that set his nerves alive. He wanted this woman even more now, and he had the edge. She didn't know he knew.

"Well, it would be nice," she said.

The elevator stopped. She hesitated, her body fit tight and warm against his. Full of promises, demands. He took out his room key, grabbed her elbow, and trotted her to his door.

"Only nice?"

He looked deep into her eyes and casually brushed his fingers above the doorknob until he found the bristle from his hairbrush he'd lodged there. It was still in place, an easy way to tell no one had opened the door while he was gone.

"Extremely nice," she modified. "Wonderfully, excitingly nice!"

He unlocked the door. "Let's experiment." He hustled her inside and locked the door again. "See if we like the idea."

"I'm game!" She dropped her purse in the middle of the floor and kicked off her pumps.

"You sure are." He picked her up and slung her over his shoulder.

"Hey," she said with interest.

He carried her to the bed and stood her on it. He took her small ankles in his hands, massaged them, then slowly slid his hands up her firm bronze legs.

"Oh, my," she said. She was very silent and still.

He stopped at her knees.

"That's all?" she said.

He started again at her ankles, rising slowly over the warm, smooth skin. This time he went to her thighs. And stopped.

"Oh!" she said.

Impatient, she pulled at the buttons of her blouse, dropped the blouse to the coverlet. He took off his shoes, pulled off his pants, the SIG-Sauer inside. And slid the pistol under the bed. She flung her bra across the room. Her small, high breasts did a perfect circle. Now she wore only a short skirt. He took a deep breath. Her body was even better than he remembered.

"More," she demanded. Again the hot up-and-down look.

He stripped off the rest of his clothes and dutifully went back to work. The ankles. The velvet legs. The kneecaps. The rounded thighs.

Higher. Up under the skirt until she gasped. She pulled him down on the bed. Her breath incendiary and sweet and compelling. He ached with the all-over need. He turned her over, around, joined . . .

And heard the faint click as the door unlocked.

Because he knew, he heard. Grabbed Tami and rolled off the bed toward his SIG-Sauer hidden under it.

The first *pop* came almost instantly. A silenced pistol. The bullet burned past his ear and exploded in the mattress. Fabric and stuffing sprayed the air.

CHAPTER
2

"No!" Tami shouted, struggling against Bolt. "No! No!"

He pulled her down with him kicking and scratching. She struggled to break loose, break away from Bolt.

The silenced shots felt like doors slamming in Bolt's head. The assassin was Japanese. He wore sunglasses and squeezed off bullets from a 9mm Beretta as coolly and calmly as if he were shooting clay ducks at a gallery. Shredded cloth and wood splinters shot into the air. Bullets thudded into walls, smashed mirrors and lamps. There was a stench of singed fabric.

Bolt held the violent Tami close against him with a grip like steel, grabbed his SIG-Sauer from beneath the bed. The Japanese guy tried to get an angle around the struggling Tami. A panic began in his eyes. It was taking too long.

Tami tried to slug Bolt, fear all over her lovely face.

Bolt fired and missed.

The guy had no choice. His Beretta honed in, blood exploded from Tami's naked breasts. Her body slumped limp, the force of the slug knocked Bolt backwards. He fired again as he fell.

Bolt's bullet blasted through the guy's forehead. A giant black hole of shattered bone and flesh appeared. And then a torrent of blood gushed out. For an instant, the guy's eyes were furious. He hated to lose. And then they were blank.

Bolt picked up Tami and held her in his arms. She was warm with life, but she had no pulse. Her chest was mangled, her heart destroyed. "Tami." Her golden face and glossy hair were beautiful, but the vibrancy, the energy had disappeared as if they'd never existed. She'd never existed. She'd set him up, but she'd been alive and now she was dead. Another of life's dirty tricks. Tragedies.

He laid her on the floor, brushed strands of the black hair from her closed eyes. He had to get out of here. Fast.

He unbuttoned the killer's right shirtsleeve and pushed it and the suit sleeve up. There it was—the signature squid tattooed on the forearm. There were many colorful tattoos on the arm, but the one that mattered was the squid. It told Bolt that this man was not only a yakuza thug, but of the same yakuza clan that had provided the muscle for the Tokyo cocaine ring he and Willoughby had wiped out.

But if they had stopped the coke operation, why in hell was this guy chasing him all the way to Kauai? Revenge? The coke ring still operating? Both? Or something else?

Bolt went through the pockets of the wide-shouldered, tight-waisted seersucker suit. The multihued tattoos, the flashy suit, the sunglasses, and the close-cropped hair were part of the unmistakable mobsterish getup of the yakuza, Japan's version of the Mafia. These oriental gangsters traced their origins to unemployed seventeenth-century samurai. Some romantics called them Robin Hoods, but Bolt had found them simply to be hoods. They robbed, extorted, blackmailed, used, abused, and pushed dope onto the weakest customers around—the impoverished. And they hired out for murder. Real humanists, he thought with disgust.

In the yakuza's pockets Bolt found nearly a thousand U.S. dollars in cash, but no identification. The guy was a pro. He'd left his I.D. in some airport locker. Bolt took the money and searched the rest of the clothes. Nothing.

Bolt threw clothes in his suitcase. He didn't want to leave anything that could be traced. The attack had been relatively quiet. Probably most of the inn's guests were at dinner, and maybe he was safe for a while longer. But only an idiot took chances.

He washed Tami's blood from his skin and thought about the young woman, the horrible way she had died. He pushed the thoughts away. He'd seen enough people die, female and male, to earn degrees in remorse and anger. No one in his business could dwell on it. Otherwise you'd have to quit. Or go nuts. Or get yourself killed.

He dressed and considered a critical question: How in hell had the yakuzas tracked him? He'd made a clean exit from Tokyo. He'd dodged even Willoughby and bulldog Olds back at Langley. Tami had set him up for the hit, yes, but how had she known who he was and where he had come from?

He grabbed her purse, dumped it onto the shattered mattress. No notebook or address book.

There was a comb, brush, folding money, coins, and a Honolulu driver's license in the name Tami Tanaka. Nothing inside the mascara. Nothing inside the first lipstick tube.

But the second lipstick was a bonanza. It also provided the connection to the Tokyo *yakuza* muscle: a neat little plastic packet of pastel pink powder. Cherry Blossom—or Sakura—coke, as the drug ring touted their ultimate snow. *Nonaddictive*! Guaranteed. A coke so powerful but harmless that it sold for a steep price to favored customers. And the favored customers happened to be in key positions in commerce, government, and the military.

But there was a problem, a snag. The pushers had failed to mention a fatal flaw in their nonaddictive formula—the drug had a cumulative poisonous effect similar to arsenic. After a few months of snorts and hits, users were still nonaddicted. But their systems overloaded and they keeled over, dead.

Just a few weeks ago a large number of important people, particularly in Great Britain, had died from the killer coke. After that MI6 agent Hugh Willoughby and, later, CIA operative Jacob Bolt had joined to eradicate the lethal drug ring.

Bolt dropped the Cherry Blossom packet into one of the yakuza's seersucker pockets. Maybe the local cops would think this was a narc killing.

He picked up Tami's compact. Inside was the standard face powder and a mirror. The mirror looked loose. He popped it with his thumbnail. Stuck with rubber cement to the mirror's back was a scrap of paper. On it was written an address in Jerusalem. Jerusalem? How did that fit into the coke racket? Or did it? He stuck the paper in his pocket, wondering.

Now he really had to leave.

Bolt dropped the last of his things in the suitcase and snapped it shut. He slung the camera around his neck. It was the tourist's coup de grace, and his only cover. He needed to get to a telephone, call his control, Clifton Olds, and report what had happened. Report the resurrection of the damn yakuzas.

He listened at the door. Footsteps and laughter echoed along the hall. People were coming upstairs. Alcoholic giggles and too-hearty guffaws. This was the after-dinner crowd. He listened longer. A moment of silence. He slipped into the corridor, didn't look back.

At an outdoor phone booth in bucolic Lihue, Kauai's seaside county seat, Bolt picked up the telephone. This was not his favorite method of contacting Olds at Langley, especially in a small town of four thousand. Too many busybodies, and too damn public.

As it turned out, the question was rhetorical. The phone was dead.

He went into a restaurant, asked to use theirs.

"Sorry, it's not working," said the distracted woman behind the cash register. Royal purple orchid leis piled high around her neck. She smiled pleasantly, but her mind was on the customers who waited in line to pay their supper bills. "I hear the phones are out all over town."

Bolt tried a small grocery store down the street, with the same result. He couldn't wait any longer.

He headed for the Lihue airport in the rented Land Rover. Overhead, stars sparkled with the brilliance only clean air and a small earthly population allow.

Damn. So much for the perfect vacation.

The flight from serene, uncrowded Lihue to bustling, hustling Honolulu was only twenty-five minutes. But those twenty-five minutes across the ocean's nighttime void separated two worlds.

There were wonderful similarities between the two cities, Bolt thought—the salty sea air and terrific scenery, for instance. But the differences gave Bolt a sinking feeling. For him, it was reentry time.

At Honolulu International he flagged a taxi and gave the driver an address near the Waikiki waterfront.

He settled into the taxi's back seat and forced himself to relax. He was an operative because—he told himself—as much as such a thing were possible, he liked the work. He also had a naive—and he knew it was naive—desire to make the world a little better. He thought a while longer, probing somewhere inside as if searching for the source of a muscle ache. Or a wound. Yes, there was one more reason. Perhaps the critical reason: he'd be at a loss doing anything else. Anything less exciting. Anything less life-threatening. He liked . . . needed . . . to test himself. He-himself-alone, against tough odds. The tougher the better.

He considered this analysis a short while longer, then dismissed it from his mind.

He watched out the taxi's windows and shook

his head. This was reentry, all right. With a bang. Polished Rolls Royces, Mercedeses, and BMWs crowded the streets. Steel-and-glass skyscrapers towered overhead. On the sidewalks, all-night stallkeepers hawked fluorescent polyester aloha shirts and muumuus. Street people offered giant parrots to pose for souvenir photos; the birds cawed nasty things in the tourists' ears while dropping nasty things on their shoulders. There was a McDonald's every few blocks.

Some things never changed, Bolt thought. In a maddening way it was reassuring.

The taxi pulled up at the door of a dark building on a quiet, dimly lighted street near the waterfront.

Bolt paid the driver from the yakuza's thousand-dollar stake, and stood at the building's door fumbling for keys until the taxi was out of sight. Then he tucked his canvas suitcase under his arm and jogged three blocks to the beach the long way, taking alleys and cross streets until he was damn sure he hadn't been followed.

At last he stopped at another dark building. This one was a three-story structure on a busy shoreline boulevard. The sign on the simple facade said HULA PRODUCTS, INC.—SHOWCASE SWIMWEAR, SURFWEAR, & SUNWEAR.

He strode around to the side door. He pressed his right palm and fingers against a wall plaque marked Private Entrance. And waited.

"Name?" a voice seemed to whisper from nowhere and everywhere.

"Jacob Bolt."

There was a pause while his voice was computer-matched. And then the door swung open. He'd passed. For a moment he wondered what he would've done if he hadn't. Then he smiled. He would've had to find some other way in, wouldn't he?

The thought reassured him. Forget Tami. Forget betrayal. Remember: He was a man who liked his work!

"Greetings, asshole."The guy inside grinned.

"Asshole yourself, Bitterman." Bolt shook his head, chuckled, and lobbed his suitcase at him. He liked tall, gangly Bitterman, not only because he was a good operative but because he liked to joke and kid. Equally important, against his boss's directive, Bitterman seemed to inordinately enjoy having Bolt around.

Bitterman almost dropped his little Star PD, one of the most compact .45s around, as he automatically caught the heavy canvas bag. The .45 was insurance in case someone had managed to dupe a cleared person's hand and voice. With Bitterman standing guard, the intruder and his success would be short-lived.

"This is gonna be entertaining," Bitterman said, held out the suitcase for Bolt to retrieve. "The boss's gonna be pissed seeing you again!"

Bolt clapped Bitterman on the back, ignored the suitcase. "Thanks, pal. Glad to hear the old boy's in." He bounded up the stairs.

"Bolt!" Bitterman said, following. "You forgot your suitcase!"

"Hey, that's okay," Bolt said. He reached the second floor and headed down the hall past the office that housed the secretarial pool. "You keep it."

"I don't want it!" Bitterman said. "What am I gonna do with *your* suitcase?"

"You'll think of something," Bolt said. He stuck his head inside the glass-doored office where Vernon White sat behind a metal desk. "Hi, dad," he said cheerfully. "I'm home."

Vernon White looked up. He had white hair, faded skin, and tired eyes. He was in his late forties, but he looked a decade older. He'd never adjusted to life's unpredictability. Bolt figured he never would.

As soon as Vernon White saw Bolt, he flushed with anger. So many things about Bolt made him furious that he couldn't decide where to begin.

He sputtered unintelligibly, then settled on: "Get the hell out of my office! Get the hell out of Honolulu! Get the hell out of *Hawaii!* Bitterman! Come here and throw this dog-breath *out!*"

CHAPTER
3

"Hey, nice to see you," Bolt said and sat on the edge of the CIA chief's desk.

"It's *not* nice to see *you*." Vernon White glared at the door and shouted, "Bitterman! Where are you!" Then back to Bolt: "Get off my goddamned desk!"

"Sure, dad." Bolt stood up. He figured Bitterman was waiting somewhere in another office until White came closer to apoplexy.

"And don't call me dad!"

"Okay, d—" Bolt said and stopped. He smiled. White sputtered again, borderline apoplectic. "Bitterman!" he bellowed.

"Good news, boss," Bitterman announced cheerfully as he stepped into the small office. "The phones are working."

"Your phones were out?" Bolt asked.

"About an hour," Bitterman said.

"Get this flea-bait out of here!" Vernon White ordered Bitterman. Then he did a doubletake, stared at his young operative. "What are you carrying?"

"Bolt's suitcase," Bitterman said.

"You're a man, not an ass. Give it back to him!"

"I tried, boss." Bitterman grinned. "You know how Bolt is. Always kidding around."

Bolt took the suitcase, punched Bitterman on the arm. Bitterman grinned and punched back.

"Do I really have to throw him out, boss?" Bitterman asked.

"You're damn right you do!" Suddenly Vernon White looked tired. But his eyes managed to shoot daggers at Bolt. "What in hell are you doing here, Bolt? You know you're not supposed to be in my territory unless Langley okays it with me first!"

"I'm on a little vacation," Bolt said innocently. "You know, the standard tourist routine—sand, sun, fun."

"Uh-huh," White said, angry again. "And wahines!"

Bolt felt a sudden jolt of pain over Tami. And instantly he ignored it. She'd been a yakuza. She'd set him up.

"I know about you and your damn wahines!" White raged on. "You get busy screwing around. Pretty soon you forget to file reports. Don't pick up your messages. You miss meetings. You know what your problem is, Bolt? You don't follow the book! You're cocky. And I won't have you in my territory mucking up my smooth-running operation!"

"What about the Adrienne Brill business?" Bolt said, unperturbed. Adrienne Brill was a gorgeous redhead who'd operated a high-class extortion business out of a Honolulu skyscraper. Because of serious international repercussions, Bolt had been sent in. Now she was doing time in a federal pen.

"And there was the weapons ring," Bitterman reminded White. "And that guy who was trying to form a Red Army Faction chapter . . ."

"Osamu Sensui," Bolt said. An interesting case.

"Yeah, that's the guy," Bitterman said. "He was a major bad dude. Every time Bolt comes here, seems to me he takes care of one of our messes, boss."

This was not what Vernon White wanted to hear. He glowered. He drilled his fingers on the desk.

"Why were the phones out?" Bolt asked Bitterman, eased his right haunch back onto the chief's sacrosanct desk.

"No one seems to know," Bitterman said.

Vernon White suddenly came back to life. "Well, go find out, goddammit!" he snapped at Bitterman. Then to Bolt: "You're on my desk again!"

Bolt stood. "I've got a problem, Vernon."

"You *are* a problem."

"And only you can help."

Bolt moved to the front of the desk. Bolt knew White's biggest quarrel with him was his lack of respect. Since routine and paperwork were vital to White, anyone who showed complete disregard for them, as Bolt did, insulted White's sense of integrity. Bolt kept that in mind when he wanted something from White.

"I've got to report to Olds," Bolt told White.

"So call him," White said grumpily.

"Right. But I've got to talk privately to him," Bolt said. "*Very privately*. What d'you suggest?" Making it appear that White came to his own decision was critical.

"We've got a couple dozen phones here," White said, stalling.

"But there're people all around," Bolt said reasonably, easing around the desk to White's chair. "And maybe bugs, too. I know you. There's no way anybody'd plant a device in *your* office. You probably sweep it every day, right?"

"Twice a week." White's eyes were narrowed. "Olds know you're reporting in?"

"He's expecting my call." Sometime in seven to ten days.

"So you *aren't* on vacation!" White said triumphantly. "You're on assignment, and Langley didn't clear it with me first!"

"Your deductive powers are uncanny, Vernon," Bolt said. He pulled White's chair back for him.

Vindicated, White stood up and brushed past Bolt. "Time for my cup of coffee."

"You're a champ, Vernon. I really mean that." Bolt sat at White's desk and picked up the phone.

White looked back. There was momentary regret in his eyes. Had he made a mistake? Was he getting soft? He seemed to decide to salve his conscious with a warning: "Stay away from my papers!" He strode stiffly out of the room and closed the door.

"Besides, Vernon," Bolt said as he watched White's back disappear, "you've got the only comfortable chair in the joint."

Bolt opened up a protected line to CIA headquarters in Langley, Virginia, and asked for a patch to Clifton Olds's home.

"You know what time it is here?" Sue Kirtt, the telephone operator, asked Bolt sternly.

"I hope so, doll," he said. He liked Sue; she kept trying to reform him. "My mother taught me to count when I was four."

"Too bad she didn't teach you manners, too!"

Bolt laughed. She sniffed. And the phone rang in the distance.

Olds's sleepy voice answered. Bolt identified himself.

"Where in hell are you?"

"A couple hours ago I was in paradise," Bolt said. "But things have deteriorated seriously since then." He described the tranquil beauty of Kauai, the aggressiveness of luscious Tami, and the yakuza attack.

Bolt got no sympathy from Olds for his ruined vacation.

"Sounds like a setup," Olds said, getting straight to the point. "I'll have our people notify the locals not to pursue the deaths. National security."

Olds's voice had a faintly aristocratic tone to it. He was a tall, wiry man with stooped shoulders, silver-gray hair, and impeccable Eastern Seaboard credentials that included ancestors in the Cabot, Lodge, and Cummings families. The only reason Bolt knew this was because Sue Kirtt had told him during alcohol-heavy cocktails one Friday night. Bolt, ordinarily a beer drinker, had mixed the cocktails himself. It's always good to know a little about your boss. In the CIA, the boss usually knows *everything* about you.

"Thanks," Bolt said.

"I've been looking for you," Olds said. "Figured you'd go to Majorca again. Or New Zealand, or Bora-Bora."

"That's what I figured you'd figure."

"And that's why I quit looking," Olds said, almost amused. "Waste of energy. I've been waiting for your call."

Bolt heard the far-away click of a cigarette

lighter. Olds smoked Camel lights, drank his Jack Daniels neat, and had been divorced four times. He would be sitting up in bed now, fully awake. Sitting like a king on a throne. He would wear monogrammed pajamas, or be stark naked. Both extremes fit his idiosyncratic personality. There were two qualities Bolt admired in Olds: He was unpredictable . . . and he was smart.

"You knew I'd have trouble?" Bolt said.

"Let's just say I suspected you might have a visitor. After you disappeared, Bando Matsumoto was murdered at home while under house arrest. Assassinated, really. Same way Bushi Nakamura was assassinated in Washington."

"Small puncture wound at the back of the skull?"

"That's it," Olds said. "A metal bulletlike projectile fired at very close range."

"It had to be someone Matsumoto knew," Bolt said, thinking out loud, "just as Bushi Nakamura must've known his killer. Someone they both knew well enough that they saw no reason to protect their backs."

"Agreed."

"How'd the assassin get into his home?" Bolt asked.

"They're still investigating that. It's beginning to look like an inside job—an employee, or someone who passed through so often no one noticed. Maybe a lawyer, a cop, or a minister."

"In Japan most likely a Shinto priest, not a minister," Bolt said automatically. He was an expert in Asian and Middle Eastern affairs.

When Bushi Nakamura was found murdered a few weeks earlier in Washington, D.C., Olds had assigned Jake Bolt to investigate. Bushi has been a top-level U.S. government computer expert with secrets foreign governments and ambitious independents would kill for.

Bushi was discovered disemboweled on a mat on his bedroom floor, apparently a victim of seppuku—ritual suicide. But the autopsy determined that the assassin had first shot Bushi in the back of the head where the small wound would be hidden beneath Bushi's thick black hair, and then he—or she—had disemboweled the computer whiz to make the murder look like suicide. The killer must've had a strong stomach and a steady hand. What had he or she been after?

Bolt's investigation led him to Tokyo, tracking an unnamed object Bushi had mailed just before his death to his cousin, Suki Nakamura. But someone killed Suki Nakamura before Bolt could reach her. By then, MI6 agent Hugh Willoughby also was checking into the young woman's death, as well as following the trail of the Cherry Blossom cocaine. Willoughby discovered that the same yakuza clan had been the muscle for both Suki Nakamura's killing and the coke operation.

Bolt and Willoughby joined forces. When they at last jailed Iwa Matsumoto, they thought they'd wiped out the whole enterprise. Bolt was never able to identify the object Bushi sent his Tokyo cousin. He and Willoughby hoped that whatever it was, it was long gone, and that its identity had died with Iwa Matsumoto, or perhaps even earlier—with Bushi. Perhaps Bushi had given up no secrets!

"Are suppliers still getting Cherry Blossom?" Bolt asked Clifton Olds.

"Nothing's going out from that coke ring. They're out of business."

"So now you're wondering again why Bushi was killed. Information? Codes? Software?"

"That's about it," Olds said calmly from his Virginia home. But Bolt detected a sharp edge to Olds's voice, worry transmitted by inflection. "Someone got to Iwa Matsumoto, someone he knew, and the same someone who got Bushi. Why? Was the killer worried Matsumoto would talk? Most likely. But what would Matsumoto say?"

"We eliminated everyone in the organization up to Matsumoto," Bolt said. "Perhaps we stopped too soon. Maybe there's someone even higher."

"My thinking exactly," Olds said grimly.

"There's a boss," Bolt went on, postulating, "someone who hires muscle, doesn't get his hands dirty. Unless he has to. With Bushi Nakamura and Iwa Matsumoto, he had to."

"And that makes me think the object Bushi sent his cousin is still out there somewhere," Olds said. "And still damn vital."

"Something else might tie in too, Chief." Bolt told Olds about the Jerusalem address he'd found in Tami Tanaka's compact.

"Check it out," Olds said immediately. Again the lighter clicked. Olds was on his second cigarette, and he hadn't brushed his teeth yet. "I don't like the international implications. Washington. Tokyo. Jerusalem. London. If there is a guy higher than Matsumoto, he gets around. Or at least his people do. Who is he? What does he have? What does he want?"

"Okay, I'm on to Jerusalem," Bolt said. Then stopped, reminded of one more piece of information by the reappearance of Vernon White outside the glass office door.

White stood frowning in at Bolt. White's message was clear: Bolt's time was up. *Move it!* he mouthed at Bolt.

"You know about the phones being down here?" Bolt asked Olds. He smiled and waved at White. White's frown deepened, and he glowered at his watch. "Down on all the islands."

"More computer problems?"

In the past few weeks, odd communication problems had been appearing around the world: A weather satellite that failed to respond to signals. In the United States, phone company computers that spit out a month's worth of bills where everyone was charged one cent. Telecommunications between Japan and Britain ceased for a short time. The Allied Kremlin listening post in Japan went out, also for a short time.

"Hold on," Bolt told Olds. "I'll find out." Bolt laid the phone on a stack of papers on White's neat desktop, jogged to the glass door, and cracked it open. "What's the story on the phone lines?" he asked White.

The grim station chief ignored him. "Finish your call!" he ordered. "I have work to do!"

"Bitterman!" Bolt called to the gangly guard. Bitterman was heading back to his post. "What about the phones?"

"Computer glitch," Bitterman said. "Something to do with the switches."

"Thanks, pal," Bolt told Bitterman. He glanced at Vernon White. "Out in a minute, dad."

"Bolt!" White warned.

"Not now," Bolt said pleasantly. "I'm on long distance with *Mister* Olds, right?"

Bolt closed the door. White's indignant glare almost shattered the glass, but Olds was higher up, and White—although a jerk—was no idiot. Bolt sat in the chair, picked up the phone, and leaned back, relaxed. "Same story. Computer malfunction."

Olds was silent, thinking. At last he said, "While you're in Jerusalem, I'll check it out from here."

"Fine. But one small problem."

White was glaring new threats through the door. Bolt smiled and waved again at the furious man. White's face was tomato red. Probably hot as hell. If White kept this up, Bolt decided, his skin would blister. Bolt smiled broadly.

"What is it?" Olds asked warily. If Bolt had a small or easy problem, he took care of it himself.

"Vernon White," Bolt said simply.

Olds groaned. "What've you done to him now?"

"He doesn't believe I was on vacation. You remember, he has that special deal with you that you have to ask permission for me to come into his territory?"

Bolt knew Olds wouldn't allow himself to get sidetracked into discussing the deal. Olds didn't like it, had never had to make that kind of arrangement before, and was still sufficiently angry at Bolt for it that Bolt would probably never receive another assignment remotely close to the scenic islands.

"What did you *do* to him?" Olds insisted.

"Nothing. I swear. It's what he does to himself."

Olds sighed. He knew what Bolt meant. "All right, put him on. But you owe me! Find out what's going on in Jerusalem so I can sleep nights!"

"No problem," Bolt said and pushed the hold button. He went to the door, opened it. "Telephone for you," he grandly told White.

"Olds?" Vernon White said. He knotted his fists. Sweat beaded on his bright red forehead. He gritted his teeth. "He broke our deal!" He charged for the telephone.

Bolt picked up his suitcase, quietly closed the door, and stepped away from the office. Behind him he heard White's muffled shouts of indignation. One thing about Vernon White, he had good lungs.

"Am I the only entertainment White has?" Bolt asked an operative at a nearby desk.

"No," the man said and grinned. "But you're our favorite. We took a poll. Come back anytime."

The other operatives scattered around the room laughed.

Bolt laughed too. He headed toward the corridor. He was feeling good, back in the swing of things. He wasn't the vacation type anyway.

He trotted down the stairs. At the outside door he stopped to say good-bye to Bitterman.

"Got your rabies shot?" he asked Bitterman.

"I don't bite people!"

"No, but White does."

Bitterman grinned, and Bolt stepped out into the starry Waikiki night.

"I'm gonna miss you!" Bitterman called and closed the door.

At the curb Bolt felt the impact of Waikiki's famous tourist trade. At any one time a hundred thousand people lived in Waikiki, and in a few days, sixty thousand of them would be on their way somewhere else. Even at ten o'clock at night the streets and sidewalks teemed. The odors of sea salt, concrete still warm from the sun, and fried foods wafted on the air. Music blared from limousines, Jaguars, and Hondas. Beautiful women strolled hips swinging from restaurant to cabaret to bar. It was an area where everyone was a minority, and the only majority was Homo sapiens.

His transition was complete. Bolt liked this tacky, talented town. Forget pastoral Kauai. He wanted the vigor and excitement of a big city.

He noted a taxi cruising slowly in his direction. He raised a hand, caught the driver's eye. The taxi pulled up to the curb.

Bolt opened the back door, readying himself to tell the driver to take him to Honolulu International. Inside the overhead light flicked on and Bolt stared down at a Japanese Service Type 64 military rifle.

The rifle was pointed straight at Bolt's heart.

"Welcome to Honolulu, Mr. Bolt," said the yakuza staring coldly up at him. "Get in, please. Slowly."

CHAPTER
4

In his elegant townhouse in Virginia, Clifton Olds remained sitting up in bed long after he'd gotten rid of Vernon White. Dressed in black pin-striped monogrammed pajamas, Olds smoked and toyed with the idea of going downstairs for a cup of strong coffee. But he might be able to fall sleep again, and he needed the sleep, so he kept pushing the craving for caffeine from his mind.

He thought about Jake Bolt. Bolt was Olds's best field operative. He was cocky, brash, brilliant. And an occasional pain in the arse. Never was Bolt boring. Particularly where women and work were concerned. Olds remembered the comment of his fourth ex-wife, Tiffany: "Jake's a bastard on a leash. But he's gorgeous, and the kind of bastard women love to tame. Preferably starting in bed." Olds found it fascinating that Tiffany never once mentioned Bolt's brain. But that's where her limitations were most obvious. Actually, Olds thought, it's a miracle their marriage had survived a year. God, was she boring!

Bolt was the antithesis. A hot-shot antithesis. A Phi Beta Kappa from Columbia, he had a double major in history and computer science. His concentration fields were modern Middle Eastern and

Asian history, and he spoke with varying degrees of competence eight languages: Japanese, Vietnamese, Chinese, Hindi, Urdu, Arabic, Farsi, and Hebrew. He was also intimately conversant with hardware and software from the most powerful multimillion-dollar Cray supercomputer to the simplest home PC.

The Company knew potential when they saw it; they recruited Bolt at Columbia. He turned out to be not only a dedicated operative but a maverick. He hated paperwork and, annoyingly, disappeared to follow obscure leads. To his credit, the leads often turned out to be important. Often enough that he acquired one of the Company's highest success rates.

But he was a control's nightmare. No one could really *control* Bolt.

Olds didn't mind. In fact, he saw a lot of himself in Bolt, what he'd been twenty years ago. Before he was benched because of heart problems. In his thirty years in the Company he'd observed that the best operatives were the ones who did the unexpected, used intuition, and forged relentlessly ahead. They also had high mortality rates, but not as high as those who turned out to be dull or stupid. And then there were the middleground operatives who were moderately intelligent and capable. They crossed their *t*'s and dotted their *i*'s—like Vernon White—and lived longest, but with only modest success.

He hoped Bolt lasted, and—especially—that he untangled this new problem. Fast.

Olds lit another cigarette and inhaled deeply. He was worried. There seemed to be someone out there—a Mister Big, for want of another name—

who'd made a fortune in regular cocaine and, with Cherry Blossom, had announced his expansion into a larger, more lethal international arena. An arena in which it was to his advantage to deliberately kill personnel in key positions in government, industry, and the military. Particularly in Britain. Yet Olds had had no direct word of this powerful man—or woman—from Company sources. Mister Big had still not officially announced himself or his intentions.

Olds hypothesized Mister Big had more on his mind than killer cocaine. Olds had seen giant coke operations regroup and resume sales within hours of being—apparently—wiped out. Yet there were no stirrings in the Cherry Blossom remains. Only the continued operation of the yakuza muscle that had also killed Suki Nakamura, Bushi Nakamura's Tokyo cousin.

The yakuza connection between Suki's death and the killer coke really worried Olds. It persuaded him that Mister Big might have something to do with the odd computer glitches that were afflicting communications around the globe. Mister Big could be the front for a foreign government. He could be an independent with a contract to a foreign government. He could be a solitaire, working for himself. Or he could be several people posing as one mastermind.

Were these global computer troubles related to something the assassin stole from Bushi Nakamura? If so, then was the assassin Mister Big himself? And what in hell had been taken?

Olds frowned and stubbed out his cigarette. He had his top computer expert, Marcus Krenchell, working on the issue right now.

He considered lighting another cigarette, but his mouth tasted like a moldy cellar floor. He stared out the bay window. Dawn was rising lavender and lemon yellow across the green Virginia horizon. Even if he could sleep, he wouldn't have time now.

He pulled on his bathrobe, headed downstairs for coffee. He had more thinking to do.

Jacob Bolt climbed into the Honolulu taxi. Warily he watched the military rifle aimed steadily at his heart. The yakuza gunman sat on the far side of the back seat, the rifle firm in his hands.

Outside, traffic passed in an oblivious, festive stream. The driver dropped Bolt's suitcase into the trunk, slammed the lid, and returned to his place behind the wheel. Bolt's enthusiasm for large cities was rapidly diminishing. Right now he needed a nosy small town. He was beginning to sweat.

"Hand over your weapon, Mr. Bolt. Two fingers, please." The backseat gunman's face and voice were impassive. He was about thirty years old and emanated a quiet assurance that guaranteed Bolt wouldn't be the first man he'd killed.

Now was no time to play stupid and loose.

"Of course," Bolt said agreeably, and removed his SIG-Sauer with thumb and forefinger from his waist holster. "Mr. ———?"

The taxi driver reached back over the front seat and picked Bolt's pistol from his fingers. The driver was a silent, sullen man with greased, spiked hair showing beneath his cap.

"Let's move," the backseat gunman told the

driver. Then to Bolt: "You may call me Maruoka, Mr. Bolt."

The taxi pulled away from the curb and joined the river of traffic.

"All right, Maruoka." As they passed beneath street lamps Bolt could see the edge of colorful tattoos beneath the guy's white linen sports jacket. "You and your driver from the squid clan?"

"We seem to keep missing you," Maruoka said, acknowledging his yakuza identity. "It is a pleasure to be the one to capture the CIA man who has given us so much trouble. We heard about Kauai."

"So you came here," Bolt said, "hoping I'd check in at the local headquarters."

"If not here, we would have found you somewhere else." The yakuza gave a humorless smile. "Eventually." His four front teeth were gold. Probably knocked out in some fight. "No one escapes us for long."

The taxi turned onto the Pali Highway heading northeast into the dark Koolau Mountains. A three-quarter moon was rising milky white above the ragged black range in the distance.

"I'll keep that in mind," Bolt said. He noted the physical symptoms of his tension; they never varied. Tight gut, sweat, and a brain that insisted he devise a means of escape, even when it wasn't practical.

"Do that, Mr. Bolt." Maruoka said coolly. "Where were you headed just now?"

"The Honolulu airport."

"Go on."

"My reason exactly," Bolt said. "I was going on home."

"Langley? Come, come, Mr. Bolt. We both

know you were headed elsewhere. Save us the exhaustion of haggling, and yourself some pain. What was your destination?"

"I'll make a trade. Tell me who you work for, and I'll tell you where I was going."

The taxi entered the mountains' first black chasm. Ahead red tail lights snaked upward. Bright white headlights streamed downward.

"You forget," Maruoka said. "I have the gun. You will tell me what I want to know, one way or the other."

"No, *you* forget," Bolt said. "You're going to kill me anyway. I have nothing to gain, except satisfying my curiosity. And you have nothing to lose by telling something to a dead man."

Maruoka seemed to think about it. Bolt judged the distance from his hands to the rifle. He was sweating more.

"No, I have nothing to gain," Maruoka concluded, dismissed Bolt's offer. "Where were you going? Tell me, or I will shoot your kneecaps. The right first, then the left. A shattered kneecap causes excruciating pain. You will scream. Weep. Beg me to stop."

"You know that from personal experience?" Bolt asked.

The taxi bounced off the highway and onto a side road. Trees and bushes closed around them, eerie sentinels in the moonlight. The taxi rattled forward. Branches scratched across the windows.

"I have myself shattered a dozen or more kneecaps," Maruoka said with pride. "Other people's kneecaps, of course."

"Of course."

Bolt was studying the yakuza, impressed by his

steadfast control of the rifle. As far as Bolt could see, he had not once relaxed, not once let his guard down. Even the taxi's bouncing didn't distract him. Bolt needed a break.

"I could tell you, but I might lie," Bolt suggested. "And you don't want to risk a punctured tire if you're forced to shoot and a bullet goes wild."

Maruoka thought about it. "How much longer?" he asked the driver.

"Now," the driver said. The taxi rocked to a halt. Maruoka remained in his corner, the military rifle trained on Bolt.

"You have no more excuses," the gunman told Bolt. He was right. They were stopped in a patch of dark, remote mountain wilderness. This was where they planned to kill him. Bolt's mind raced, searching for escape.

The driver turned off the motor and got out. The gunman waited until the driver had Bolt's side of the taxi covered, then he stepped out of the back seat and stood next to his door.

"Get out on your side," Maruoka told Bolt. "I will come around." He was going to wait until Bolt was safely out of the taxi. He would take no chance that Bolt would slide across the seat and escape out the other door.

Bolt obediently climbed out, facing the taxi driver and his Japanese Service rifle. There was a break in the trees behind the driver. The land spread out in knee-high foliage—flowers and ferns, it looked like—and then the shadowy area ended abruptly. A wind whipped up over where it ended and gusted across the ferns and flowers toward Bolt. That told Bolt there was a precipice out there where the land stopped. Judging by the wind, a deep one.

"A thousand feet straight down," the driver said. His teeth flashed in a wolfish grin. "You'll fly like a bird!" He laughed. "A dead bird!" He laughed harder and backed beyond Bolt's reach, waiting for Maruoka to join him. Maruoka's steps sounded around the rear of the taxi. Bolt turned just enough so that he had both men in view.

"Now you will tell me everything I wish to know," Maruoka said as he closed in. In the pale, glowing moonlight, there was a sheen of anticipation on his cold face. "Where were you going next? What clue were you following?"

And then Bolt saw it. For about four seconds as Maruoka rounded the taxi and headed toward the driver's side, Bolt would be between the two men. If they fired, they risked shooting one another. That would slow their responses. Maybe enough.

"I'm paid to keep my mouth shut," Bolt stalled. "What's in it for me?"

"A less painful death," Maruoka said and, unknowingly, stepped into the position Bolt was waiting for.

With the swiftness of years of practice, Bolt rotated and crashed a *mae-giri* karate kick to the driver's jaw. The driver's head snapped back. He dropped his rifle, staggered, and fell to the ground.

Maruoka stepped aside to avoid shooting his downed driver. He aimed. He was taking his time, a mistake. Bolt smiled and directed a powerful *yoko-geri* side kick at Maruoka's chin.

But Maruoka saw it coming. He moved like lightning now. He ducked and shoulder-rolled away, untouched.

And fired from a half-crouch.

Bolt scrambled back toward the driver and his

rifle. The driver groaned, still unconscious. Bullets sliced through the night air. Vegetation exploded beside Bolt, covered him with sticky spray. He grabbed the rifle.

Maruoka's rifle was honing in. The yakuza gunman squatted in the moonlight, making himself a small target. He kept shooting, no longer caring about his driver. He wanted Bolt. The price was unimportant.

Bolt raised the rifle and fired. Moonlight was deceptive. Targets wavered, faded. The odd light often ruined precision.

Bolt's first two bursts went wide.

A bullet screamed past Bolt's ear so close it burned. He felt more than saw the taxi driver's unconscious body jolt as it absorbed the impact. No sound came from the driver.

Bolt concentrated on the gunman crouched ahead in the luminescent light. He waited. It didn't do him a damn bit of good to fire at something he couldn't see well enough to hit. Another bullet screamed past, this one farther off. And then for a moment his target seemed stationary.

It was what he'd waited for. Bolt squeezed the trigger.

The gunman flew back, arms widespread.

Bolt waited a count of ten. There was no movement or sound from either of the yakuzas. No movement or sound anywhere except the rustling wind that gusted up over the cliff and swept above and through the dark ferns and flowers of this lush open area.

Bolt padded toward Maruoka. The yakuza was drenched in blood. The wound was through the top of the head, the back of the skull gone. Bolt checked the guy's pockets. Another wad of bills, but no I.D. or anything else of use. He slid the cash into his pocket. His expense account was going to please Olds—so far the yakuzas, not the CIA, were the major financial backers of this mission. He carried Maruoka to the edge of the cliff. He could see down about ten charcoal feet to where bushes clung to the sheer face, and then there was nothing. For all he could tell, the void might drop all the way to the center of the earth.

He heaved the gunman over the side. The body crashed out of sight. It continued to roll and bounce, the sounds growing more and more distant until there was silence again.

Bolt checked the taxi driver. He was dead from a massive gut wound. His pockets were clean, too. Bolt took his keys and cash, and dumped his corpse over the cliff.

Bolt waited on the edge until the mountain's silence enveloped him again. There was no serenity in the silence, only questions. Who had sent the yakuzas after Bolt? And why?

Israel was born in 1948 of dreams and bullets. Today little had changed, Bolt thought as he drove through the spring-warmed countryside where rusting war vehicles rested among greening vegetable fields. Dreams and bullets still fueled the small nation.

In the early days, kibbutzniks irrigated the merciless desert by day and danced the hora by firelight, and the fierce Irgun took on the Arab enemy with the same vigor and intelligence with which David had challenged—and slain—Goliath.

United with statesmen and poets, garage mechanics and housewives, they'd forged Israel.

Bolt drove into the golden, crumpled Judaean Hills where Jerusalem, the ultimate urban survivor, had been built and rebuilt for thousands of years. Three hours ago he'd arrived at Ben Gurion International at Lod and picked up his SIG-Sauer, ammo, and new I.D.s from a diplomatic courier. Then he'd rented a car and now —eighteen miles later—entered scenic Jerusalem on the Sederot Weizmann.

Before him across the low hills spread crumbling arches, dusty limestone walls, and ancient domes accented by the long shadows of afternoon. The tiny metropolis thrived, quarrelled, and did business amid the venerable architecture that testified to its endurance as the Holy City, sacred to three of the world's major religions—Christian, Jewish, and Muslim.

The address that had been in Tami's compact was on the city's outskirts, where vendors hawked brass vases, ceramic animals, Bedouin daggers, and olive wood sculpted into both crucifixes and Stars of David. The street was wide and busy with trucks hauling produce, home furnishings, and clothing. Although Jerusalem had no heavy industry, light industry flourished. And of course there was tourism; visitors from all over the world, curious about this famous rectangle of Earth.

Bolt drove past stores and stalls until he reached the address. He studied the big building as he continued on with the traffic. It was a warehouse with a sign that said, in Arabic, GLOBAL IMPORTS AND EXPORTS.

The warehouse looked deserted, a chain padlocked across the receiving doors. Bolt parked and strolled alongside the building. Once it had had first-floor windows, but now they were boarded and painted the same undistinctive dirty tan as the rest of the siding. The second-story windows still had their glass, but they were barred. A large padlock hung from a side door. The small yard was weed-choked, and the tall, healthy weeds in the cracked concrete drive and parking lot indicated that it'd been weeks since vehicles delivered and picked up goods.

Bolt stopped in shops along the street, learned from some of the storekeepers that packing crates had been stored in the warehouse. A few thought the crates might have been labeled dishes, gardening tools, or linens. They said there was never an on-site warehouse staff. Trucks came at irregular hours, often at night.

By this time the sun was setting and the air was turning cool. Bolt drove a few blocks away to buy a flashlight and some tools, then sandwiches and a thermos of tea at a delicatessen. He returned to the warehouse's street and parked at a curve where he could watch the deserted building and parking lot. He turned off the motor, ate, and drank tea while surveying the area. This could take a while.

By four a.m. the street had long been silent, empty. Bolt snapped alert from his half-doze. It was time.

He stepped from the car. The moon glistened in the black sky, and shadows fell deep and eerie among the buildings. No one had arrived at the warehouse, and now in the depths of the night when only night workers, insomniacs, criminals, and the desperate were about, Bolt would investigate more closely.

He circled the building. The only doors were those that were padlocked and faced the street. The only usable windows were on the second story and barred too narrowly for a man to squeeze through. In the litter that edged the building, there was no evidence that anyone had been here recently.

But all of this could mean nothing. A professional could be waiting in there now.

He returned to the warehouse's front, took from his pocket the heavy wire that he'd bought earlier that evening. His back to the street, he picked open the lock. He crouched, SIG-Sauer in hand, waiting for anyone inside to react to the small noise. He heard nothing.

He swung open the door, slipped through, and closed it. The odor hit him first—dust and staleness, the close mustiness of day after day, night after night of no fresh air. He listened, allowing his eyes time to adjust to the blackness. No sounds, and nothing moved among the shadows. Faded moonlight filtered gray through the high, greasy windowpanes. He clicked on the flashlight.

The bright beam was a narrow finger in the vastness of the empty warehouse. There were no boxes or crates, no machinery, no tables and chairs. Nothing.

Across the expanse, stairs climbed to a second-floor balcony where doors stood ajar. Silently Bolt ran across the concrete floor and up the wood stairs. Lining the balcony were three offices. Marks on the wood floors showed where desks and chairs had stood for years. Nails protruded from the plastered walls where pictures had hung. There were no clues to the histories of the empty offices in the dust that remained.

Bolt returned to the first floor, set up a pattern, and walked the length of the warehouse, back and forth, until he'd covered the entire area. All he found were several piles of wood where crates had broken and been kicked aside. What had been stored here that was so secret that no one in the neighborhood seemed to know what it was? Or so frightening that no one would tell?

He spent the rest of the night watching from the car.

Just before dawn the city began to come alive. Bells rang across the rooftops, calling worshippers to prayer. Trucks rumbled on the streets, delivering milk and fresh bread. Sleepy storekeepers opened their shops. And no one gave any particular notice to the empty warehouse.

For two more days Bolt staked out the area, leaving only to grab food and quickly return. He moved his car every few hours, parking it on the side streets. He watched the warehouse from cafes, benches, and doorways. At night he moved the car back to where he could view both the warehouse and its parking lot. He slept in the car, if you could call it sleeping. This was the boring—and lonely—part of the job. He was beginning to think the stakeout had been a lousy idea.

And then in the dead of the third night, around three o'clock, he saw a shadowy figure dressed in black circling the warehouse. He'd hoped for a shipment. Instead it looked as if he'd gotten a burglar. But in this business, assumptions were dangerous. They could get you killed.

Bolt slipped out of his car and quietly followed.

CHAPTER
5

The figure hesitated in front of the warehouse's side door, and then disappeared inside.

Bolt pulled out his SIG-Sauer and ran quietly toward the building, his adrenaline pumping. The padlock lay on the ground; it'd been picked again. He listened at the door, cracked it open, listened again, and slid into the musty interior.

Silently he closed the door behind him.

The only sound was of feet moving rapidly away. The figure was heading toward the back, straight through the shadows close to the wall. Had he heard Bolt? Didn't look as if he had.

Bolt sped after, feeling the old exhilaration. His stride ate up the distance, and the pure, rarefied high hit him. It came from running, any running, and the length didn't matter. In school he'd run the one hundred meter and two hundred meter. He'd trained with the rhythm of those distances engraved in his mind. And he'd won. Set records. It was something you never forgot. The running. The winning.

Following the wall, he closed in on the figure as he was about to enter the blackness beneath the balcony. It was a dead end for the guy—no doors, no windows, and nowhere to go but back into the warehouse's cavernous heart. As the figure darted into the darkness, Bolt realized there was something about the way he moved that seemed familiar. What was it?

Now Bolt also slipped into the umbra beneath the balcony. He paused, giving his eyes time to adjust. He studied the area, then the shadowy main warehouse where moonlight from the second-story windows made rectangles on the floor and walls. There was no movement, and no sound.

There was no one, nothing.

The figure had vanished.

Bolt padded through the blackness. He turned back and forth, the SIG-Sauer waist high, looking for a target. There had been something familiar about the way the guy ran? Did Bolt know him?

Bolt continued forward, rotated, and stepped again, searching.

Then there was sudden shock. Pain. Heavy weight crashing down onto his shoulder.

Bolt staggered back.

The figure! It landed catlike on its feet and lashed out with a karate kick to Bolt's other shoulder. And then it tore away, escaping across the long shadowy floor.

Bolt fell, surprised and off-balance. But he was grinning. Hiding in rafters was one of her favorite tricks.

"Sarah!" he bellowed into the warehouse. He stood up, the image perfect in his mind of the last time he'd seen her: Stark naked on the edge of a steamy Jacuzzi in Tel Aviv. Only a man with formaldehyde in his veins would ever forget how Sarah moved.

"Sarah Maizlish," he boomed again.

There was a pause, then her voice echoed back, astonished. "Jacob?" She turned and ran toward him. Dressed head to foot in tight black pants, jacket, and knit cap, she was almost invisible in the faint light.

He grinned wider. There was no one quite like Sarah. And it wasn't just the pyrotechnic body. He opened his arms.

"Hey," he said, "it's been a long time."

She slammed a solid *age zuki* rising punch to his chest. Rotated. And blasted a *ushiro kekomi* kick to his chin.

"Not long enough!" she told him, furious.

Pain shot through his ribs, connected with his jaw, and shot through his skull. He dropped to the floor again. Down, but not finished. His eyes cleared. His hand snaked out. He grabbed her ankle. He jerked. She'd caught him completely unawares. Females did that to you sometimes, he thought ruefully.

"What the hell's wrong?" he asked.

She fell beside him. "You don't remember? You *are* an asshole!" A dusky smell of roses radiated from her. He knew it wasn't perfume; it was his memory. She kept rolling, aimed a scissor kick at his head. He ducked, only a moment to spare. She was a top Mossad agent, and great at karate.

She slashed a fist at his jaw. Before she could connect, he grabbed the arm, then the other, and flipped her over onto her back. She struggled against him, trying to break free.

"I give up," he said, straddling her hips as he tried to keep her arms pinned. "What'd I do?" She was soft and round and tough, all at the same time. Irresistible.

"You stood me up!" Saying the words reminded her again of how angry she was. She broke free enough to swing a fist at his jaw.

"I stood you up?" He ducked, incredulous.

"Delhi," she snapped. "Arunachal Pradesh."

Well, he'd learned one thing: When she was talking, she quit trying to hit him.

"Delhi," he echoed, encouraging her to go on.

"The Indians were conducting exercises, and the Chinese were getting mad," she said irritably.

Now it came back to him. He and Sarah were gathering intelligence on a military build-up in the Arunachal Pradesh, a disputed area between China and India on the strategic watershed of the Brahma Putra River. They'd made a date to meet at a cafe they knew for dinner, drinks, and whatever developed. Their stay at the Tel Aviv Jacuzzi was the time before that. And she was right: He'd stood her up. And he'd forgotten.

"Langley changed my assignment," he explained. "Suddenly."

"Right," she sniffed. "Tell me another one."

"Langley tracked me down to a tank, for chrissakes!" Bolt said. "They sent a helicopter to pick me up on the field. I couldn't even get my stuff out of the hotel. And then they flew me straight to Macao. They went to a lot of trouble to keep it secret. How in hell could I get in touch with you?"

"You're the hotshot. Isn't communication your specialty?"

"You know damn well that's not the point."

"Ah, then you admit you don't communicate well," Sarah purred.

"Sarah," he warned.

He wished he could see her face, but the light was too faint. He imagined her blue eyes blazing.

She had a hell of a temper. He chuckled. It was time to change tactics.

"I apologize," he said.

"What?"

"I'm sorry."

"I can't hear you."

"I'm sorry!" he shouted into the warehouse.

"We-ell," she said.

"Besides," he continued, "you're gorgeous. Brilliant. And when you're not mad at me, very nice." He felt her relax under him. This was more like it.

"Hmmm," she said.

"I've missed you, Sarah. Really."

"How much?" she said, lifting her lips.

He looked down at the face veiled in darkness. In his mind he could see every contour of it, and every plane and curve of the body that was trapped, no longer struggling, between his legs. He remembered Tel Aviv, the Jacuzzi, and their three days in bed. The only time they'd gotten up was to eat and go to shows. And then they'd come directly back. To bed. Three perfect days. Desire spread warm up from his groin.

He kissed her roughly and pulled her up. Reluctantly, but both of them had to be on their feet nevertheless. He had work to do, and so did she.

"Hey," she said, disappointed.

"You on assignment?" he said.

"And if I am?" She dusted herself off.

"What was stored here?"

"*Was* is the operative word, isn't it?" she said, accepting the need to do business. "You've searched?"

He nodded. "Completely empty. Even the pictures on the walls are gone."

They strolled back toward the door. She took his hand. He squeezed hers. They were in the same profession, and even if they had despised one another, which they didn't, that unity of the work, the danger, the pressure was a bond that set them apart from others. Add to that genuine respect and hot, explosive sex, and you had an affair that resumed whenever their work brought them together. They had been doing this off and on for more than five years, and would probably continue until one of them died or left the service. Of which they never spoke.

"We figured that might be the case," she said, "but I had to check to make sure."

"If Mossad is interested," Bolt said, "then whatever was here must've been important." Such as . . ."Weapons?"

"Right. One of our people heard that a new Muslim terrorist group has something big planned, and it's related somehow to this warehouse. They apparently used the building for storage and transfer. Probably won't be back again." She stopped and kicked a pile of wood that had once been a crate. "What about you?"

Bolt leaned over. He hadn't searched through any of the shattered crates. He took his flashlight from his belt, turned it on, and lifted wood pieces. He examined them in the light and then set them aside, making a new pile. She knelt beside him and, using her flashlight, did the same.

"Put simply," he said, "I'm tracking the assassin of one of our computer experts. The assassin—man or woman, I don't know which—also killed a Japanese agent who was bossing an international cocaine ring. Have you heard of Cherry Blossom?"

"Tell me."

Bolt was halfway through the pile and had found nothing yet. He described the killer coke ring. "This guy—whoever he is—killed both Bushi Nakamura and Iwa Matsumoto."

She was disgusted. "The guy's vicious. He disemboweled Nakamura *after* he killed him? That's sick."

"Not one of our finer human specimens," he agreed. "Then the yakuzas came after me in Hawaii."

"Hawaii?"

"A little vacation," he explained.

"Oh." She knew Bolt and his vacations. "Who was she?"

He heard the warning in her voice. Jealousy on the rise. She could explode in another tantrum. He didn't want to deal with it now. And he wanted to keep her in a good mood; he had plans for them later.

"She's dead now," he said. Short, factual, and to the point. "She was a yakuza, and she set me up for a hit."

They moved to another woodpile and continued searching.

"Was she pretty?"

"Pretty, but not beautiful like you."

"And she's dead now?"

"Very."

"Good."

Altogether there were seven piles. They checked six and then moved onto the last.

"She's how you came to this warehouse?" Sarah said.

"I found the address in her compact," he confirmed. He told Sarah about locating the warehouse, questioning shopkeepers, then staking out the building.

"As always, you're thorough, Jacob." She set aside a cracked board from the last crate. "This looks like a bust. For both of us."

"Maybe not," he said. He picked up a piece of crumpled, dusty paper from beneath the crate's rubble.

"What is it?"

"Don't know." He held it up to the light. "Good rag bond. Got a lighter?"

"How about a match?" From a pocket she took a small, flat waterproof container. Inside were a half-dozen wood matches.

"My beautiful heroine." Bolt struck a match and moved it beneath the paper. If there were a message written on the paper in an organically based colorless ink—milk, lemon juice, vinegar, saliva, even urine—heat would make the ink burn. What would be left would be a carbon-based substance, a natural byproduct of combustion, and what had been invisible would then be readable.

The edge of the paper smoked and caught fire. "Damn." Bolt blew out the match and tamped out the fire. He lit another match and moved it beneath the paper. A spot on the paper turned brown from the heat. Then another spot. The spots smoked.

"Heat's not going to do it," Sarah observed.

"Come on." He blew out the match and stood.

"Where?" she bristled. Sarah didn't take orders from *him*.

He laughed and grabbed her arm. "Your HQ." He pulled her toward the door. "We need infrared or ultraviolet light."

CHAPTER
6

Sarah Maizlish drove through the silent nighttime streets of Jerusalem. Behind her Jacob's solitary headlights followed.

Jacob Bolt. He was like her, all fire and competition. And yet he had coolness, distance. It enabled him to stay where others lost their nerve. She envied him that ability to separate himself; she was always in the midst of the flames, the chaos, part of it herself. She didn't know why it had to be that way for her, only that that was the way it was. Like a junkie, she needed her fix. And Jacob, with his own ambitions—was it ambition?—sometimes got in her way.

Overhead the crescent moon was just past the three-quarters stage, and Jerusalem's worn stones and historic streets glowed with an ashen, moonlit luminescence. Maizlish sighed and felt the old pull. The timeless city, its graphic reverence for the past, its daytime hustle into the future, made her think of Masada, that long-ago settlement carved atop a mountain plateau above the Dead Sea. The memory of Masada lived uneasily in her soul, and in the collective soul of all Israel.

Tragedy had become inevitable in 70 a.d. when the Romans besieged Masada, a small Jewish Zealot town. After three years of fighting and the Jews' famine, the Tenth Legion finally broke through Masada's stubborn defenses. Defeat was certain, so the Jewish commander encouraged 960 of his followers to commit suicide rather than surrender to the Roman infidels and become slaves. The men agreed, first killing their parents, wives, and children. It was a shock of monumental proportions; even hardened Roman soldiers wept when they saw the self-inflicted massacre.

Nineteen centuries later, Israel's birth reminded the world of that refusal to succumb. Nowadays Israeli army recruits went to the ruins to swear an oath: "Masada shall not fall again!"

Sometimes Maizlish thought it was a disease, this preoccupation Israel had with the past. Yet it seemed necessary so that the tiny nation could forge into the uncertain future. It kept them working together, despite their differences. They built weapons, created state-of-the-art technology, cemented political ties with the West, and crafted an economy that constantly strove for independence. Military service was compulsory for men between ages eighteen and twenty-one, and for women between eighteen and twenty. All men were in the reserves until fifty-five, with at least a month a year on active duty.

Israel was everyone's responsibility, Maizlish had always believed. And so she'd spent her two years of service as a rifle instructor and occasional combat soldier. Afterwards she'd earned a bachelor's degree in archaeology at Hebrew University. Restless, eager to *do* something, she'd sought out the Mossad, the Institution for Intelligence and Special Assignments, one of the world's foremost intelligence agencies. Without realizing it, she was perfect for the job: The child of Polish holocaust victims, she had a remarkable memory, combat skills, and an intuitive flexibility that made her a survivor like her parents. Quickly she discovered that intelligence gathering, with its occasional need for the kill, suited her.

And now she was on a new important assignment, and part of it had become bringing Jacob Bolt back to headquarters.

Professional courtesy, yes. But more, too. He was the ultimate operative. She wanted him—his lean runner's body, his quick mind, his honed skills, his hidden soul. Everything. Being with him was like being with the finest in herself. If times had been different, she would have spent the rest of her life with him.

But now she alternated between wanting to take him to bed and wanting to prove she was better than he. Both desires seemed perfectly natural to her. When they were separated, she stored his memory in a distant part of her busy brain. When she saw him, she ached for him. And sometimes denied the ache. He was, after all, competition. In her own way, she was in love with him.

She drove into the parking lot. The sky was turning gray. Soon dawn would cast a pink haze over the ancient city. She turned off the motor, got out, and stood beside her car, watching Jacob as his wary gaze swept the parking area and the building with professional thoroughness. His face had a compelling intensity, the kind that made a woman's belly tighten when he focused on her.

"Ready?" she said as he climbed out of his car.

"Always ready for you."

He walked toward her with that predator stride she loved. He looked deep into her eyes. She felt the hot impact straight to her toes.

"Let's go." She led him into the building, smiling, then frowning. He was a problem. What did a woman like her do with a man like him?

At this early morning hour, Mossad headquarters was quiet. Telephones rang occasionally. Voices talked in tired tones. The computer consoles in most rooms were dark. A few agents strolled down the halls, nodded at Sarah, and stared curiously at Bolt.

As Bolt passed, he had the sense the agents memorized his face and filed it away for future reference. There was no laxity here.

Sarah walked ahead. She'd pulled off her black watch cap, and her blond cornsilk hair fell loose to her shoulders. In her snug black pants and leather jacket she looked part professional agent and part sex vixen. It was an irresistible combination, Bolt thought as they headed downstairs. She paused to open a door marked *Laboratory*. He followed her through. She was tall and steely slender, and her movements were liquid.

"Hal Kalin will be in in an hour," she told him. Kalin was, Bolt suspected, the number two or three man in the secretive Mossad organization. No outsider would ever know for sure any Mossad member's rank.

"Kind of early," he said.

"Not really."

She turned on a switch and opened a booth.

They went in and closed the door. Beyond them in the laboratory several technicians and scientists worked at tables, in cubicles, at computer consoles, and in booths.

"He must be worried about something," Bolt said. "Or honchoing an important project."

She didn't answer. Instead she turned on the infrared light.

He held up the paper from the warehouse. And there it was, appearing on the paper: a single word, *Dimona*, and a hand-drawn map of some kind of facility. The map was very detailed.

"So that's it," Sarah breathed.

"This your nuclear research center near Dimona?" Bolt mused. "Maybe why Kalin's coming in early?"

She snatched the paper and left the booth. "Jonathan," she called a technician. He came to her, a young, eager puppy. She handed him the map. "See what you can learn about this, will you? Fingerprints, paper source. You know what we want."

"Yes, Sarah," he smiled, happy to help. He went to work at a table where a microscope, a Bunsen burner, and rows of bottles stood.

"The weapons that passed through that warehouse have something to do with your Dimona installation?" Bolt asked.

Sarah went to a telephone and dialed. Impatiently she tapped her foot on the floor.

"And with the new Muslim terrorist group?" Bolt went on, thinking aloud. "Nuclear weapons and conventional weapons both? In the hands of terrorists? If I was dealing with that, I'd come into the office early, too."

"Hal?" she said into the telephone. "I've found what we needed." She glanced at Bolt. "Jacob Bolt's here. He had the warehouse staked out. He's guessed part of it. Shall I fill him in?"

"Now," Bolt said, "the question is, which Islamic country is going nuclear?"

Sarah shook her head. She whispered, "Not here. Come on." She led him back upstairs and into a small, spartan office in which there was a desk, chairs, computer terminal, and political maps of the Middle East spread across two walls.

"Your office?" Bolt wondered as he sat in a canvas chair.

"All mine." She sat behind the desk. She had no window, and the barren room seemed unlived in, as if she were seldom here. Which was probably accurate. She was a field agent. A full-time desk would be a tombstone for her.

"Which is it?" Bolt probed. "Saudi Arabia?"

She smiled grimly. "Iran."

He let the implications sink in. Iran, a nation fueled by hatred and zealotry. Even with the Ayatollah Ruhollah Khomeini dead from cancer some months ago, and the Iran-Iraq war at a supposed standstill, Iran constantly teetered on the sharp edge of violence. The nation's fundamentalist leaders continued to pray for the deaths of other world leaders, and they executed internal political opponents with blood-chilling ease. Iran was not Bolt's idea of a responsible repository for keys to global conflagration.

"Let's be very clear about this," Bolt said slowly. "Iran has nuclear capability?"

"Either has or is very close to achieving."

"You're certain?"

"Our satellite studies show a new underground installation in the mountains north of Tehran, camouflaged to look like a small village in a valley. But there are signs that give it away. Also its location and purpose have been confirmed by a disillusioned Khomeini follower who, unfortunately, is now dead."

"Executed?"

She nodded, her eyes cool. "By Mohammed Masumian's government." The Ayatollah Masumian was Khomeini's successor. "And we've learned about blueprints stolen from a facility in the United States, heavy water taken from a secret European source, and various scientists and engineers kidnapped from Britain and France."

"Where does Dimona fit in?"

Sarah sighed, suddenly tired. "Our source, the one that Masumian executed, had confirmed intel that this new terrorist group was planning to kidnap a top Israeli scientist. The map tells us the scientist targeted is at the Dimona installation. The problem is—which scientist?"

"You—"

A knock at the door interrupted Bolt. Before Sarah could acknowledge the knock, the door swung open.

"Sarah." It was Hal Kalin, Sarah's boss. He nodded brusquely at Bolt, shook his hand. A small, energetic man with thinning gray hair and a sad mouth, he held a lighted cigarette and punctured the air with it as he announced: "Our military computers are down!"

Sarah jumped up. "The whole system?"

When a technologically sophisticated nation like Israel lost its military computers, it lost its defense.   Everything was computerized, from communications to guidance systems. Despite its state-of-the-art Merkava tanks, Uzi submachine guns, and Kfir fighter jets, the country would be a helpless target. Three-quarters of Israel's population, all its major cities and airports, and most of its industry lay within range of Muslim artillery.

Although not officially at war, Israel was always in a stage of siege.

"The computers are down from the Sinai to Lebanon!" Kalin snapped.

He swung away down the hall. Sarah and Bolt were right behind him.

CHAPTER
7

Mossad headquarters was a controlled madhouse. Phones rang up and down the corridors. Technicians ran back and forth, reported readings, answered questions. Agents stopped Kalin to confirm the terrible news.

"The prime minister's on the phone," a bald-headed man with a hawk face announced. The man was standing outside the door to a large meeting room, waiting for Hal Kalin.

Kalin nodded briskly, and he, Sarah, and Bolt entered the room.

A huge world map extended the length of one long wall. The acrid stench of cigarette smoke and tension filled the air. Several men and women were sitting around a conference-size metal table, talking worriedly, their voices rising. The bank of computer consoles was dark, testament to the trouble that had brought everyone here. Coffee perked and tea water steamed on a filing cabinet at the end of the room.

Kalin gestured, and the hawk-faced man closed the door and handed him the phone. Sarah sat at the table. Bolt went for coffee.

"Yes, sir," Kalin said into the telephone. "I'm afraid so. We're on it. No indication what the

problem is. I'll report as soon as . . . Yes, sir. Good-
bye, sir." Kalin handed the phone back to the
hawk-faced man and turned to the world map.
"How long?" Kalin asked, his back to the table as
his gaze settled on the Middle East.

"The computers went down . . ." —the hawk-
faced man checked his watch— "twelve minutes,
ten seconds ago. We called you immediately, but
you'd already left home."

Kalin nodded. "More?" he asked those gathered around the table. He still didn't look at them.

Bolt sat down silently next to Sarah. He handed
her a cup of black coffee and drank his. It was hot
as hell. He noted that she simply cradled hers as if
trying to warm herself from a deep chill.

"It appears to be a problem in the central
system," a woman with a halo of curly iron-gray
hair reported.

Kalin turned to face the table. "Hardware?
Software? What?"

"As you probably remember," lectured a man
with horn-rimmed glasses, "our military and intelligence machines are physically and electronically
isolated from other nonclassified computers."

"Yes, yes," Kalin said impatiently. "I know.
To keep intruders out."

"And the rooms are lined with copper mesh so
eavesdroppers can't pick up radio emissions," Sarah
reminded him.

Which was critical, thought Bolt. Classified
computers were used for everything from designing nuclear weapons to guiding photo-intelligence
satellites. The computers stored information that
Israel's enemies would risk anything to acquire.

"There's no way to dial into a secure computer

by outside telephone," the man in the horn-rimmed glasses continued. "You have to phone from another secure facility and use encripted communications—"

"What are you getting at?" Kalin interrupted.

"What he's saying," Bolt explained, "is that it seems to be an inside problem. That it's in the programming, which under less secure conditions could've been tampered with from an external source." The council watched Bolt attentively, waited to hear what else he'd say. "The problem's not in the hardware—not in the wiring or the chips, for instance. It's in the software."

"That's what I was leading up to," the man in the horn-rimmed glasses confirmed.

"Is it sabotage?" the hawk-faced man demanded.

"Did Syria or Iran or Iraq break into our system?" asked the gray-haired woman, her voice rising self-righteously with each word.

"Has one of our people been compromised?" said another man, his sun-leathered face tight. "Has someone betrayed us!"

The phone rang, and the hawk-faced man snatched it up. He listened, and turned agitated to Hal Kalin. "The media's heard about it, sir! They want an explanation!"

Kalin grimaced and shook his head. "Tell them everything's under control. We're conducting . . . computer experiments. They'll have a full report soon."

The hawk-faced man spoke calmly into the phone, relaying his chief's message in reassuring tones while his own nervousness throbbed in a vein on his forehead.

"They won't buy that for long, Hal," the man in

the horn-rimmed glasses warned. "We're a nation besieged by neighbors. Our people could panic!"

"Hal," the gray-haired woman said, "we can't let the Arabs take over our system! Can't we do a manual launch?"

"First strike, Hal!"

"If they've got our computers, they've got us!"

"We have to get them first! We learned that lesson in '67!" The voices clamored for action. The tension was electric. Some would call the Israelis' response realistic, others paranoid. Yet the tiny nation had remained alive because of its constant battle to maintain technical and informational superiority, and its bloody wars to defeat and humiliate its enemies. But these days the future seemed to be slipping away from Israel. The country was losing its technological edge, and recent skirmishes showed that the Muslims—through fighting one another—had acquired the materiel and the know-how to win. It was only a matter of time until they turned their new expertise against the hated Jews.

"We don't know that there's another nation involved!" Kalin insisted. "And even if there were, which one?"

They hesitated, seeing Kalin's logic. Maybe it was simply a system failure. But if it were sabotage, which of their many enemies? How did the saboteurs get access? What did it mean? Unless they had more information, they could do nothing!

And then the unexpected happened.

"Look!" Bolt said, astonished. And yet somehow he'd suspected . . . It was the same pattern as the other failures worldwide.

The group turned to stare speechless at the

bank of consoles. Colored lights were blinking as merrily as if the system had never been off.

"It's on again!" the hawk-faced man said unnecessarily.

"It must've been a system failure," the man with the horn-rimmed glasses decided.

In relief, the group continued to watch the bright lights. Somewhere a printer clicked on and began automatically to feed out data.

The group turned to stare across the table at one another, fighting to calm the adrenaline that could have sent them into a first strike. Except that their eyes promised one another they hadn't really meant it, that they would never agree to something so irresponsible. But beneath the promises, Bolt saw two thousand years of fear and disenfranchisement—the homeless Jew wandering from shtetl and ghetto to the prayed-for salvation of "next year in Jerusalem."

"Be nice to know what happened," Bolt told Kalin. But privately he was already comparing the sudden computer stoppage and resurrection to the telephone interruption in Hawaii and the series of other recent, odd electronic phenomena that had been afflicting computer and communication systems around the globe. What in hell *was* going on?

Hal Kalin nodded. He took a deep breath and gestured for the telephone. Bolt waited silently while the room emptied of all but Kalin, Sarah, and himself.

Kalin dialed, announced himself, listened at length, and at last hung up. He took a handkerchief from his pocket and mopped his face while Bolt and Sarah waited. His sad mouth seemed even sadder.

"The security people will get back to me,"

Kalin told them. "I know you want to know what caused the problem, Jake, but I doubt I'll be able to tell you. It'll be need-to-know. You understand. Unless there's something you can help us with, of course." He smiled wryly and turned to his agent. "Now, Sarah, at least *you've* brought me some success. Tell me about the Arabs' warehouse." He went for a cup of coffee.

Sarah described the empty building, their search, and Bolt's discovery of the map. It seemed a long time ago now.

"The map's in the lab?" Kalin said. He held his cup in one hand and dialed with the other. When he hung up, he said, "There's a set of prints, but no match to any in the computer. The paper and ink are common, probably from Egypt. The message appears to be one to four weeks old."

"Not much help." Bolt paused. "So, Sarah, when do we leave for Dimona?"

"You're not going!" Sarah said instantly.

"I found the map," Bolt said reasonably.

She turned to Kalin. "He's *not* going!"

Bolt drank the rest of his coffee, which was now cold. Still, he wanted the caffeine. Needed it.

"I guessed what was happening with the nuclear business," he continued. "You told me the rest. Seems to me you'd better keep me under surveillance so I don't spill the beans or accidentally muck up your plans." He grinned at Sarah. "Personal surveillance."

She rolled her eyes.

"He's got a point," Kalin said.

"He *always* has a point. He's maddening that way when he wants something. Him and his logic!"

"I have other attributes," Bolt promised.

Her eyes widened and narrowed. Bolt thought he detected a certain softness. Maybe even come-hither sexiness. But it was quickly gone. The blue eyes were steely again. He smiled. She was one beautiful, hard-nosed lady. But she was going to have to put out a lot more rejection than this to discourage him.

"*You* watch him," she told Kalin and headed for the door. "I've got work to do."

"Take him, Sarah," the Mossad man said. "He may be useful to you."

"Hal insists," Bolt said. "Don't you, Hal?"

Hal Kalin laughed. "I'll have a Jeep ready for you here at six tomorrow morning. Sharp. It's not a bad drive, but better to do when you're rested. Get some sleep, Jake. You look dead." He waved them toward the door and picked up the phone to make more calls.

Bolt waited for Sarah to exit into the hall. When she was out of hearing, he stuck his head back into the room. "Send the Jeep to Sarah's place," he told the Mossad man.

"You're sure?" Kalin said.

"Positive."

"She's not easy."

Bolt chuckled. "And I've got the bruises to prove it."

He wanted her. Intended to have her. Exhausted or not. As soon as possible. As often as possible. But first he had to break through her bristly guard. She'd been like this before, and he figured it was only a matter of time until he wore her down.

He left Kalin shaking his head, and he trotted after Sarah.

"Let's get breakfast," he said when he caught up with her. That seemed like a safe opening. "I'll buy."

She kept walking but looked at him. A big concession.

"You're filthy," she announced rudely. "You'll scare donkey drivers and offend Mercedes owners. No one'll serve you."

"Oh."

He looked down. He hadn't changed since he arrived in Jerusalem. Dirt and grease from the warehouse caked his clothes. But all was not lost. This was a perfect opening for a better plan.

"We'll go to your place," he amended. He thought: take a shower together, see what develops. He said: "Get cleaned up, then get breakfast."

She looked startled, then suspicious.

"Haven't had a chance to get a hotel room," he said quickly. "Been living out of the car."

It was every agent's pain in the ass. You're bored, uncomfortable, you sweat from inactivity and fear of activity, and eventually you stink. But you're on stakeout. Sometimes Bolt thought that intelligence organizations lost more agents to boredom and discomfort than to incompetence, death, or transfer. Anyway, it was an explanation Sarah would understand.

"Okay," she said, hesitated, and added sternly, "but don't try anything."

"Wouldn't dream of it," he lied.

CHAPTER
8

In Hebrew, Jerusalem is Yerushalayim, "City of Peace." In Arabic, it is El-Quds, "The Shrine." Bolt considered this as they drove west past the city's walled and divided sectors and up into picturesque countryside on the slope of a hill. Sarah was driving. Bolt's car remained back in the Mossad parking lot where one of the agents would return it to the rental place.

Beneath them in the distance lay the square-kilometer heart of the town, the historic Old City, while around it the modern metropolis jutted, sprawled, and climbed over forty-two square miles. This City of Peace, this Shrine had been, ironically, the cause of more warfare than any other piece of comparable real estate on Earth.

"Here we are," Sarah announced and parked at the side of a rocky street. "En Karem. John the Baptist's birthplace. I live up there." She waved at the second story of a white-washed building where pink geraniums bloomed in window boxes.

"*En* means spring," Bolt said, scanning the scenic village, "and *karem* means vineyard. Looks like you've got both."

"Now it's a big artists' colony, too."

They got out of the car. Bolt took his suitcase

from the trunk. Up and down the street villagers
came and went from galleries, cafes, stores, and
restaurants. The pungent odor of cardamom tea
and baking breads sweetened the air. Handmade,
sun-bleached wood tables and chairs stood outside
the houses. Curtains fluttered in the warm breeze.

"I like En Karem because it's . . . different,"
Sarah said as she led Bolt up wood steps to a balcony.

"Looks like a good place to come home to,"
Bolt agreed politely. He was watching his manners.

On the balcony, she stopped at the door and
flipped through her key ring. Sunlight shimmered
platinum in her pale hair. A scent of roses surrounded her. It was his memory again. He considered tossing her over his shoulder and kicking in
the door.

Instead he said, "Need some help?"

"You've got to be kidding." She unlocked the
door.

"Yeah, I was kidding."

They walked inside.

The small studio was crowded, the opposite of
her spartan Mossad office. It was if she'd com-
pressed a full, secret life into the sanctuary of these
four walls.

She liked comfortable old things—there was a
worn wingback sofa with a crocheted afghan folded
over the back, two cane chairs, scarred end tables,
antique lamps, and a small campaign bed pushed
into a corner. A neat, practical kitchenette filled
another corner. She was a great reader—books and
magazines crammed a ceiling-high bookcase and
overflowed onto every surface. Her family was

important—framed photographs of a bald-headed man, a thin, smiling woman, and herself as a freckle-faced child growing to womanhood filled a wall. He remembered she'd told him that her parents were both dead now. An heirloom silver menorah stood in an arched alcove. And there was a final clue to the mysteries of the elusive woman who lived here: dust covered everything, preserving through neglect what was obviously a cherished refuge.

"Coffee?" she said, shucking off the leather jacket and heading for the kitchenette, hips swaying nicely in the snug black pants. An interesting, complicated lady. "Or do you want to shower first?"

"Shower," he said. Enough was enough. He dropped his suitcase and headed toward her. "With you."

She backed off, eyebrows raised, indignant. "You said you wouldn't try anything!"

"Hey, be practical." He grinned. "You've got enough dirt on you to make the Missouri River look like purified drinking water."

"Jacob!" she warned, circling away backwards around the sofa.

"Imagine how good it'll feel," he said, following. "The shower, I mean."

"And I've got a bridge I'll sell you, if you think I believe that's what you're up to!" She backed toward the front door. "I shower alone!"

"I remember a few times you didn't."

Her eyes flashed sultry blue. She fell back against the door.

He slammed his hands down on the doorjamb, trapping her. She wasn't fighting him, not yet. But she could attack in an instant.

"Do you remember?" he asked quietly.

She stared up at him. Beneath the angry expression of her face some inner battle raged. Something to do with him, and her, and them.

"Khartoum," he told her. "Remember the Lord Nelson, with the sandstorm shaking the windows?" Frustrated Libyan agents had searched for them for hours. "And Cairo? Dinner on the Nile?" AK-47 bullets ripped out the yacht's hull beneath them, and they'd escaped drowning to spend the night in hot sex in sweet-scented hay in the remote countryside.

Her lashes flickered. "I remember."

He touched her hair. "You always smell like roses," he told her.

"There were roses in the room at the Lord Nelson." She lifted her lips, the conflict over. Now her eyes smoldered sapphire with memories, promises. Desire.

He slid his fingers through the thick, silky strands, pulled the face up to his. His mouth devoured hers. The wet honey taste of her.

Her tongue darted hungrily over his teeth, through his mouth. Heat exploded in his groin. She tugged at his shirt, fumbled at the buttons, at last pulled it off. He peeled her turtleneck up over her head, undid the black lace brassiere. The porcelain breasts swung free, pink-nippled. His fingers fanned over the round, satin flesh. She shivered, moaned, leaned against him. Hot naked chest to hot naked chest. The skin on fire.

"No shower," he said gruffly.

"Later," she whispered, unzipped his pants.

They went to the bed.

Afterwards they slept, showered, and slept again, arms and legs entwined in deep comfort. Bolt had no dreams or nightmares. When he awoke in the long shadows of that same day's late afternoon, he was revived. Vigorous. Beside him, Sarah stirred. He turned, tenderness welling in him. He studied this strange, lovely woman who was among the toughest in their business, yet so vulnerable in bed.

She had an elegant face with high cheekbones, full pouty lips, tiny shell-shaped ears, and soft, tanned skin over fragile-looking bone structure. She was almost too beautiful to be true. Like one of those airbrushed mannequins enshrined in slick magazines. Or a hybrid hothouse flower with no hope of surviving in real sunshine, air, and rain. It made you wonder how she could have a brain in her head. Or lead a useful life. Or be luscious, exciting, and so damn wonderful to sleep with.

Now she lay in the last rays of the day's sunshine. Her dark lashes cast shadows onto her cheeks. He closed his eyes and instantly was back a few hours ago, standing in her tiled shower stall. The water sprayed, beat on them. He picked her up. She locked her slick legs around his hips. He crushed her against him. She kissed his cheeks, his eyes, his lips, his throat. He thrust up into her moistness...

"Jacob?"

He opened his eyes. "Yeah?"

"You're daydreaming again," she told him. "About me, I hope."

Her hand slid down his side to where the sheet thudded up and down. Her cool fingers encircled his furnace-hot cock.

"Baby, you'd better believe it," he said. And rolled her over.

She bit his neck, opened her legs to receive him.

"Did you know," Sarah said later as they finished dressing to go out to dinner, "that Moses was a stutterer?"

"Never heard that before," Bolt said, clipping his SIG-Sauer holster to his belt.

"Well, he was," she continued, her eyes twinkling. She clipped a small holster for her Colt to the waistband of her silk trousers. "So when God asked Moses which country he wanted to take the children of Israel to, Moses stuttered, Ca-ca-ca-na-na-na... Of course, God thought he meant Canaan. By the time Moses finished what he was saying, God was gone and everybody was headed to Canaan. And poor Moses had to hustle his butt. After all, he was supposed to be leading." She smiled and wrapped a shawl around her shoulders. "That's how we ended up in this miserable godforsaken Middle Eastern war zone, surrounded by sand and bloodthirsty Muslims."

"So where'd Moses want to go?" Bolt said. He shrugged into a sports jacket.

"Canada!" Sarah joked ruefully. "Imagine, we Jews could've had Canada!"

They laughed and headed for the door.

"Jacob," she said. "Tell me again how you got that scar on your ear."

"Automobile accident. Got cut by flying glass."

"I didn't remember that."

"Well, it's been a long time since we were together."

"Too long."

On the balcony the night air was cotton-soft and cool. Overhead the black sky sparkled diamond-bright with stars. Somewhere off in the distance, cow bells tinkled, the sound carried across the earth-scented hills on a light wind.

"There's a restaurant I know in the next block," Sarah began.

"Anywhere you want to go," Bolt said.

He took her hand. They walked down the steps.

"You don't have any problems here with ultra-Orthodox sects?" he said.

"Why?" She hesitated. "Oh, because I'm wearing slacks. No. Not in En Karem. Our ultra-Orthodox live mostly in Jerusalem's Mea Shearim district. But you're right. They're very serious about enforcing the *halakah*, the rules that govern everyday life. Women have to wear long-sleeved, high-necked, long-skirted dresses. So if you're a woman—Jewish or not—and you walk through their district, you'd better be dressed respectfully, because if you're not, you're likely to get hassled, and if you're not properly contrite, stoned."

Bolt nodded. "Interesting that Israel's fundamentalists are arising at the same time Islamic fundamentalists are increasing."

"Our ancestors' paths have been tied together for millennia."

They strolled off down the ancient rocky street.

"Here in the Promised Land," Sarah went on, "we've got civilization piled on civilization. Hebrew, Assyrian, Babylonian, Persian, Greek, Maccabean, Roman, Byzantine, Arab, Egyptian, crusader, Mameluke, Ottoman . . . Have I left anyone out?"

They passed a dark, closed pharmacy at the mouth of a narrow, shadowed alley.

He laughed. "You're the student of archaeology, not me." And then, out of the corner of his eyes, he saw movement in the alley.

Instinctively he turned.

Too late.

Black cloths fell over Bolt's and Sarah's heads. Iron hands wrenched back their arms, and the round barrels of revolvers rammed into their ribs.

CHAPTER
9

General Akbar Salehi, commander-in-chief of Iran's armed forces, stood at the open office window of his villa and looked out with satisfaction at the slender, towering minarets of Tehran and the scenic, rugged Elburz Mountains in the distance. Smog had collected at about midpoint on the mountains, but the morning air was cool and refreshing. He inhaled deeply and savored the view of the city. His city. Today was an important day. The beginning of the final stages of his plan.

General Salehi was a beefy man with a handsome swarthy face, large liquid eyes, and a cruel mouth. He knew these physical things about himself with the same dispassion that he knew the world. His world. Iran, the Middle East, the very globe itself. At forty-eight, he assessed himself to be at his intellectual, physical, and sexual prime.

Akbar Salehi was a Shiite Muslim, as were ninety-seven percent of those in Jomhori-e-Islami-e-Irân, the Islamic Republic of Iran. He could be nothing else. Just as a falcon must fly, Salehi must stand before the one and only Allah, Islam's Allah. Only a fool turned his back on who he was, what he was. Salehi drew great strength and determination from his self-knowledge. Already an erect, solid man, he stood even straighter at his office window as he thought about this.

But there was a difference. He smiled, and the cruel mouth took on a look of menace and cold pleasure. It was the difference that now governed his destiny—and Iran's destiny. Unlike most of his countrymen, he had the advantage of a religious commitment tempered by earthly experience.

He'd had the good fortune to be born the only son of Shah Reza Pahlavi's oldest and most trusted military adviser, General Bozorg Salehi. The old general had been a hard master, but young Salehi had respected his legendary father and absorbed the beatings, knowing that with each blow he drew closer to success for Allah—and for the Salehi name.

In the early 1960s, fresh out of Tehran University, Akbar Salehi had begun his career by enlisting in the army. Almost immediately the shah had sent him and other hand-picked young warriors to the United States for sophisticated combat and officer training. For the next fifteen years, Salehi had moved steadily up the ranks, voluntarily leading jungle patrols in Vietnam with a multinational U.N. force, successfully putting down Iran's bloody border skirmishes with the Kurds and the Iraqis, and eventually serving as top military officer at Iran's embassies in Paris, Bonn, and Washington.

Then in 1978 Salehi's father died. About the same time, the shah saw that technology had changed radically, skyrocketing the superpowers' military forces into the computer age. Iran was being left behind. The shah called Salehi home to his father's job, to his father's villa. To his father's unfulfilled dreams.

Salehi remembered with pride his return—the somber ceremonies, the lavish parties, the extravagant promises. Akbar Salehi was considered a hands-on combat fighter, a hero, and the most internationally knowledgeable, the most forward thinking of all the shah's generals. Youthful General Salehi would never question his shah by disputing such an advantageous, if slightly exaggerated, reputation.

As a member of the shah's inner circle, he had the prerogatives, power, and possibilities reserved for a select few. And he had plans no one knew about. After all, back in the 1920s the shah's cossack father had been a simple military officer until he'd deposed the last of the arrogant Qajar dynasty to become shah himself.

In time, Salehi believed, he would do the same. He would oust Shah Reza Pahlavi, who grew more imperious each year, antagonized more supporters, and insulted Allah with his obscene displays of wealth. With the certainty of known destiny, Salehi would take over the Peacock Throne for himself and his sons. *He* would be shah.

But soon after his return, General Salehi's world turned upside down. Street protests and antigovernment demonstrations erupted, directed from Paris by the exiled fundamentalist leader Ayatollah Ruhollah Khomeini. By late autumn Iran was in a state of civil war. In January the shah fled. And so did nearly a million professionals, military leaders, government officials, and their families.

General Salehi acted decisively. He didn't have enough support to take over the monarchy, so he offered his services to the ayatollah. After all, he explained through intermediaries, he'd been outside the country five years. He'd not known how far the nation had strayed from Islam, the extent of the shah's corruption, or the brutality of the shah's secret police, the dreaded SAVAK, which had tortured and killed hundreds of the country's clerics.

The ayatollah's people held General Salehi and his sons under house arrest while they investigated his case. It was a time of bad nerves, terror in the streets, and wrenching screams that echoed through long, wintry nights. Each time his fundamentalist inquisitors interrogated him, General Salehi answered with the diplomatic calm and patience—some would say coldness—that had characterized his highly effective embassy service. He assured them he wished only to serve a man whose piety he could respect, the Ayatollah Ruhollah Khomeini himself.

Meanwhile General Salehi also quietly called in favors owed him and his late father. Two refused. There was no time for persuasion; their remains were buried in his back gardens. Allah would understand; it was all to his glory.

Soon the ayatollah's troops routed the elite Imperial Guard, the last of the shah's resistance. Festive crowds gathered to welcome the Ayatollah Khomeini and his aides as they drove victorious into Tehran.

But by this time Salehi's own miraculous coup was complete, and he stood shoulder to shoulder with the ayatollah's long-time supporters on the steps of the capitol, stood with them as if he'd always been one of them, and greeted the ayatollah as if the ancient cleric were his own beloved father.

It was then that Salehi knew his decision to stay had been right. Zealous and puritanical, the

long-bearded, raspy-voiced, hypnotic Khomeini
cursed the heathen United States as the Great
Satan and prayed for the death of its evil president,
Jimmy Carter.   Yet when the anti-American
Khomeini arrived so gloriously in the capital, he
was riding in a Ford truck.

The irony confirmed General Salehi's observa-
tion of the world.   Successful rulers were more
practical than they let their ideological followers
know. The Ayatollah Khomeini might hate non-
Shiite nations, but he would use them when he
needed them.

Named *velayat faqih*, Khomeini became Iran's
top religious leader, charged with overseeing the
new Islamic government.   In hoarse, whispered
rhetoric, he promised a righteous new day for Iran.
He issued directives restricting life-styles, food,
clothing, schools, and banks. The sexes could no
longer mingle or speak in public.   All Western
influences were eradicated, especially music, dance,
and free speech.

Salehi watched all this come to pass with little
interest because it was business as usual in the
only area that interested him: power. Under the
Ayatollah Khomeini's rule, life was the same as it
was everywhere—no rules. Survival of the fittest.
Which Salehi understood, preferred.

And so while other leaders in the military were
purged, General Salehi survived. He lived through
the long years of the war with Iraq, again working
his way into a position of trust, and, at last, of
power. Now pragmatic General Salehi had the
support he needed. The mad dog Khomeini was
dead, and the less-effective Ayatollah Mohammed
Masumian was Iran's new supreme religious au-

thority. But that would change soon, too.

The buzzer on his intercom sounded.

"Yes?"

"The colonel's here, sir."

"Send him in."

General Salehi, commander-in-chief of Iran's armed forces, smiled his cruel smile and contemplated the simplicity, the perfection, the inevitability of his plan.

His top aide, Colonel Ahmed Rizvi, entered Salehi's villa office and bowed.

"How are you today, my general?" Rizvi asked in Farsi, although he could just as easily have asked in English or Arabic. He was a small, weasel-faced man with a thin beard, dressed in the same crisp, tan army uniform that Salehi wore.

"Very well," Salehi answered, also in Farsi. "And you?"

"Well enough to look into the future with pleasure."

Salehi nodded acknowledgment. Rizvi was telling him he brought good news.

"Welcome to my home." Salehi gestured graciously at Rizvi's usual seat, and sat himself behind his long rosewood desk.

The small man sat, too, crossed his legs. Over the years the two had acquired certain rituals establishing that they were more than superior and inferior, but that they knew, as friends knew, what to expect from one another. By watching his father, Salehi had learned that to bind another person through emotions into one's service was to have more than a friend, but to have a willing slave. Rizvi had and would again kill for him.

They had met when they were both students at

Tehran University. Rizvi had attached himself to Salehi, seeing that Salehi could fulfill the ambitions Rizvi would never do more than imagine. In turn, Salehi had quickly realized Rizvi's potential. He had convinced his father to intervene with the shah to send Rizvi to train with him in the United States. After that, Rizvi had followed Salehi from post to post, sometimes spending a year or two under another commander, but always coming back to Salehi. Rizvi had aged well, growing narrow, mean, bullheaded, and tireless in service to Salehi, his future shah.

"Are we ready?" General Salehi asked.

Colonel Rizvi nodded. He seldom showed emotion, but now he allowed himself the indulgence of a thin-lipped smile. "The installation is complete."

"Tell me."

"Everything is ready," Rizvi reported. "We've checked the instrumentation. The computer system is in place, hooked into your system here and in the capitol. The foreign engineers and scientists have done their jobs . . . just as you said they would."

General Salehi had chosen the site carefully. Most of the complex was buried beneath the ragged surface of the Elburz Mountains north of Tehran. The installation had the convenience of being roughly a hundred miles from the city yet hidden in a valley, dug into a stable mountainside in a virtually uninhabited wilderness. The general often watched the mountains from his office window, imagining with pleasure the work that went on in this vital installation.

"And the foreigners?" Salehi rested his elbows on his desk and made a triangle of his fingers. Some of the foreigners had thought they could resist, but all of them cooperated—eventually.

"Once the installation is running, they think they will be returned to their countries."

Salehi rotated the fingers to his chin and then back, pointing at Rizvi. "And?"

"When we no longer need them, the Falcons will execute them, of course. No one must know what we are doing, the extent of our triumph. Until you wish it known."

"Exactly. So. We are ready . . . as they say . . . to pull rods?"

"Start up the reactor. Then we can arm our long-range ballistic missiles as well as some of our battlefield weapons. Put nuclear warheads on everything from shoulder-fired antiaircraft missiles to advanced anti-aircraft, air-launched surface-attack, and ground-launched anti-ship missiles."

The general's broad face thickened with satisfaction. "Few places in the Middle East, Europe, Asia, or Africa will be beyond our grasp. Our missiles will arrive with little or no warning. There'll be no defense against them. And with nuclear warheads, our attacks will mean annihilation." He spread his fingers on his desk and looked at them as if they pointed the way to heaven.

"Once you have given Iran nuclear capability, the Majlis and *mullahs* must honor you," the colonel added softly. "The nation is dispirited. Iraq grows stronger, Israel laughs at us, the superpowers want only to talk about oil . . ."

The general and his long-time aide locked gazes,

almost affectionately, thinking of what the future held. For both of them. For Iran.

The Majlis and the *mullahs* were the two groups Salehi needed to convince—or defeat—to become shah.

Iran's parliament, the Majlis, was the legislative body that in 1925 had elected Reza Pahlavi's father shah. The mullahs were Shiite Muslim clerics whose underground war more than a half century later had deposed Shah Reza Pahlavi, brought the fundamentalist Khomeini to power, and created a nation ruled by religion. With the Ayatollah Mohammed Masumian as Iran's new head, the unbending mullahs continued to preside over Iran with brutal fists, leveling death sentences on their political opponents and on those who offended what they perceived to be Allah's law.

Neither Majlis nor mullahs would be easy to deal with. But General Salehi had four advantages: As commander-in-chief, he had the control and the backing of Iran's military. He also had his own private, unimpeachable, elite force—the Desert Falcons. The Falcons had overseen the building, staffing, and equipping of the nuclear facility in the Elburz Mountains, so secret that neither the Majlis nor the mullahs knew of its existence. That was his third, very convincing weapon—the nuclear facility, a project every commander-in-chief had tried to put together since Prime Minister Ali Razmara's government in 1950. And then there was his fourth advantage—his will. If necessary, he would mount a bloody coup.

"You've picked the Falcons for tomorrow night?" the general asked.

"Of course. Two dozen. Fine soldiers for Allah.

They've memorized the map and the face of the scientist. We fly into Jordan, and Jeep the rest of the way across the desert. Afterwards, helicopters will fly us out. The Israeli installation is a few miles outside Dimona."

"This scientist is our last key," the general said. He stood and paced around his desk. "He will start up our facility correctly, and then he will train our people to run it."

The general circled back to his chair. His home office was large and cool. He preferred it to his capitol office, but soon he must leave and go there anyway. There would be paperwork to read and calls to make. He must make small talk with the ayatollah and the prime minister, the leaders of the mullahs and the Majlis.

He must listen to complaints, sign orders, oversee the continuing problem of reintegrating veterans from the Persian Gulf War and finding husbands for the widows.

Perhaps the worst repression of the religious regime was the requirement that all women must wear full-length black *chadors*. This the general regretted. They moved anonymously along Tehran's sidewalks like invisible shadows. You could never get a look at them. He missed blond women, a rarity even in the shah's time, since they were either tourists or foreigners married to Iranian men. Yes, he preferred blonds to all others. It had been a long time since he'd had a blond woman, a real all-over blond woman.

He sat in his chair. Tomorrow would be different. A good day. Tomorrow he would be with his Falcons. That night they would mount the raid at the Israeli installation. For a brief time he would be a soldier again. The most honorable of all professions. Yes, tomorrow was a day to look forward to.

"Come along," he told the colonel. "I want to see them."

He left his chair and headed for the door, Colonel Rizvi following. They moved briskly along a tiled second-story alcove and down open stairs past a large inner courtyard. The old, elegant villa stood on six acres on a shady, tree-lined street on a rise above the center of Tehran. It was secluded and wellprotected by patrolling Falcons armed with AK-74s.

The sentries, with their distinctive shoulder badges of gray falcons in flight, snapped to attention and saluted as the general and colonel passed.

At last the general stepped inside the barracks. Two dozen men leaped to their feet, saluted. They looked as sleek, muscular, and intelligent as the bird whose name they bore. Salehi had great admiration for the predatory falcon, its endurance, its courage. He had great admiration for these men.

"There is no god but God, and Muhammad is the Messenger of God!" the general greeted them in a ringing voice. It was the *shahada*, the confession of faith professed by all Muslims.

"And Ali is the Friend of God!" the Falcons shouted in return, reaffirming their passionate claim to be Shiite, not Sunni Muslims. "*Allahu-Akhbar*! God is great! *Allahu-Akhbar*! God is great!"

General Salehi shouted with them, encouraging them, feeling the thrill of Allah, of power, the future, deep in the marrow of his bones.

"*Allahu-Akhbar*! God is great!"

"*Allahu-Akhbar*! God is great!"

CHAPTER
10

That night in the alley in En Karem west of Jerusalem, Jake Bolt felt a fleeting moment of panic. It
was instinctive, visceral. The pitch-black cloth
suffocated him. He was immobile, arms pinned.
And painfully aware of the gun jammed into his
ribs. As Clifton Olds, his Washington control,
would observe dryly: "The odds stink, my boy."

But his attacker had made a mistake. He'd let
Bolt know where the gun was.

In a single swift motion Bolt grabbed the muzzle
and slammed an arm back in a *ushiro hiji-ate*
elbow strike into the guy's belly. The man gasped,
choked.

At the same time, Bolt heard a thud and groan
nearby. Sarah!

The attacker's gun felt like a rifle. Bolt twisted
it aside, yanked off the black shroud, instantly took
in the situation.

There were two men. Japanese. Damn! The
yakuzas again! Why in hell were they after him?
In the shadowy alley, their faces were smooth-
cheeked masks of determination.

Near him Sarah ripped off her black hood and
slashed the hard flat of her hand at the throat of her
yakuza thug. Her pale hair flew. Her face glowed.

She was in her element, moving with the strength and agility of the trained karate fighter, of the warrior who loves the fight.

Bolt's attacker staggered back, swung the rifle up to aim again at Bolt.

Bolt kicked a *mae-keage* snap straight at the rifle. But the yakuza recovered. He stepped nimbly out of range. Bolt charged. This time he saw the man's eyes. They were cunning eyes, eyes that deduced he was overmatched.

The yakuza spun on his heel. He raced away down the alley.

Bolt tore after him. He could have shot, maybe killed the yakuza, but he wanted him alive. He wanted to know why in hell they were after him.

The yakuza, shouted something back in Japanese to his companion. Something Bolt couldn't quite make out. A clan code perhaps? Behind him Bolt heard feet pounding—running the other way! Was it Sarah and her yakuza?

Bolt tore out of the alley just in time to see the thug jump into a sleek little MG and zip away through the faint lamplight. Bolt stood there only a second, breathed deeply, and ran again, retracing his path back through the dark alley.

Sarah was waiting. Alone. She stood on the street near where they'd been attacked, holding her evening shawl limp to the ground in one hand, the two pieces of black cloth in the other.

"He got away," she told Bolt, disgusted. "The other one came roaring around the corner in an MG and picked him up. I couldn't stop them." She glared at Bolt. "What's going on? Those two were *not* our usual Japanese tourists. And the Red Army Faction is supposedly moribund in the Bekaa Valley."

"It's a long story."

"I'll bet."

"It's classified."

"You want to go to Dimona?" she said. "Talk."

"And you complain about *my* maddening logic."

"A fair trade. Dimona for those two." She gestured off as if encompassing En Karem, all of Jerusalem, and Israel itself. Which was about as fair a guess as any as to where the two thugs would disappear.

Or maybe they were already heading back. To try again.

"Deal," Bolt decided. Following the lead to Israel's nuclear installation was important. "But we've got to leave right away. As is."

"For Dimona?" She was astonished.

"Anyone ever tell you you're cute when you're surprised?" He walked away down the rocky street.

She sputtered a moment. Then she trotted after.

"First, my car's the other way," she said, controlling her temper. "Second, I want to change clothes, maybe even do a normal little thing called packing. Third, there's no reason to go tonight when Hal's scheduled us to leave in the morning. Fourth, don't ever—*ever*—call me cute!"

He studied the line of cars parked ahead in front of a restaurant.

"First," he said, "we're not taking your car. The guys who attacked were yakuzas, and for some reason I haven't been able to fathom, their gang's been tracking me the last four or five days. If they found me here, that means they know about you. And your car. And your studio. Which takes care of arguments two and three. We're not going back to your studio, so we might as well go straight to Dimona. With luck we'll lose them."

He stopped next to an army Jeep.

"And fourth," he continued before she could interrupt, "you *are* cute, although probably more 'beautiful' than 'cute.' Your cuteness is an unassailable fact, known by all men of the civilized world, and besides it's better than being ugly." He pointed at the army Jeep. "We'll take this one."

She was silent, digesting. "But . . ."

"You know how to drive a Jeep?"

"Of course."

"Then I'll hot wire it." He took her by the elbow and deposited her in the driver's seat.

"I don't like this," she said.

"You'll get used to it."

He stuck his head under the hood. The motor roared to life.

"Hey!" a man's voice bellowed.

"What're you doing!?" yelled another.

Bolt dropped the hood. "Sorry, fellows." He jumped into the front seat. "Let's go!" he told Sarah.

Two Israeli soldiers ran from the restaurant doorway toward them. Sarah hit the accelerator, and the Jeep leaped ahead like a scared rabbit. Shouts and then gunfire echoed behind them.

"We'll stop somewhere," Bolt told her. "Get Hal to call off the army."

"We'll stop all right," she said grumpily. "But *you* phone Hal." She drove for a while. She chuckled. "Maybe now he'll believe me when I warn him about you!"

In the north of the triangular wedge of glistening wasteland called the Negev Desert stands Israel's top-secret nuclear research center. Israel is the world's sixth largest nuclear power after the United States, the Soviet Union, Britain, France, and China.

Bolt stared ahead. Barbed wire and antiaircraft guns surrounded the distant cluster of shoebox buildings, cylindrical towers, lookout posts, and solitary gray dome. The dawn rose pale over the flatlands and encircling sere hills. Already the air was dry and warm. It would be a hot day.

Armed soldiers stopped them and carefully checked Sarah's credentials and called Mossad headquarters to confirm that Bolt was who he and Sarah said he was.

Apparently Hal Kalin was still angry at Bolt for stealing the Jeep and leaving him a mess to explain to the army. So he ordered the soldiers to take Bolt into the squat building that served as a sentry post and frisk him thoroughly, imposing as many indignities as possible.

Bolt suggested they might want to take precautions since he had a loathsome social disease, and—even though they didn't believe him—they stopped their investigation of his orifices and hustled him out of there. It was a triumph of sorts, Bolt supposed. An ancient weapon—suggestive viral warfare.

Sarah was drinking a Coke in the shadow of the building.

"That didn't take long," she said, heading for the Jeep.

"Efficiency," Bolt said. "The mark of the Israeli military."

"Do I detect sarcasm?" she said.

He again hot wired the Jeep, jumped aboard, and they took off down the dusty road toward the nuclear complex.

"Nah. Love it. Think any of your hotshot nuclear scientists can make us some keys for this tin can?"

She was silent. "Just what did those guys do to you back there?"

"It's our secret. I'll take it to my grave."

She was silent some more. "Hal Kalin?"

"He was still pissed. But I escaped, my reputation unsullied."

"They didn't . . . ?"

He smiled. "I told them I had a social disease."

She snickered. Then she thought about it. Suddenly it wasn't funny. "Jacob . . . ?"

"Not a chance, baby." He patted her thigh. Nice long thigh, slightly rounded. Delectable. "I check in with my urologist regularly. Company standards, you know."

She nodded. She knew. All part of the business.

Daniel Lambert, noted physicist and head of Israel's nuclear facility, met them in the air-conditioned, glass-and-concrete lobby of the administration building. He was of medium height and build, fit-looking, with a fringe of gray hair over his ears. Somewhere in his sixties, he exuded health, vigor, and incurable optimism. Bolt liked him immediately.

They shook hands and the trio walked away down the hall. Quietly Sarah told Dr. Lambert about the detailed map they'd found, what little they knew about the Iranian terrorist group, and

Mossad's suspicions that the terrorists planned to kidnap one of the installation's scientists.

"I seriously doubt anyone could carry off a kidnapping here, my dear," the physicist said. He spoke with the faint remnants of an Oxbridge accent. Born in England or educated there, or both, Bolt figured. "We're extremely well-guarded. Almost overguarded, you might say. And there's been nothing to indicate outside surveillance, nothing at all. All reports cross my desk. No unusual incidents. Our security's intact."

"Didn't your computers go down yesterday?" Bolt said.

"Well, yes. Everything in the military went down, as you know. But it was internal. They're still investigating."

"No footprints?" Bolt asked.

"Footprints?" Sarah echoed.

"Traces of an unauthorized user entering or attempting to enter the system," Lambert explained to her. He turned to Bolt. "We have checks to detect anyone trying out codewords. A caller gets three chances to remember his code and encryption numbers. Three strikes, he's out. Or almost. The system notifies security, and security plays along, lets the caller in, follows him around, encourages him to come back until we can determine who he is. We're sanitary, believe me, old boy. No one's tried to enter the system in over a year. And the last one we caught easily. A nineteen-year-old hacker from West Berlin. Something of a genius, I'd say."

They stepped into a long, narrow room with a wall of windows that looked down into a much larger room where white-coated scientists worked at computer consoles that rimmed the walls. The air was cool, odorless, filtered. There was little sound.

"This facility opened in 1964, I understand," Sarah said.

"That's right," Dr. Lambert said. "We started small. Just a twenty-six-megawatt nuclear reactor supplied by France. Eventually we upgraded to one hundred fifty megawatts. Enough to produce plutonium for ten nuclear bombs a year."

"Do you make ten a year?" Bolt asked.

"Perhaps." The scientist smiled.

"Ah," Bolt said. "Hmmm."

"How do you start a nuclear reactor?" Sarah asked curiously.

"First you pull rods," Lambert explained, leading them out the door. "The control rods are made of graphite to slow the reaction. In fact, if we were to have an accident, God forbid, unlike Chernobyl, we have a protective dome to prevent radiation from accidentally releasing into the atmosphere."

They walked down the hall again. Bolt read door titles, noted the cameras at the ends of each corridor, the alarm boxes, the red, blue, and green lights that flashed messages to staff members.

"The rods are just the beginning of very delicate manipulations, of course," the physicist went on. "They absorb neutrons. By controlling neutrons we can control the fission and the chain reaction that result when free neutrons bombard the nucleus of uranium 235. The fission and chain reaction create thermal energy."

"And lead to plutonium and nuclear explosions," Bolt added.

"Exactly," Lambert said.

"Bombs and warheads," Sarah added, understanding.

They followed Lambert out a side door and to
another building.

"Here's our tritium facility," he told them.

They stepped inside. Scientists turned, smiled
at their director. Dr. Daniel Lambert seemed to be
very popular. He joked, teased, shook hands, exchanged greetings, asked about families, introduced Sarah and Bolt, and kiddingly urged his
colleagues back to work.

"Tritium's a radioactive form of hydrogen,"
Bolt remembered. "It's used in nuclear detona-
tions and lasers."

"Ah, yes. This building is where we recover
and purify the tritium that's made in our reactors,"
the scientist said. "Have you visited your Los
Alamos and Lawrence Livermore laboratories where
your people design nuclear weapons?"

"Some time ago," Bolt admitted.

"Good, good. Well, then you'll know that this
is as much as I can show you. National security and
all that. Yes, we must analyze the tritium to make
certain it's the required purity and amount. We use
state-of-the-art, light isotope mass spectrometers
manufactured in Tel Aviv."

They stayed a short while longer, Bolt keenly
aware that he had no idea what the white-coated
professionals were doing.

They left. The sun had risen into a clear azure
sky over the dusty gold hills. Birds circled high
above, riding the heat currents.

"You don't know the purpose of the kidnapping?" Dr. Lambert asked. "We have the finest
physicists, chemists, and engineers in all Israel

here. Good, decent people. If you knew what
specialist the Iranians wanted, we would concentrate security there. Although I still doubt very
much anyone can get beyond our defenses."

"I wish we did know," Sarah said. "The only
intel our informant had was 'a scientist.'"

"I hope your defenses are impregnable, Dr.
Lambert," Bolt added. "No one likes to lose a good
man."

At his villa in Tehran, General Akbar Salehi
sniffed the crisp dawn air. His meteorologist had
predicted clear weather for twenty-four hours across
the Middle East, and it looked as if the information
would be accurate. There were only a few wispy
clouds high in the sky, and no odor of coming rain.

It was a good day for travel. It would be a good
night for battle. And the weather would hold until
tomorrow. At least. Salehi knew. Allah would
provide. Tomorrow the heavens could open in a
massive downpour; Salehi didn't care. But it must
be tomorrow. Not today. Not tonight.

In a few minutes General Salehi, Colonel Ahmed
Rizvi, and their two dozen Desert Falcons boarded
trucks to drive to the airport. There they loaded
onto a transport plane. In its hold were two
helicopters. They flew northwest across Kurdistan
in northern Iraq. They took the shortest route
possible and watched for Iraqi jets. Even though
the war was over, there were still border problems,
and the Iraqis were a restive, unpredictable lot.
Salehi wanted no delays.

At last they crossed into Syria and turned south.
More hours passed and they flew into Jordan where

General Salehi had received permission to land on a flat desert edge of the Rift Valley near the Jordan-Israel border.

It was late afternoon when they arrived at the desolate spot, and the sun's shadows were long across the dry, hard earth. Loaned by the Jordanian military, Land Cruisers were parked in a line, a modern-day caravan waiting to cross the desert.

General Salehi, Colonel Rizvi, and the Falcons left the pilot and copilot to guard the plane. The small, eager force boarded the Land Cruisers and took off toward a seldom-guarded crossing on the invisible line between Jordan and Israel.

As they rode, General Salehi felt himself fill with the old thrill, the exhilaration of the hunt. Soon he would have his prize. The last piece he needed before successfully pulling off his coup. One of the world's greatest nuclear facility administrators. Dr. Daniel Lambert.

CHAPTER
11

It was midmorning at the Israeli nuclear facility, and the heat was intensifying. Bolt and Sarah were still wearing their dinner clothes from the night before. As soon as they stepped back outdoors, Bolt started to sweat. Dr. Lambert led them over concrete paths through the maze of buildings. He pointed out offices, labs, barracks, guest quarters, the cafeteria, and central security.

"Other . . . facilities are underground," said Lambert vaguely. "Sorry," he apologized to Bolt. "Not the sort of thing I can show—or talk about—even to our good friends in the CIA."

"How about security?" Bolt asked. "After all, that's why we're here."

In his office, the security chief, Abbe Hilton, gave them a rundown of the installation's system of computerized surveillance, cameras, monitors, sentry posts, guard schedules, mortars, and rocket launchers. He also described the placement and use of the barbed wire, antiaircraft guns, and minefields on the installation's extreme perimeter.

As usual the Israelis left little to chance.

In fact the thorough security reminded Bolt that in 1981, as a precaution, Israeli jets had bombed Iraq's only nuclear research reactor. The reactor had had a fatal flaw—it was designed to use weapons-grade uranium, which meant that Iraq could soon have been pointing armed warheads at Israel. When the jets had finished, the facility was a pile of rubble.

Bolt wondered whether that would be the fate of Iran's installation, once Israel had confirmed its existence and intent. But perhaps not. Perhaps the balance of power had shifted so much that they would no longer dare such an audacious attack. In 1981 Israel's conventional arsenal and expertise were far superior to the Arab world's. Today the Jews and Muslims were on nearly equal military footing. The Arab's reprisals would be extreme and costly.

"You might want to sort through personnel's files," Bolt suggested to the security chief. "Look for disgruntled employees who've been fired, quit, or maybe even are still working here. The map we found was so accurate that it must've been drawn by someone who knew the facility well."

"Like an employee," Hilton said. "Past or present. What else d'you suggest?"

"Change everything you can," Bolt said, pacing. "Especially your guard schedules. Make them random, so that not all posts change at the same time every day. Randomly rotate the overall schedule every three or four days. Also, tie everything you can into your computer for checking and crosschecking. Is a staff member where he's supposed to be? Is materiel? The computer will know. Put scanners on your antiaircraft guns so that you've got some idea of what's going on at ground level out there. Looks to me by the way you've got the guns placed, scanners would cover your entire perimeter. You'd spot intruders quickly."

"But the area in front of the guns is mined," the security man said. "Anyone who tried to get through would be blown sky high!"

Bolt shrugged. "Looks like this Islamic group's got a hell of a good map."

The security chief stared at Bolt. "I'll order the scanners. Tel Aviv should deliver them tomorrow."

It was noon when they left security. Bolt was dead tired. Every once in a while Sarah seemed to stumble. Bolt took her arm. Lambert suggested they go to the cafeteria. They ate sandwiches accompanied by fresh fruits and vegetables from a garden tended by the kitchen staff. In a way, the facility was a kibbutz.

"Now I think you should sleep," Dr. Lambert told them. "I've taken the liberty of having two of our cottages prepared for you. I assume you'll be staying?"

Sarah nodded.

"For a while at least," Bolt confirmed.

"I must return to my duties," said Lambert. "This young man will take you." He beckoned, and a uniformed youth appeared at his elbow. He held Lambert's chair as the older man arose, his eyes twinkling. "By the way, there's no rule you must use both cottages. Sleep well."

The young man walked ahead, and they followed—out the door, past sand-colored buildings rimmed with grass and flowers whose existence depended on irrigation, and at last to the outskirts of the compound where the glistening desert swept out to the hills. A thousand yards away were anti-aircraft guns and the first stand of barbed wire fencing. Farther yet were the minefields, more barbed wire, and signs in Hebrew, English, and Arabic warning trespassers to stay off. *Government Property. Minefield Ahead*!

With unspoken agreement, Bolt and Sarah went straight into the first cottage.

"The other one's very comfortable, too," the young man told their backs, disappointed. "You might like to see it." He wasn't doing his job if he didn't show both.

"This'll do," Bolt said curtly.

"Thank you," Sarah said. "Please thank Dr. Lambert." Bolt locked the door.

Sarah started stripping. She walked through a small living area toward what looked like a bedroom. The shawl first, then her blouse, trousers, and undergarments in a trail of aromatic silk and lace. This was the hardnosed Mossad agent and karate fighter? Bolt never ceased being amazed—and entranced—by the apparent contradictions in her character.

"They've left jumpsuits for us," Bolt called to her. "An assortment of sizes." They were spread on a small sofa.

The toilet flushed.

He went into the bedroom. She was naked, climbing into bed, pink all over with exhaustion.

"Come to bed," she demanded and closed her eyes.

Amused, he stripped, slid between the cool, clean sheets. She turned on her side, backed up to him.

"Hold me," she told him.

He wrapped his arms around her, buried his nose in her loose hair. It smelled of flowers and soap. She wriggled closer, her smooth buttocks pressed against his groin. His penis rose hard against her back. She sighed.

"Nice," she said.

Almost immediately her breathing became regular, even. She was asleep.

Bolt decided he was too damn tired to be disappointed. He closed his eyes. Soon he fell asleep, too.

Sometime in the late afternoon he felt her warm, wet tongue probing inside his ear.

His cock rose, instantly demanding. He sensed sunlight, dusty outdoor heat. He kept his eyes closed. It was as if he were in a languid erotic dream, and he stayed unmoving in the dream as she flicked her tongue down his neck, his chest, his belly, and enveloped his hot hardness in her soft moist mouth.

And then suddenly the mouth was gone, and she was on top of him. Locked onto him. Teasing. Pulling from him the need . . .

Still in the dream, his breathing grew ragged, deep. His crescendo built.

She gasped, cried out.

He awoke, exploding deep in the steamy valley of her.

Panting, hearts pounding, they broke apart.

Fell back asleep in each other's arms.

The sun sank lower. General Akbar Salehi and his Falcons ate sandwiches and drank from their canteens as the Land Cruisers jarred and rattled cross -country. It was a long day, and would be a longer night. But they had had days of rest and preparation in anticipation of this raid. Now they were eager.

Bolt and Sarah sat side by side eating dinner in the cafeteria, which served breakfast, lunch, and dinner twenty-four hours a day. They were wearing Lambert's jumpsuits, dark blue in color. After six hours' sleep, a shower, and clean clothes, Bolt was feeling human again. Sarah looked wonderful, as usual.

"You look terrific," Bolt said, drinking coffee.

"This old thing?" Sarah kidded. "Aw, shucks."

"Actually," Bolt continued thoughtfully, "you look best in nothing."

"We already did that," she reminded him.

"Yes, thank you. I'd almost forgotten."

"Jacob!" She whacked him in the chest. "You didn't forget!"

After dinner, they separated for a more thorough investigation of the complex. She went through the areas he was forbidden to see, while he retraced the tour Lambert had given them earlier in the day.

They interviewed engineers, scientists, technicians, and sentries. They checked logs for inconsistent entries. Already new guard schedules were posted, effective immediately as Bolt had suggested.

Bolt learned that personnel stayed round-the-clock at the facility for four days, then had three days off to return to their families. With three eight-hour shifts a day, the barracks was always partially full of sleeping staff. Top personnel stayed in private studio apartments adjacent to the barracks. There were at least one hundred employees here at any one time.

Sometime past midnight General Salehi and his men arrived at the place where they were to leave their vehicles. They piled out, formed a straight line in the desert night. The air was cooler, the sand warm beneath their feet. The moon rose ghostly white on the horizon.

The drivers turned the Land Cruisers around, heading back to the plane.

"Who has a hypodermic?" the general asked his elite troops. Four hands shot up. They carried hypodermic needles loaded with a fast-acting tranquilizer, but most likely only one would be necessary. The tranquilizer would sedate Dr. Daniel Lambert so he could be moved out of the installation as fast and as quietly as possible. As a precaution, Salehi carried one also, in case the unexpected happened. You could never be overprepared. He'd learned that in Vietnam.

"Remember, our target will be sleeping in his quarters," General Salehi said. "If an alarm sounds before we reach him, he will go to his command center. Who remembers the location of his quarters and the command center?"

Two dozen hands instantly raised. All remembered. He gazed at his black-clothed men standing tall and brave-hearted in the starry wasteland. Pride filled him. Pride in them, and in himself. Now he must speak. Inspire them as they inspired him.

He chose favorite lines from the Holy Koran. These lines would remind them of their birthright, and that heaven waited for the righteous on the other side of this difficult life:

> *Ye are the best*
> *Of Peoples, evolved*
> *For mankind,*
> *Enjoining what is right,*
> *Forbidding what is wrong,*
> *And believing in God.*

They nodded. Their young faces were radiant. They believed, understood Islam's responsibility and that they were helping to teach the globe to respect their religion. General Salehi offered his Falcons a new, forward-thinking Iran that, nuclear-armed, would once again have status in the Middle East and in the world.

They marched off, carrying their West German G-3 rifles. They wore ammo pouches and fragmentation grenades clipped to D rings on their belts. General Salehi strode sometimes at the front of the line, sometimes at the back. Colonel Rizvi hustled to stay by his side.

As the miles disappeared behind them, the Falcons grew excited. Salehi could feel it. Unleashed from the prison of the airplane and the Land Cruisers, soon they would face their enemy, the Israelis. Like dogs scenting a fight, they geared up psychologically for battle.

Although if all went well they would be in and out of the Jews' facility without detection long before anyone realized Lambert was missing.

They arrived in the dead of night, as planned. It

was the long, dark time when a sentry's boredom accelerated. About two hours before dawn, it seemed to those who must stay awake that the night would never end. The edge needed for watchfulness grew dull. The desire to sleep grew stronger, more compelling, near impossible to deny. The sentry's most consuming job was not to watch, but to fight sleep.

It was General Salehi's favorite hour to mount a hit-and-run raid.

Using their memorized maps, the eager Falcons snipped the first row of barbed wire, slipped through, and separated into two single-file lines. Slowly they weaved among the mines. One step at a time. In the silver light of the nearly full moon, their trail in the sand would guide them back out, making their exit much quicker than their entrance. The two helicopters that the plane had carried in its belly would meet them in the desert out of sight of the facility and fly them back to the plane for the ride home to Tehran.

They cut through more barbed wire and padded on, hunched close to the ground, past the antiaircraft guns. The big guns pivoted, useless as they searched the sky for a target. Just as useless as the informant had promised.

General Salehi raised his hand. It was time for the next part of the plan. He gestured and one group followed him, running toward the guest cottages. Colonel Rizvi took the other group, racing toward the administrative building. Each would circle back toward Dr. Lambert's sleeping quarters.

Suddenly General Salehi's heart thundered. Ahead was a sight he hadn't expected. He gestured his Falcons back into the shadows of the tritium facility. What was the Israeli sentry doing here? He was too soon! According to the informant, the sentry should have passed this point fifteen minutes ago!

The general caught his breath. He sensed the men next to him knotting their hands with frustration. It would be so easy to kill this lone guard. So satisfying. But they must not. The sentry's corpse might be discovered, or his presence missed when he failed to check in at his next point. And that could lead to the Falcons' discovery, and failure!

They stood resolutely in the black shadows as the sentry passed, so casual, so tired. He'd hardly glanced their way.

But just to be sure, the general waited until the man's steps were only a distant, hollow echo. Then he gestured the Falcons back to their work. They ran onward. The general was nervous now. Wondering what else unexpected lay ahead.

Colonel Rizvi was waiting at the structure that housed the senior staff sleeping quarters. His men were spread through the shadows. General Salehi brusquely nodded approval, took two Falcons, unlocked the door with the key the informant had supplied, and took the stairs two at a time to the second floor. His men breathed lightly behind.

This time he had no choice.

Illuminated by the overhead hall light, another sentry stared at the three Iranians. The youth was shocked. Absolutely frozen with astonishment that intruders could have come so far. As if he'd found a snowball in hell.

"Who are you?" he managed to croak, still not believing his eyes.

The general nodded to his two Falcons. They

approached the youth on either side. The youth backed off. His Uzi grew steady, his training resurrected.

"Stay where you are!" the boy warned, one hand reaching above and behind to pull an alarm.

The general snapped his wrist.

The knife sliced between his men and straight into the boy's gut. The youth dropped the Uzi, grabbed his belly. His wide boy eyes were again startled, this time by betrayal.

Quickly one of the Falcons knelt, pulled out the knife, made a clean deep cut across the jugular. Blood gushed onto the floor. The boy tried to talk, gurgled.

No time to waste now. The Falcon handed the knife back to the general. They leaped over the body as the eyes glazed in death. General Salehi wiped the knife on his pants and slid it back into the sheath on his belt. They ran to the door. The general unlocked it. Quiet as shadows, they moved inside.

Daniel Lambert was a small, thin figure lying on his side in a narrow bed. One Falcon yanked back the covers. The other held the physicist's legs. The general closed a hand over his mouth, sat on his chest. As the scientist struggled, the first Falcon injected the tranquilizer into his hip. Within sixty seconds Dr. Lambert was limp.

The general nodded. The Falcons wrapped their prize in the dark bedspread. One hefted him over a shoulder like a sack of rice. They ran out the door and down the stairs. Colonel Rizvi was waiting. He gave a toothy wolf's smile in the moonlight. *Congratulations!*

A moment of triumph surged through General

Salehi. Quickly he repressed it. It was too soon, he told himself. Instead he went over again in his mind their exit, retracing their paths to the installation's perimeter, then the jog through the desert to the meeting place a mile away.

Before dawn had lightened the sky, the helicopters would land at the meeting place. He and the Falcons would pack their prize aboard and fly back to Tehran. And then the general promised himself he could enjoy what they'd accomplished this night. He would savor it. It was sweeter for the difficulties. Victory!

CHAPTER 12

Bolt and Sarah met at four a.m. at the cafeteria. Tired of coffee and needing to talk privately, they left to stroll through the serene, moonlighted desert.

"Nothing," Sarah told him as they walked alone. "Everything looks perfectly normal. They keep good records. Morale's high. No one's seen or heard anything suspicious. No one's been approached off duty. No one thinks he or she's been the object of unwarranted curiosity."

"I got the same thing," Bolt said. "Seems like a well-run, boring place. Just what one would hope for a nuclear installation."

Overhead the stars twinkled brightly. Far away from smog or city lights, this grand wilderness showcased stars so clear they seemed close enough to touch. Thousands of years ago, Bolt thought, the Earth must have enjoyed displays like this every night, before metropolises, electricity, and polluted atmospheres.

They continued walking across the sand, enjoying the peace.

"I'm getting tired again," Sarah said. "Talk about interrupted sleep."

They headed back toward the compound.

"You talk about it," Bolt joked. "I'll enjoy it."

"You liked that then?" she asked. "This afternoon?"

He stopped in the shadow in front of their cottage, remembering the dreamlike sex.

"What?" she said, turning.

He kissed her. "This." He kissed her again.

She moved against him, lean and sensuous. God. She could make a dead man come to life.

And then he heard the rustling. No. It was light running.

She ran her fingers down his chest. He caught them, held her still.

"Jacob?"

"I think our kidnappers have arrived," he said softly.

Unmoving in their shadow he studied a cluster of dark, silhouetted shapes approaching through the moonlight. They were racing away from the central facility and toward the cottage and the perimeter beyond. He pulled Sarah back into the doorway. The intruders must've entered through the minefields. Now they were headed back. There were about a dozen, dressed all in black.

"We can't let them get away!" Sarah whispered.

"We're not," Bolt said.

He opened the cottage door. They slipped inside. She closed the door and he picked up the phone, punched security's number, spoke rapidly. In response, an ear-splitting alarm screamed across the complex. Soon soldiers would come.

They ran to the windows on the back side of the living room. He took out his SIG-Sauer, she her little Colt.

"Sarah?" he said over the siren's continuing blast.

"We'll cover more territory if we separate," she shouted.

He knew she was right. He nodded, worried.

They slid open the windows. Now there were two groups of about a dozen figures each. They were humping at full speed toward the compound's outskirts. Bolt and Sarah jumped out the windows. Sarah took off after one group, Bolt the other.

Bolt's stride ate up the distance, closing in. Had the intruders succeeded in kidnapping the scientist? If they had, the victim was moving with them, indistinguishable. That seemed impossible to Bolt. If it were a kidnapping, the scientist would be resisting, stumbling, running slower.

Some of the intruders turned, fired over their shoulders at Bolt. But they were running and couldn't aim. Their shots went wild.

Maybe the scientist was in the other group? Sarah's group?

Bolt's feet pounded onward. Damn. Too late to switch with Sarah. Parallel to him he caught a glimpse of her, the moonlight glinting on her hair. And suddenly it didn't matter. There was nothing he could do about the others. Not now. But he was gaining on those he pursued. The exhilaration of the race hit him, that natural high he loved.

Behind him the siren stopped. Silence echoed across the vast, lonely desert for one long moment. Then came the dull buzzsaw of approaching Jeeps. Off to the left six Jeeps bristling with soldiers and rifles appeared in the moonlight, careening toward the group Bolt chased.

At the sound, four of the intruders stopped,

spun, and raised their rifles. Bolt hit the ground. The four fired. Bullets peppered the sand. Granules sprayed up, stung his face and hands. He ignored the biting pain, squeezed off rounds. He got lucky, picked off the two in the middle. The two on the ends turned, running again to escape with their comrades.

Bolt stayed where he was. He aimed carefully, compensating for the unreliability of the moonlight. He pulled the trigger once, twice more. One intruder, then the other pitched forward. It seemed easy when it happened right.

Instantly Bolt was up and running again.

Now the awesome blast of many powerful rifles thundered. The soldiers were in range. The Jeeps rushed past Bolt. The Israelis were firing their 5.56mm Galil assault rifles at the small, fleeing band.

Two of the intruders fell immediately. Another two stopped and knelt, firing back at the Jeeps. But it was hopeless. Within a minute, faced by all that firepower, the kneeling two were dead.

Bolt changed directions, heading after Sarah. The Israelis would take care of his group.

Two of the Jeeps seemed to hesitate, then hurried past Bolt, following his line of sight.

They got there first. When he caught up with Sarah, she pointed wordlessly at the minefield ahead where what was left of her group had disappeared. The two Jeeps screeched to a halt at the edge, next to an antiaircraft gun. Black-clothed bodies lay sprawled in their wake, some moaning.

The soldiers moved restlessly up and down the minefield rim. Bolt found footprints, a narrow weaving trail. He moved slowly, then with increasing confidence along it toward the last barbed wire fence and the empty flatlands beyond. Sarah and the others followed through the minefield.

"There must've been three or four," she told his back "maybe more who got away."

He nodded. They passed through the barbed wire. There were more footprints, but the prints were jumbled, massed. They found several branches that led to or from the compacted area and followed all of them. The paths seemed to lead nowhere.

Bolt, Sarah, and the soldiers searched as dawn rose iron gray and then metallic bronze across the hilly horizon. Where had they gone?

General Akbar Salehi boarded the helicopter at the desert landing site. Daniel Lambert lay unconscious on the floor, still wrapped in his bedspread. They'd had to give him a second injection.

The rotors whirred and chopped. The helicopter lifted off, a cumbersome swaying bird. Empty, the other chopper followed them up into the clear dawn. The casualties back at the facility had been heavy, protecting the rear and flank as the general and his prize had escaped.

But all were martyrs for Allah. As martyrs, they would go directly to paradise.

"It's a good day," Colonel Rizvi said.

"An excellent day," General Salehi agreed.

The two surviving Falcons nodded. They showed their respect by not speaking.

"The beginning of many excellent days," Colonel Rizvi went on. "Many excellent years."

"Yes, the beginning."

General Salehi smiled. His dark liquid eyes

burned, and his cruel mouth was almost a grimace.
His satisfaction was enormous. This battle was
his. Victory.

At the Israeli installation, Bolt, Sarah, and the
soldiers continued their search.

"Dr. Lambert is missing!" A woman from security brought the news to them in a hushed, frightened whisper. Soon the information spread among
the searchers. The popular director, the man who
had shepherded the facility from birth to success,
had been kidnapped. Upset, worried for him, they
muttered angrily among themselves. Bolt felt the
old sickening sensation of loss. Quickly he dis-
tanced himself from it. He must work.

A recon group found a flat piece of wasteland
about two miles away where helicopters had landed.
So that was how they'd managed it. A few men
from Sarah's group had been far enough ahead—
probably deliberately ahead—to escape through
the minefields to the landing site, carrying their
quarry, drugged.

Sarah had told Bolt she'd spotted one of the
intruders with a body-size bundle over his shoulder. Bolt believed her, doubted they could have
kidnapped the physicist any other way. Beneath
Lambert's mild, optimistic exterior Bolt saw stubborn will. Had to be, he figured, to build this
installation, fight the Knesset members who'd
been against it, keep the supporters happy, and
most important, find the personnel who could
grow the facility from a twenty-six-megawatt dream
into a world-power reality.

There were no Muslim survivors. The corpses

had no identification. But they did wear the emblem of a gray bird in flight on their shoulders.

"A hawk of some kind?" Sarah wondered.

"Or a falcon," Bolt said. "Look at the long wings."

"They're what?" Bolt couldn't believe what he was hearing.

"Down, I'm afraid." The security chief, Abbe Hilton, was embarrassed. He stood before monitors that encircled the room with views of the interior and exterior of the nuclear complex. He'd had a bad night. First his impregnable perimeter had been bridged, now his telephone lines were on the blink. "Obviously we can't call out." He shook his head, almost in disbelief. "They beat us. You were right, Bolt. We had to beef up the security, but it was just too late."

"It happens," Bolt said. "Now it's our turn."

He flicked on a computer. He searched the facility's library for information about terrorist groups using a hawk or falcon for a signature, but the local library was limited, containing information mostly about nuclear matters.

"You need a line out," Sarah told him.

"Damn right I do." He was growing short tempered.

"You need to tap into our central military system. They have the records you want."

"I should report to Langley, too," Bolt grumbled.

"I should call Hal," Sarah said. "Do you know what time it is?"

He didn't answer.

"One o'clock," she went on. "We haven't had

breakfast or lunch. Abbe can get us the information we need when the telephone lines are working, can't you, Abbe?"

The security chief nodded. "No problem. I'll ring you at your cottage." Helping them would salve his shock at the terrorists' breach of his system.

Bolt looked up. Sarah was right. They were both tired. You made mistakes when you were tired. They'd better get some sleep.

"Okay," he agreed reluctantly. "But be damn sure to call us. Immediately!"

"You're crabby." Sarah laughed a light, amused laugh. She was sitting on the edge of the bed, pushing her navy jumpsuit down over her legs. "I've never seen you crabby."

He went into the bathroom, stood in the middle of it trying to decide what to do, and wandered back out.

"It's heartening," she continued. "You're human after all." She stepped out of the jumpsuit.

He decided he might as well take off his clothes and go to bed. That's what he was here to do. He wasn't going to save Lambert until he had some intel. He began unbuttoning.

"I mean, Jacob," she went on, removing her underwear, "you're intimidating. You always do everything *right*. With so much panache. And you have such a high success rate. Even Hal thinks you're tops. Never mind the business at the entry gate. He'd hire you in a minute if you'd come over."

It hit him suddenly. She was standing in the

middle of the room naked. Tanned, sleek, and very naked. Blond and gorgeous all over. What was wrong with him?

"Sarah." He sat to pull off his shoes, shove down the jumpsuit. Christ. His cock throbbed.

She got into bed.

"Now take me," she said.

"I plan to," he said.

She ignored his words. "I let some bastards get away with the man I was sent to protect," she went on. Suddenly her tone turned sad, guilty. "*I* should be the one who's crabby."

She lifted her head, and with a brisk, business-like motion flipped her cornsilk hair out in a spray on the pillow. It was a charming motion, he thought, almost schoolmarmish, prim. Virginal. The light caught in the smooth silky hollows of her model's cheeks. She seemed to be upset about something.

He got in bed. "Baby, you can be anything you want to be."

"I intend to get Dr. Lambert back."

He kissed her throat. "You've got me. Right here. Now." He slid his hands up the slim hips, past the waist, up the deep chest.

"No, Jacob," she said seriously. She shivered delicately as his hands brushed her nipples. "You don't understand."

"You don't want me?" he said. He kissed her ears, her eyes, the salty hollow of her throat.

Her breathing was growing ragged. "Of course I want you," she said.

"Good," he said, rolling her over. "Let's do something about it. Now."

That evening General Salehi's plane landed safely in Tehran and the trucks, all empty but the first, returned his small group to the villa on the tree-studded rise in central Tehran. The weather was still clear, the stars twinkling high above in a dramatic display of the universe.

Daniel Lambert's eyes fluttered where he lay curled in a fetal position on the truck's rubber mat. One of the Falcons grabbed his legs and dragged him to the door. He groaned. The other Falcon threw him over his shoulder. The physicist made a deep guttural sound of unconscious pain. They were handling him roughly for a purpose. It was important he learn quickly he had nothing to gain, everything to lose, if he refused to cooperate.

"Take him downstairs," General Salehi said as he strode to the comfort of his upstairs villa office. "You know where."

CHAPTER
13

Bolt felt the mattress rock. He was deep in sleep, but still he recognized that the movement was more than Sarah just turning over.

He forced himself to the surface of consciousness, slitted his eyes, watched as she crept naked and silent toward the jumpsuit and underwear flung over the back of a chair. Sunlight made narrow slices through the blinds and wide across the room. The low angle told him the hour was late.

In the dusty afternoon light she was all planes and sumptuous curves. But her face was almost sexless, deep in thought, plans. What in hell was she up to?

Unmoving he watched her. She dressed quickly, with an economy of action that showed training and was far different from the provocative strips she'd performed in the past. He almost smiled, thinking about that, the sex, *their* sex.

But the way she moved, the concentration on her face sobered him.

He eliminated possibilities. If the phone had rung, he would have heard it. Therefore security had not called. If someone had knocked on the door, he would have heard it. Therefore no one had delivered a message. If she'd received no external summons, then her own internal mechanism had gone off. Either she knew something she hadn't shared with him, or she had suspicions.

Dressed, she picked up her evening wear from two nights before, patted the Colt on her waist, and passed out of sight through the bedroom door and into the living room. He sat up. He heard the front door click so softly that unless he'd been listening for it, he would have missed it.

He pulled on his jumpsuit, holstered his SIG-Sauer. Waited a moment at the cottage's door, listened, then stepped out into the desert's afternoon heat.

It was almost dusk, the sun so low over the hills that the whole western sky was a cauldron of reds and oranges, reflecting in brilliant colors the repressive heat that had settled over the complex.

Sarah disappeared around the tritium facility.

Sweating he strode after her, fast enough to make time but not so fast that he'd attract attention. She went into security. He ducked into a doorway, pretended to admire plantings recovering from wilt in the shade.

After a while she came out, and he followed her over baking sidewalks to the motor pool. A corporal had started a Jeep. He slid off the seat, just warming up the engine for her. She chatted with him to show her appreciation, hopped aboard, and drove off toward the installation's entrance.

No way Bolt could follow her undetected now, not on a narrow road with little traffic. She'd spot him in a heartbeat.

He returned to security. Abbe Hilton was gone,

but his assistant, Loren Singer, was at his desk, leaning over a pile of paperwork.

"Telephone lines back up?" Bolt inquired innocently.

"Just started working," Singer said, signing a page. In his late forties, he had faded red hair, freckles, and a distracted manner.

"No one called us."

"Sure did," Singer said. "A few minutes ago." He picked up another paper, scanned it. "No one was there. Ms. Maizlish picked up the message when she came in."

"Which was?" Bolt was trying to be patient.

"The message? To call her boss."

"Uh-huh. What about the check Abbe was going to run on the terrorists? You remember, the hawk or falcon insignia."

"Came up negative." Singer looked up from his paperwork. "Sorry. Was it important?"

Bolt stared at him. Singer's mind was buried under a mountain of bureaucracy. So intense was Singer's preoccupation that if the complex were on fire, someone would have to bring it to his attention. Or if Abbe Hilton had wanted Singer to be ignorant of something—say, the hawk or falcon business—Singer would know only what he was told.

Bolt smiled. "Nah. Just curious. Anything new on Dr. Lambert?"

"Not a thing unfortunately. A real tragedy. The investigation's continuing."

Bolt was silent. "Say, mind if I use one of those babies?" Bolt gestured casually at two computers whose screens were dark. Near them, security staff monitored other screens where data continually appeared with up-to-the-minute reports of the facility's security.

"No problem." Singer's nose disappeared as he leaned down to his work.

"By the way," Bolt said as he headed toward the computers, "did Sarah phone her boss?"

"Ummm? I think so."

Bolt sighed. Singer didn't like to be bothered with talking. He wasn't going to get a thing from him. Bolt turned on the computer, called up the central system's library—probably located in Jerusalem—and got a barrage of questions about his code, security clearance, and encryption number. Which he had for United States military computers, but obviously not for Israel's.

"Hey, Singer! Can you come here a minute?"

Bolt explained the problem: He needed the security man to clear him so he could check again for the terrorist group. He stood up.

Singer sighed and sat down. "Okay." He glanced back at his desk, at the work that called him. "But I'll have to stay with you. You're allowed to know about the terrorists, nothing more."

Bolt stood impatiently as Singer logged in and called up the library files on terrorists and terrorist groups. At last Singer arose, pulled up a second chair. Bolt sat at the console and entered questions on hawks, falcons, Iranians, and Shiite Muslims. No matter how many ways he asked the questions, the library denied having anything on Iranian or Shiite groups with falcons or hawks for emblems, or about any terrorist group at all using the birds for symbols.

"Guess that does it," Singer said at last, relieved he could return to his work. "I'll log you out."

"Thanks." Bolt walked away, disappointed. "Where did Sarah go?"

"Ms. Maizlish? To Jerusalem, I assume."

"She didn't say?"

"I didn't ask."

Mentally Bolt threw up his hands. He headed for the door. If Sarah had simply returned home because it was time to go home and she knew nothing more, she would have told Bolt. And not because his suitcase was still in her En Karem studio; she'd probably forgotten that. No, a return to Jerusalem would signal retrenching, looking for new leads—something they would do together.

He believed Sarah had something right now. He considered calling Olds in Washington to report in, but decided that without a secure line there would be too many opportunities for someone to eavesdrop. He thanked Singer and marched back out into the hot air.

The sun had set and the purple sky was deepening toward black, waiting for the rising moon. The temperature had dropped a couple of degrees, but not enough. The air was still oppressive. Sweating, Bolt made time toward the motor pool.

The corporal who had prepared the Jeep for Sarah was drinking beer in an air-conditioned office with two other soldiers. His hands were clean, but his face was smudged and his nails were black with grease. His priorities were clear—clean hands for beer, the hell with the rest.

He grinned up at Bolt. "You the guy that hot wired the Jeep?"

Bolt nodded. "Sure would like some keys to it."

The guy laughed. "Bet you would. Sorry I can't help you out. Don't have the equipment."

"Hey, you're the guy that helped wipe out the terrorists?" one of the others said.

"Yeah. He *is*!" said another, eyeing Bolt respectfully.

"Wish we could've taken them sooner," Bolt said. "Before they got Dr. Lambert."

There was silence in the little room, sadness, regret.

"Yeah," the corporal agreed solemnly.

"I was supposed to meet my partner here," Bolt went on. "You know Sarah Maizlish? A beautiful blond. You seen her around?"

"No," the corporal said.

"Yeah," said one of his friends at the same time.

The corporal shot him a blistering look of disapproval, told him rapidly in Hebrew, "She said she had to go secretly to Dubai. No one is to know where she goes. She's Mossad. This one is CIA!"

The friend blinked slowly, comprehending. He turned to Bolt. "I was mistaken. That was another woman. I haven't seen your . . . partner."

Bolt nodded and thanked them. Hebrew was a language he knew fairly well, a dormant ancient language whose resurrection had been another of Israel's brilliant strokes. Constantly renewed and invented, the tongue had been the prime source of communication in the early days among settlers from such disparate places as Poland, Morocco, Ethiopia, Mexico, and the United States. With Hebrew the new nation had created a functioning society and democracy, and today along with Arabic and English it lived on as one of the nation's major languages.

So Sarah was going to Dubai. But why?

Bolt left, headed for the Jeep he and Sarah had stolen in En Karem. As he hot wired it for the third—and he hoped final—time, he thought about Dubai. It was a colorful, bustling city, often called the Hong Kong of the Persian Gulf. What was there for Sarah?

He got into the vehicle, drove toward the complex's front gate, noted with relief someone had had the foresight to fill the gas tank. And then as the sentries waved him through and out toward the Negev wilderness, he remembered.

Dubai's biggest single customer was Iran. Iranians were constantly flying back and forth between their country and the hustling Dubai port near the Strait of Hormuz. Something was happening in Dubai that had attracted Sarah's attention. Something . . . or someone.

Late that night Bolt drove into Tel Aviv. After a short argument with the tense marine guards, he was allowed—minus his SIG-Sauer—to enter the U.S. embassy on Hayarkon Street. There he found an assistant to the assistant to the military attaché who agreed to make the appropriate phone calls clearing him.

Soon he had his pistol back, a suitcase with tourist clothes of approximately his size, and an upstairs bedroom where he could sleep. Tomorrow he would be on the first flight out of Ben Gurion International at Lod, eventual destination Dubai.

During the night, someone in a basement office would create credentials and credit cards for Australian journalist Jake Bolt, on assignment for *The Sydney Times*. In the Persian Gulf states, citizenship in the United States was often more than a liability. It was dangerous. Australia, however, maintained a useful neutrality.

The embassy bedroom upstairs was unpretentious but equipped with a shower. Which, next to answers, was what Bolt needed.

He stripped and headed straight for it. He stood in the blast of stinging hot water, trying to wash off the feeling of betrayal, guilt, anger. Damn Sarah. First he'd let the bastard terrorists take Daniel Lambert. Then he'd let Sarah drive off with information he probably could use.

What in hell was he thinking when he watched her drive away? Must've had his head up his ass.

And why in hell hadn't she confided in him? Which was probably what was really pissing him off. Except, he knew, that if he'd had to move on—for whatever reason—and couldn't tell her, he would've gone, too. The way he had to admit he had left that time in India.

It was part of the business. She was an agent, not his woman. He decided to think about something else. Anything else.

He turned off the shower, stepped out, and toweled off. He picked up the phone, asked to be connected to information services. He told the sergeant on duty to look through their computer library for information on terrorists, probably Iranian, who used a hawk or a falcon for an emblem, and a connection to Dubai.

Then he signaled the operator and asked for a secure line to CIA headquarters in Langley, Virginia.

Sue Kirtt was her usual kidding self. "You're doing better, Jake. It's only five o'clock. Another half hour and you would've interrupted Mr. Olds's cocktails."

"Thank god," Bolt told her, "I've finally done something right."

"Probably by accident anyway," she laughed and clicked off.

"Actually," he told the ringing phone, "it was."

Clifton Olds's aristocratic voice was curt, worried. "Where in hell have you been, Jake?"

Bolt brought him up to date, from the warehouse in Jerusalem to Mossad headquarters and their downed computers and to the Israeli nuclear installation, Lambert's kidnapping, and the telephone lines that were inoperable for several hours.

"Iran's going nuclear?" Olds said, shocked. "You're certain?"

"The Mossad's certain," Bolt said.

"Jesus."

"Yeah."

They were silent. Then Olds said, "You're checking on the terrorist group?"

"The embassy is. I should know something shortly."

"Good. I want a copy of the file. And you're going to Dubai?"

"First thing in the morning," Bolt said. "What about these communication problems, sir? The computers and telephones. What's causing them? Are they related?"

"Our expert is checking. You remember Marcus Krenchell. He says they appear to be individual events. He's looking for a link."

"Strange," Bolt mused.

"Get back to me when you have something."

"Yes, sir."

"And be careful." Olds hesitated. "As you know, Dubai is fairly civilized, but parts of the United Arab Emirates are medieval . . ."

The only place worse Bolt could think of was Iran. He knew what Olds was leading up to, and that Olds was required by conscience to voice it.

"Our idea of law—and justice—doesn't exist there," Clifton Olds continued. "If you get into trouble . . ."—a long pause—"if they get you for whatever reason, you're on your own."

CHAPTER
14

In Moscow, Viktor Markov listened quietly.

"*Nyet, Ya apazdal,*" he said into the telephone. "That won't do."

As he talked he rotated slowly in his chair, left to right, right to left. Pictures of Gorbachev and Lenin hung side by side on one wall of his KGB office. On another was a calendar, featuring a springtime photo of Gorky Park's graceful linden trees, with picturesque old men in their worn black suits sitting beneath the greening branches, playing chess. It was a quaint photo, overly sentimental. Markov had no time for sentiment. The photo always irritated him.

"Send the package up. Immediately," he ordered. "I will not come for it." He hung up.

Viktor Markov was a stout man with a thick lower lip and overly bright, intense eyes. He wore eyeglasses and dressed fastidiously in a navy blue suit, pale blue shirt, and striped tie—the new, more stylish uniform for KGB agents since *glasnost*. Certainly far closer to Markov's tastes than the dark baggy suits and dingy white shirts of previous administrations. His shoes were polished to a high shine.

His brilliant eyes swept his office as if it were

the globe. Surrounding him was a bank of computers, his domain, his specialty. Gone were the days when brute force ruled. Now real strength—real command—lay in silicon microchips, coaxial and fiber optic cables, and software programs that did everything from writing simple business letters to designing rockets.

In the United States alone, he mused, thirty million computers linked the nation in a vast, interlocking maze. So much of everyday life depended on computers, even grocery store checkout registers, that technological strength could quickly be turned into devastating weakness.

And that would work to his advantage.

A few days ago he'd destroyed the blueprints revealing that Iran was building a nuclear facility. Destroyed them so he could use the secret to his advantage. Yesterday he'd succeeded in resurrecting one of his old identities—Swiss banker Horst Renssauer. And in an hour he would be in the air, flying to meet General Akbar Salehi, commander-in-chief of Iran's military.

Markov had selected General Salehi as his best link to Iran's military system. General Salehi was a man who could be influenced. He was a pragmatist and a romantic. A pragmatist since he was eager to deal with other countries and enjoy civilization's comforts, and a romantic because he believed too much that man had a destiny.

Viktor Markov knew better. Man made himself.

Destiny was created, not bestowed.

And there was no God, no Allah to give or to take away, to be blessed by or to be cursed by.

Markov had learned about the nuclear facility

from one of his most reliable sources, and then that the information was still unknown to the mullahs and Majlis. This made Markov think General Salehi was planning a coup.

That would leave the Iranian leader even more vulnerable to Markov's overtures.

There was a knock on the door.

"Come," Markov boomed.

An obsequious KGB clerk sidled in, dropped on the desk the package that contained the Horst Renssauer identity, and sidled back toward the door.

"It's all here?" Markov asked sternly. He was aware he tended to slur his sibilants when he spoke. His words made a slight hissing sound.

"Yes, comrade." The clerk edged closer to the door.

Markov watched the man squirm, the gaze fixed on the floor as if he could burn a hole and drop through to safety.

Markov cleared his throat. The clerk jumped. Markov smiled, waved his hand.

"Get out!"

Viktor Markov stood, put on his cashmere overcoat, picked up the package, and walked through the doorway. Compared to himself, Markov thought coolly, General Salehi was an unambitious man.

He mulled over his plans and the events of the last few weeks. Through General Salehi, he would access Iran's military computers and infect the system with Bushi Nakamura's virus. He was enormously pleased by the insidious disease called a computer virus.

Different from other kinds of computer sabotage, a virus was a small software program that secretly cloned itself and spread. Like a biological virus, an electronic virus carried genetic codes recorded, in this case, in ADA. Once activated, it could stifle networks with dead-end tasks, print out false data, erase files, erase entire disks, and even destroy equipment.

Hidden in other software programs and secretly inserted, a virus was extremely difficult to detect, and even more difficult to stop. This made it an ideal weapon for Markov, if it could be controlled. And Bushi Nakamura's was a work of art. It altered weapons' controls and put them in the computer-expert hands of Viktor Markov.

But Bushi had not seen the future Markov's way. The U.S. government computer scientist had been a pacifist. He had developed the virus as a private crusade, his goal to freeze all nations' military weapons systems, make them inoperable. By doing that, he believed he could bring a forced nuclear disarmament and, ultimately, peace to all.

Bushi had confided all this to Markov, and Markov had secretly made adjustments to the virus. These adjustments were advantageous to a man of vision.

Bushi had suspected Markov's tampering, but kept to himself the means of stopping Markov cold. Bushi had created the antidote to his own virus. Without that ultimate control, Markov remained vulnerable to Bushi and to the virus itself, should it contaminate his own computers. His first reaction had been to halve the threat. Markov had gone to Bushi's Washington apartment, delivered the small gunshot to the back of the head where it wouldn't be noticed beneath the dark thick hair, then disemboweled him to make the death look like ritual seppuku. A messy but necessary job.

Then there was the problem: The CIA had assigned Jake Bolt to investigate. Searching for the identity of the killer, Bolt had traced a parcel Bushi had mailed to a cousin in Tokyo. Markov had sent his men after it, too. It was far more important than his Cherry Blossom coke operation. Far more important than the yakuza thugs he'd hired to go after it and Bolt.

The parcel might contain Bushi's antidote.

But no one had been able to find it, and today it still remained undiscovered, unopened. Perhaps only the dead knew what it looked like, or what was in it, or where it was.

So although Markov still worried, he'd ceased to actively look for Bushi's parcel.

Instead he'd methodically returned to his original plans. Without method, a man was lost. With method and vision, a man could build an empire, as he had.

An empire of drugs, weapons, and fortified military installations. Money and power. All concealed beneath his bland, chameleon official status as a government computer consultant.

And now in the last few weeks, using contacts and covers, he'd planted Bushi Nakamura's altered virus in the military systems of the nuclear powers. He'd been testing the results—all surprisingly satisfactory. With a few codewords and instructions, he easily controlled everything from telephone communications to bank deposits and military computers themselves.

Iran would be the last country to be infected.

The last country whose computers would become his. As an unstable nation, it could be particularly useful to him.

Then he would, quite simply, assume techno-logical command of the world.

In Tel Aviv, Jake Bolt lay in bed in a pool of yellow lamplight and read the short embassy report:

The Desert Falcons are an elite Iranian special force unit founded approximately two years ago by commander-in-chief Akbar Salehi. Similar to Iran's religion-based Revolutionary Guards, the Falcons are not officially considered a terrorist force, although they may provide materiel and support for jihad activities.

To receive combat experience, they are assigned to patrols along the Iran-Iraq border. It is rumored they have successfully conducted several raids. (See *Shatt-al-Arab*.) They are trained, highly motivated para-commandos and, like the Persian Immortals and Alexander's Companions, serve a secondary function as a 'palace guard' to General Salehi. This is tolerated because of the general's prestige and, since the disappointing and inconclusive end to the Iran-Iraq war, the renewed faith he has given the Iranian people in their military.

Bolt read the report once more, turned off the lamp, and closed his eyes.

There was no way the Mossad or Israeli military could be ignorant of this information. Sarah had found out about it, or been told about it. And she had erased it or hidden it so he couldn't find it.

Once known as the Pirate Coast, modern Dubai strove for the title "City of Merchants." With a wide-open trade policy and taxfree incentives, it thrived in a scenic waterside setting on the turquoise Persian Gulf. Goods from Asia and the Middle East flowed through Port Rashid's containerized cargo terminal; nearly three-fourths were reexported to India, Pakistan, East Africa, Saudi Arabia, Kuwait, and other nations. About fifty airlines used the emirate's airport.

Bolt felt Dubai's entrepreneurial fever spark and crackle in the brilliant sunshine. He walked past the Shiite mosque through the teeming covered *suqs* to the bustling ferry landing near the ruler's office. There was an exotic, dangerous ambience about this place, he thought. Here backgrounds collided, mingled, and sometimes disappeared amid the strength and fervor of this multicultural, multinational port.

Since early morning he'd been walking. For eight hours he'd been checking hotels, circling the mosque, and roaming the streets looking for Sarah, or the gray Desert Falcon emblem on clothing, store signs, and ships' sails. He was getting damn tired.

He strode along the ancient harbor—called the Creek—that wound among glass-and-granite office towers. He watched sweating longshoremen shepherd aboard cargoes of Japanese video players, Korean truck tires, cars, vans, pickups, and Taiwanese telex machines.

Bolt boarded a slender wood *abra*, a water taxi, and for only twenty-five *fils*—about seven cents— he was ferried across the harbor. Taped recordings of the Koran's scriptures rang out from small portable cassette players. The smell of cardamom tea mixed with the sea-salt air.

Again he walked. This was where intuition mattered, he reminded himself. Discouragement came from what seemed to be long, unproductive hours. The key word was *seemed*.

"Forget not the Day of Judgment!" bellowed a short, heavy imam in a long gray robe with billowing sleeves. On his head he wore a red fez wrapped in white as he shouted his warnings from a tall pulpit. "Repent your sins! You cannot escape Allah's book. *Wallahi! Wallahi!* It is written! It is written!"

And then he saw her. Not the embroidered Desert Falcon sewn onto a shoulder or sail. But her. Sarah's blond hair shone silver in the sunlight, a beacon as she hurried through the darkhaired crowds. She wore a burgundy-red Western business suit, pink silk blouse, nylon hose, and high-heeled pumps, and looked as if she were going to a company meeting. The men she passed, whether in Bedouin robes or European sports jackets, turned to stare. In London or Paris she would have been just another beautiful career woman. Here in this exotic part of the world *she* was exotic.

She was flaunting her presence. Obviously she was not worried Bolt would find her. Perhaps she was making herself noticeable so someone else would. But who?

He tailed her past stalls selling spices, intricate metalwork, and hand-knotted Iranian carpets. Past hawkers crying their wares, and veiled, subdued women shopping. He held back, never getting too close. With her pale hair she was easy to follow. Occasionally she glanced back over her shoulder as if *her* intuition warned something was wrong.

But she never saw him. And at last, looking all around, she walked purposefully through the front doorway of an old brick hotel. The hotel was seven stories and rimmed with mature palms. Its bricks had faded brown-orange with the years. The sign in Arabic above the front door read *The Gulf Hotel*.

He strolled along the sidewalk outside, saw her through the window. She sat in the lobby, took a copy of *Cosmopolitan* from her large handbag.

Bolt knew all the signs: the feigned relaxation, the magazine, the gaze that constantly swept the lobby. Sarah was on stake-out.

General Akbar Salehi stood before the seventh-floor window of his hotel. The Gulf Hotel, it was named. Once it had been called the Persian Gulf Hotel. Then the Arabian Gulf Hotel. Now in acquiescence to the easily excited political atmosphere, it was simply the Gulf.

His family had been coming here for years. Each time he arrived the owner met him with fresh dates and coffee. The owner was sensitive; he discretely met all the general's needs, as he had his father's. It was well worth the cost even though it was an old hotel with little of the beauty and lavish comfort to which the general was accustomed.

"I can no longer be silent," Horst Renssauer told him in Farsi. He sat on the sofa, an impressive, dignified man. "My conscience is greatly troubled."

Renssauer's slim leather briefcase waited at his feet. A little under six feet tall and rotund, he wore an expensive, impeccably tailored three-piece suit, a diamond ring on the ring finger of his right hand, and a diamond stick pin in his rep tie. He seemed to hiss slightly as he talked. Perhaps he had a speech impediment of some kind.

"I am here," the general said. He spoke kindly, as he would to one of his Falcons. Or someone from whom he wanted something. "Unburden yourself."

As he spoke, General Salehi continued to study the man who had been the cause for this sudden trip to Dubai. Horst Renssauer had phoned the general from Switzerland two days ago, twenty-four hours before the successful raid on the Israeli facility. Renssauer said he was an official with a Lucerne bank; his request to meet the general had been urgent and imbued with hints of large sums of money—and a need for sensitivity about publicity. Hence the Gulf Hotel, where delicate matters were more easily arranged.

"It has to do with money," Renssauer said.

"*Naleh*. You had led me to believe that."

"A rather large amount."

General Salehi sat down in the overstuffed chair next to the window. Sunlight streamed through and across his feet. He was relaxed, thoughtful. It was important not to seem too eager.

"Yes," he said. "You mentioned that. I wonder if you can now tell me how much we are discussing?"

"Five million U.S. dollars," Renssauer said morosely. He seemed riddled with worry and guilt. "Approximately."

"Ah." General Salehi was silent. A large figure indeed. A very *fine* large figure. "And what does this have to do with me?"

"As you know, the late shah, Reza Pahlavi, kept accounts in Switzerland. After the . . . change . . . in leadership and his death, some were turned over to the Pahlavi family and some to Iran's new government."

"I remember. He kept accounts with your bank?"

"Several. But . . . we missed . . . one."

"And it was in your department?" Which would explain Renssauer's request that the matter be kept quiet. Neither he nor his bank would want the adverse publicity.

"I'm afraid so."

"The five million U.S. dollars?"

"Interest has grown the account to that approximate sum, yes."

"It belongs to Iran," the general said immediately. Always establish your territory. "No word of this . . . embarrassment will get back to Switzerland." And there might be a way to funnel the money to Salehi's personal treasury before it reached Iran's.

Renssauer nodded, relieved. "*Teshekoor.* Thank you."

"For what purpose did the shah keep the account?" Already General Salehi could see a dozen uses for the money.

"It was opened twenty-four years ago," Renssauer said uncomfortably, again reminded of his error. "The funds had been transferred from another Swiss bank. I believe the shah used it to pay for the upkeep of his mistresses. It appears he

bought several of them houses or apartments—
Paris, Vienna, London, New York City."

General Salehi laughed. A man was a man!

He said to the banker, "I hope you brought a
check with you."

"Nothing would please me more than to give
you the money now," Renssauer said sincerely,
"but before I can order the check drawn up, I must
fulfill the needs of my bank's record-keeping department, as well as Swiss privacy and banking
laws." He leaned over, took a thick sheaf of papers
from his briefcase. "These must be read and signed
by the Ayatollah Mohammed Masumian himself. In quadruplicate. I appreciate your smoothing
the way so that this can be done with dispatch
and . . . sensitivity."

"My pleasure." General Salehi reached for the
papers.

Renssauer pulled them back against his slop-
ing, well-fed chest. "Only the ayatollah," he explained. "In my presence."

"Ah." General Salehi reevaluated his approach.
In this world, nothing was easy. "Come to the
ayatollah's office tomorrow afternoon. Tehran.
We will see that all is done properly."

Horst Renssauer stood, beaming. "I am greatly
relieved."

The general walked him to the door. "Consider
the matter closed."

They shook hands, and the general watched as
the Swiss banker headed for the elevator where two
Falcons stood guard. As always, the general had
taken every room on this floor as a precautionary
measure.

General Salehi returned to his suite. Immediately the door to the adjoining room opened. His

little assistant, Colonel Ahmed Rizvi, stepped forward.

"You heard?" the general asked. "It is good news, is it not?"

The colonel nodded. "Money we can use to Allah's glory!"

General Salehi inclined his head reverently. "All to Allah's glory!"

Downstairs in the hotel lobby Sarah Maizlish endured the bald, rude stares of the men who passed through. Only her clothes—her blouse and business suit—kept the doorman and deskman from assuming she was a prostitute. They would have liked her to be a prostitute. Since she hadn't been cleared by the owner and was not cutting him in, they could have picked her up and thrown her out into the street. For them it would be an interesting interruption to an otherwise boring workday.

She ignored them. All the men.

If her information were correct, General Akbar Salehi was upstairs in his room. If he followed his usual routine, he would sweep downstairs soon for a night on the town. For a fundamentalist Shiite, the general had very Westernized tastes. Including, according to the Mossad report, a preference for blond women.

His plans for tomorrow were to attend camel races outside Dubai, then board his jet back to Tehran. Except, if all went well, he would not board the jet. Nor would he leave the camel races with his usual contingent.

Her heart rate increased as she saw the elevator go up to the seventh floor, pause, and head back down again. The general and his people were housed on the seventh floor.

She watched the elevator as it descended, opened into the lobby. She glanced casually toward it, her heart pounding.

But it wasn't Salehi. She would recognize him instantly from the photos Mossad had provided. This man was large, rotund, wearing an expensive three-piece European suit. He strode out the elevator, through the lobby, and out the front door. He had an arrogant air about him, as if he owned the hotel and everything else in Dubai. She wondered briefly if he were the hotel's owner. Then dismissed the question as irrelevant.

Again the elevator climbed. She ordered her heartbeat to return to normal. This seldom worked, but it took her mind off whatever imminent problem had triggered the pounding.

Again the elevator stopped at the seventh floor and paused. It descended to the lobby. As it opened she glanced casually toward it, but now she allowed her gaze to linger a few seconds.

And there he was, in full medaled uniform. General Akbar Salehi, surrounded by men in handsome tan uniforms with Desert Falcons embroidered on their shoulders. He was a big man, barrel-chested and strong-looking, with dark liquid eyes and a narrow cruel mouth.

Suddenly she was calm inside.

She stood, stretched modestly, slipped her magazine back in her bag. She glanced at her watch, allowing the tiniest bit of irritation to cloud her face. Just as General Salehi was crossing the lobby in front of the registration desk, she walked toward it to ask a question.

CHAPTER
15

In the lobby of the Gulf Hotel, Sarah Maizlish looked back over her shoulder. Had she forgotten something on her chair?

She collided with General Akbar Salehi.

"Oh!" she said, stumbling in her precariously high heels.

"Pardon me!" he said and grabbed her shoulders to stop her from falling. He spoke in formal, nearly unaccented U.S. English. "Are you all right?"

"I'm so sorry!" She was embarrassed, couldn't meet his gaze.

"No, it was my fault," he said smoothly.

She could feel those large moist eyes burning over her flesh, assessing the potential as he would a horse or a recruit. He continued to hold her shoulders, even though the danger of her falling was past. Around them his men smiled and shuffled their feet. They knew their leader, knew he had weaknesses, and that Allah might have to forgive him once again if he strayed with this blond foreign woman.

"It's just that my . . . friend . . . is late," she said lamely. "I mean, I thought there might be a message for me at the desk . . . explaining why he is . . ."

"Late," the general finished for her. Slowly his fingers uncurled. She was not trying to get away, so he held her more loosely. It was the way you trained a favored animal. "I will ask for you."

"No! I don't want to be any trouble!"

"Of course I will do this. What is his name?"

"Drew Cunningham. He's with Aramco."

"Drew Cunningham," he repeated, took her arm, led her toward the desk. "And your name?"

"Sally Mather."

"And you, too, are with Aramco?"

"No, actually. With General Motors."

"Ah, yes. And you are American. You sell Cadillacs?"

"Uh-huh. Would you like to buy one?" she said daringly.

He chuckled. "Perhaps."

The general turned his gaze to the fellow behind the registration desk. The clerk looked as if he weren't sure he approved of the turn of events, but General Salehi was a long time customer, and he had orders to do whatever was necessary to keep the general happy.

"Yes, sir?" the clerk asked.

General Salehi inquired whether there was a message for Miss Sally Mather and whether he knew a Mr. Drew Cunningham.

"Sorry, sir," the clerk said.

"Have you been waiting long?" the general said, pivoting her by the elbow back into the old lobby.

"More than an hour now," Sally Mather said forlornly.

"Well, we cannot allow this," the general decided. "A beautiful young woman like you. Were you going to have a meeting with this Drew Cunningham? Was he going to buy many Cadillacs from you?"

She laughed a light, tinkling laugh. "Oh, no. I wouldn't sell a car to a *friend*. I had company meetings all day, and tonight he and I were ... going out to dinner."

"First," the general instructed, "you must always sell to friends. Always. They will appreciate your fine products, and your friendship will encourage them to buy more. Second, *I* will take you out to dinner. What would you prefer? French? Italian? Chinese? Perhaps hamburgers almost as good as you make in the U.S.A.?"

Her eyes sparkled with excitement. "How wonderful!" She hesitated. "No, I couldn't impose!"

But he was already guiding her across the lustrous old hardwood floor toward the hotel's front door. Two of his men strode ahead to open the door and stand outside. The rest fell into double file behind.

She looked forward and backward in awe at the retinue. "You must be very important," she decided. "I can see you're a general. Are you a king, too?"

He laughed a deep, guttural laugh. His cruel thin mouth bowed in real mirth.

"Not yet," he laughed. "Not yet."

Outdoors on the sidewalk Jake Bolt had a most interesting experience. He watched another CIA agent come out of the Gulf Hotel, a special agent he hadn't seen in quite a while—Marcus Krenchell.

As far as Bolt knew, Krenchell was—or should be—back in Langley, working on the problem of the odd worldwide computer and communications glitches that had been so prominent lately—and so frightening.

Rotund and expensively dressed, Krenchell looked more like a high-powered tycoon than a government computer expert. He walked with a long, springy stride that ignored his indulgent soft weight, and that showed far more physical agility than one would have supposed. He held his head in an arrogant chin-high tilt, and his eyes dismissed traffic and pedestrians as so much flotsam. Only those people and things that directly affected him were important.

Krenchell worked under Clifton Olds's direct supervision, but now he looked as if he were undercover. Strange, but not impossible.

Bolt was tempted to make contact, although that was usually not advisable in the field. He watched Krenchell walk down the street and into a glitzy South African bar called the Johannesburg.

As Krenchell disappeared, three white stretch limousines with darkened windows drew up to park in front of the Gulf Hotel. The elegant automobiles seemed to fill the whole block. Impressed pedestrians slowed to stare and gawk. Three chauffeurs liveried in gold and royal purple got out, stood erect and proud on the curb beside the passenger doors.

Bolt looked in the hotel window. Sarah was gone. He moved his angle, saw her talking in the lobby to a barrel-chested man in an Iranian general's uniform. She must be undercover, too; she wasn't acting like herself. Too innocent and dipsy with the big eyes and shy, hanging head.

He stared at the general, realizing with a shock he'd missed the gray falcon insignia on the shoulder. That came from paying attention to Sarah, not business. The falcon was also on the shoulders of the dozen or so soldiers clustered around the general.

The Desert Falcons. Seeing them gave Bolt a cold feeling of satisfaction. At last.

He studied them, their self-assured postures, their polished muscular movements. They looked like just what they were—elite special forces. Sleek and dangerous as hell.

Bolt had never seen a photo of General Akbar Salehi, but he had a feeling he was looking at the general right now. And the general and the Falcons must be the reason Sarah had come to Dubai—to track Dr. Lambert through them.

But why was General Salehi in Dubai? And what was Sarah planning?

General Salehi looked as if he could eat Sarah for dinner. If he'd had fewer manners, he'd be drooling. The general escorted her out of sight, toward the hotel's front door.

Bolt backed into a shop's window alcove and watched from its cover as two Falcons, Sarah, the general, and the rest of the Falcons streamed through the doors and piled into the waiting limos. This worried Bolt. The general had a reputation for ruthlessness; he was a soldier who murdered political opponents. And he had a reputation for being an opportunist; he was a politician who became a Shiite fundamentalist not for any great belief, but so that he could stay in Iran and attain power.

What in hell had Sarah gotten herself into? If the general found out she was Jewish, and a Mossad agent . . . and since Israel was one of Iran's most hated enemies . . . But that was the point. She was a Mossad agent, and a damn good one. Bolt had to assume she knew what she was doing.

Their passengers safely inside, the splendid white limousines drove off down the street at a stately pace.

Bolt strode into the hotel, to the reception desk. He'd better confirm the general's identity.

"General Akbar Salehi, please," he told the clerk.

The clerk looked up. "I'm sorry, sir. You've just missed him."

Bolt hesitated, pretended to be disappointed. "Damn. Guess I'll have to wait until tomorrow."

"Come early, sir," the helpful clerk said. "He's scheduled to check out by nine at the latest."

"Thanks for the tip."

Outdoors again he headed for the Johannesburg bar where a gold neon nugget flashed over the sidewalk, beckoning passersby.

Soft twilight was settling in a lavender mantle over the city's sparkling lights. Foreigners from every part of the industrialized world jostled among Dubai citizens, hurrying to hotel rooms, homes, and places of entertainment for the night.

Indoors the dim bar was decorated in black and dusty gold in homage to the South African mines that had skyrocketed Johannesburg's wealth. Music whispered from overhead speakers. Little black, glossy tables filled the room. Tall, spindly stools stood at the bar. Patrons bustled noisily in.

Next to the wall Marcus Krenchell sat at a table talking to a small man with a scar down the left side of his face. A glass half full of ice and amber liquid sat on the table in front of Krenchell. There was no glass in front of the little man. Either he didn't drink, or he wasn't staying long.

Bolt went to the bar, ordered a beer, watched Krenchell. Eventually Krenchell's gaze would wander toward him, reconning the room. Yes, now he was looking. The casual, all-encompassing sweep of the professional.

Bolt's and Krenchell's eyes met. Krenchell seemed shocked. It wasn't just surprise. There was suspicion, maybe anger, too. Very odd. Krenchell quickly recovered, returned to his usual self-assured demeanor.

Bolt waited. He had questions for Krenchell.

Krenchell seemed to have the same idea. He talked animatedly, increasing the pace of his business. Soon he took a drink and dismissed the little man. Bolt waited until the fellow was out the door, then took his beer to the table.

Krenchell nodded a greeting. "What the hell are you doing here?" he demanded. Moisture glistened on his thick lower lip. "You could destroy my cover!" He took a large white handkerchief from inside his suit jacket and dabbed the lip, fastidious. And nervous. He seemed to be evaluating Bolt.

"Ah," Bolt said, understanding. Krenchell seldom worked in the field. He would be shaky for a while, even the most innocent event churning up fear and questions. Either he would adjust, or get out. "Yes, but I'm taking an equal risk," Bolt reminded him. "There's my cover, too."

Krenchell's brows raised, apologetic as he saw Bolt's point. Why was it, Bolt asked himself as he studied the computer expert, he always had the feeling Krenchell was playing a role? Now that he was sitting across from him, the arrogance was subdued, almost missing, and the overweight body seemed incapable of anything more strenuous than carrying a PC to the car.

"Of course," Krenchell said. He drank again, emptied the glass, wiped his lip. "Olds didn't send you?" He hissed slightly when he talked, a problem with sibilants, if Bolt remembered correctly.

"In a manner of speaking," Bolt said, "yes."

"To check on me?"

"Tell me what you've been doing," Bolt said.

Krenchell opened his mouth, closed it. His eyes narrowed. "You first."

They stared at each other, a standoff. Bolt summoned the waiter, and Krenchell ordered whiskey and water while Bolt chose another beer.

"Perhaps we can help one another," Bolt said reasonably.

"Perhaps," Krenchell said, his voice doubtful.

"You came out of the hotel where General Akbar Salehi is staying. I'm interested in the general. In fact, Olds is, too. Perhaps the general is the reason you are in Dubai."

Krenchell was silent, but he didn't dispute what Bolt was saying.

"As you may know," Bolt went on, "the general has an elite force called the Desert Falcons. I'm also interested in them."

This seemed to relieve Krenchell. "The Desert Falcons are of no interest to me."

Their drinks arrived. Krenchell imperiously waved the waiter away. He would pay later. Bolt peeled a five-dollar bill from the roll in his pocket and laid it on the table. He was still living off the yakuza money.

"Perhaps we *can* be of service to one another," Krenchell decided. He eyed Bolt speculatively, pleased with his decision.

They drank.

"Why are you here?" Bolt asked again.

"Checking out Iran's military computer system." Krenchell told Bolt about his cover as Swiss banker Horst Renssauer. "I'm hoping General Salehi will get me close enough to check through their system. I have a feeling that perhaps Iran's behind the computer problems we've been seeing."

"Iran?" Bolt was astounded.

"It's possible they could have stolen the capability," Krenchell continued. "Just as they apparently have stolen right and left to put together a nuclear facility."

"You know about the installation?" Bolt said. "Olds didn't."

"I don't tell Olds everything. Do you?"

Bolt was silent. Of course he didn't. "You told Olds you thought the problems originated from several sources, not one."

Krenchell nodded. "That's what I thought then. Now I have a report from a very reliable person..."

"You know about Israel's military system going down, and then their telephones?"

"Olds didn't tell me," Krenchell said, studying the glass on the table. "I haven't checked in with him for a couple days. You fill me in."

Bolt obliged, describing the uproar at Mossad headquarters and then at the nuclear facility.

Krenchell seemed strangely excited. He drank and dabbed his lip. And drank again.

"Do the two events mean something special to you?" Bolt asked.

Krenchell looked up, smiled. "Nothing special. Wouldn't it be ironic if Iran attained world domination? A nation with a history of oppression, an ancient culture most people have forgotten?"

"Not ironic. Highly dangerous. Iran thrives on violence. Look at the young boys they sent in, the *basij*. The kids were ordered out front in human waves. They absorbed Iraqi fire and exploded the mines and boobytraps so Iran's regular troops could survive to fight."

"Ah," Krenchell said, "but the *basij* were martyrs. Khomeini promised them they'd go straight to paradise."

"Right. I wonder where Khomeini went."

"Who cares?" Krenchell shrugged.

"So you think Iran is smart enough to put together some diabolical weapon to screw up communications and computers?" Bolt asked.

"I'm beginning to think so," Krenchell said seriously.

"Let me get this straight," Bolt said. He crossed his arms, reciting. "Iran entered Israel's top-secret military system, screwed up our communications satellite, screwed up Israel's telephone system, and sent electronic junk mail throughout the United States, and . . . Well, you know the other incidents. How? Why?"

"That's what I'm going to Iran to find out."

"Well, for starters, I'd say *computer virus*. This sounds like a natural for it. A difficult-to-detect, self-perpetuating electronic disease that can erase files, restructure data, change control and entry commands . . . the sky's the limit."

"There's one large problem: access."

"No problem really," Bolt said thoughtfully. "It copies itself secretly from disk to disk within the same machine. It travels over telephone lines when one agency sends data to another. It's hand carried by disk or portable computer from the office to home, or vice versa."

"You're suggesting that what we've been witnessing is the result of an accidental, out-of-control computer virus?" Krenchell seemed to like the idea. Or perhaps he was simply amused by it.

"I don't think I'm far off," Bolt said. "That would explain how Israel's military computers were affected. One moment of carelessness, one thoughtless exchange of data—that's all it would take for the virus to infect a system, even a protected system."

Krenchell rubbed his chin. "All right, you've got a point. Maybe it's not Iran. But I've still got to check it out."

"Sure you do. Your job."

Bolt and Krenchell drank.

"Why are you here?" Krenchell asked. It was his turn.

Bolt gave an abbreviated version of his investigation of Bushi Nakamora's murder and how it had led him through Tami Tanaka to Dubai.

"You never found the package in Tokyo . . . " Krenchell mused. "Strange. Have any idea what was in it? Where it is now?"

"Not a clue," Bolt said.

"Too bad. So I am here investigating computers, and you are here tracking this Sarah Maizlish in hopes of retrieving Dr. Lambert."

"And ultimately solving Bushi Nakamora's

murder," Bolt reminded him. "A matter of national security. Until we know whether his job played a factor in his death, the case is open."

"Of course."

They finished their drinks.

"You may end up going to Tehran," Krenchell decided. "Perhaps we will meet there."

"If not, then at Langley."

"At Langley."

They stood. Krenchell paid his bill and they walked out the door into the glittering city night. They strolled along the sidewalk back toward the Gulf Hotel, where Bolt would resume a stakeout, wait for Sarah and the general.

In the street the colorful flow of Dubai's exotic four-wheeled and four-legged traffic streamed by. Behind them a car's tires squealed as it rounded a corner too fast.

"I think I will stay overnight here," Krenchell said. "Much easier to find a suitable room in Dubai than in Tehran. Nothing has been right there since the shah left."

The tires' squealing was an ordinary city sound, nothing to be concerned about, Bolt thought. Except that the squealing continued too damn long.

He looked back. Horns honked. Angry drivers yelled out their windows, shook their fists. A black Toyota sedan was weaving through the traffic, much too fast. It looked brand-new, as if it'd just rolled out of a ship's package. And been stolen.

Bolt stared. The sedan was headed straight toward them. In it were four men. He saw the two in the front seat. Japanese. Again, dammit!

"What is it?" Krenchell was alarmed by Bolt's sudden change in demeanor, intensity.

Bolt pushed Krenchell across the sidewalk toward the safety of a pharmacy's wall. Krenchell was field-inexperienced, likely to get himself killed. Bolt felt responsible.

"Yakuzas," Bolt snapped. "Keep out of the way. We've got to get out of here!"

CHAPTER
16

In Daniel Lambert's dream it was the early 1900s. He was with Robert Peary slogging through the bitter cold, the ice and snow toward the North Pole. His teeth ached from chattering. His fingers were immobilized. He hadn't felt his feet for days. So cold was the blinding white day that the dogs whimpered and the rubber rimming his snowshoes cracked brittle as a dry leaf. Peary had advised him not to choose those snowshoes.

Lambert was trying to resolve the snowshoe problem when he felt the rough hands on his shoulders again. He was making a serious attempt to think, and some imbecile was yelling in his ear.

"Wake up!" the voice demanded in accented English. "Up! Dr. Lambert, you must open your eyes! *Stand!*"

His lips formed the word *no*. He didn't hear his mouth say it. But he must have, because someone was terribly angry about his refusal.

This puzzled Dr. Lambert. Who was angry? He'd spent his lifetime in a constant state of negotiations—with politicians, government officials, townspeople, technicians, engineers, chemists, other physicists, even his wife. Once, perhaps twice in the past forty years someone had been so angry that he'd lost his temper. Lambert had considered the occasion a defeat.

The mark of his success had been to make deals in which everyone got something, and people shook hands afterwards with their dignities intact. There was no anger. No need of it.

"Dr. Lambert!" The voice and shaking again. "Get up. You have slept long enough. You have work to do!"

This last interested the doctor. Work was what his life was about. He opened his eyes.

He didn't recognize any of the men standing over him. They wore uniforms, and a small angry man with a knife slash on his left cheek and wearing a lieutenant's uniform seemed to be in charge. What was that insignia on their shoulders? Some bird. He didn't recognize it, or this place with its concrete walls. So tiny. A cell. No, it couldn't be a cell. It smelled of mold and . . . something frighteningly human he couldn't quite identify.

"Where am I?" Dr. Lambert rasped. His voice was odd. Suddenly he shivered. The cell was freezing. He shivered again. Had he been kidnapped? But when? How? He couldn't remember . . .

"You will come with us," the scarred lieutenant said. "Get up."

Lambert studied the lieutenant and his soldiers. They were not Israelis. The words above their shirt pockets were in Farsi.

Iranians! A knot of fear lodged in his chest.

"I will stay here," Lambert announced. His voice cracked. He ached all over with the cold.

The lieutenant's face thickened with color. The scar turned from white to bruised purple.

"You will get up!" the lieutenant snarled.

Lambert couldn't move. For a moment he looked straight into the lieutenant's eyes and saw the animal inside. He could not work with this man, with people who hired this man. There would be no negotiations with them.

"No," he said.

The lieutenant made a deep guttural sound in his throat. He grabbed the neck of Lambert's nightshirt and hauled him straight up off the floor from where he'd been lying. The soldiers cleared a path. The fabric cut into his neck. He closed his lips to keep from groaning. The fear in his chest suffocated him.

The lieutenant dragged the scientist across the cell and threw him out into the stone corridor. The doctor's shoulder smashed into the wall. Pain enveloped him like a shroud. Somewhere in the distance someone cried out, begged for mercy.

In Dubai, Marcus Krenchell slammed against the pharmacy wall. The impact jarred him to the marrow. Christ. The damn yakuzas. They had failed him. Not only had Bolt survived their attacks, he had managed the improbable success of bumping into Krenchell in this out-of-the-way Middle East port.

"Move it!" Bolt bellowed, shoving Krenchell down the street. Bolt thought he was *saving* him, Krenchell realized, startled, then amused.

Krenchell wasn't ready to compromise his cover, so he dutifully ran alongside Bolt, who raced as if they were both Olympic marathoners.

There was one good thing that came from the encounter, Krenchell told himself as he huffed along. And that was Bolt's confirmation that the CIA was still ignorant of Bushi Nakamura and Iwa Matsumoto's killer. And equally ignorant of the package Bushi had sent to Tokyo. Which meant Krenchell might still locate the antidote to the virus . . . if it was out there somewhere.

Horns honked behind them. Furious drivers shouted obscenities in a multitude of languages at the black Toyota as it hurtled toward Bolt through the traffic and screeched to the curb. Pedestrians scattered.

The four yakuzas jumped out, doors hanging open, motor still running, and rushed across the sidewalk. Two flung themselves at Bolt and two attacked Krenchell.

Bolt whirled, feet and hands swinging in powerful karate blows.

Krenchell pulled out his Mauser. His two yakuzas hesitated. Krenchell backed away. The two attackers followed, their menacing gazes focused on him and the gun, waiting for him to make a mistake, falter.

He growled loudly in Japanese, "Leave us alone or I'll kill you!"

"No!" Bolt shouted. "I want them alive!" He jammed an elbow strike into the yakuza behind him.

Krenchell was impressed. Bolt was a good man to have on your side. In fact, Bolt might prove useful in Tehran.

"Sakura Shogun says forget Bolt!" Krenchell whispered urgently to his two men. Sakura Shogun—Cherry Blossom Chief—was his code name within the Japanese coke ring.

The two stared at Krenchell a long moment. They had been hired by an intermediary, had never seen or spoken to Krenchell, didn't know anyone above their clan boss.

"I am Sakura Shogun!" Krenchell told them.

Their black eyes blinked once, twice. Abruptly they spun, obeying. They wouldn't bother Bolt again until they received counterorders. They touched the shoulders of the other two yakuzas, and the four raced back to the car.

Bolt stared after them in astonishment. He straightened up.

"What in hell?" he said.

The yakuza driver gunned the motor, the doors slammed closed, and the car shot out into the traffic.

"Did you do something?" Krenchell asked Bolt. "Did you frighten them away?"

Bolt looked at him suspiciously. "Your two split before my two."

"I thought there might have been some communication between them. Some agreement to desist."

"Not that I saw," Bolt said.

"Well, you must have done *something!*" Krenchell insisted. There was an interesting honesty about Bolt that made him susceptible to the lies of those he thought he should trust.

"The only thing I did was try to take them," Bolt said.

"You wanted to ask questions?"

"Goddamn right!" Bolt stalked down the street toward the Gulf Hotel, leaving Krenchell behind as if he were a hopeless child, or an idiot.

"Such as?"

"Why in hell are they after me? Who in hell sent them!? Get the picture?" Bolt pivoted and leaned up against the limestone wall of a bank. Across the street and one structure away stood the Gulf Hotel. This was as good a place to wait as any, his slouched posture seemed to say. For a while.

Krenchell sighed a weary sigh. "Of course. Well, personally, I'm relieved they changed their minds. I thought I had you to thank for that. Obviously I was wrong. But I do appreciate your spotting them."

Bolt waved him off, no longer interested in talking to Krenchell. Krenchell watched Bolt study the cars and trucks that droned steadily up and down the street. The traffic was lighter. Bolt's cool blue eyes assessed the vehicles, probably looking for more yakuzas and watching for Sarah Maizlish.

Krenchell hailed a taxi. As he climbed in, he glanced back over his shoulder at the tall, lanky CIA operative. Krenchell had a sudden insight that he wouldn't fool Jake Bolt long. It was an odd sensation—a chill, something like respect.

He hoped Bolt would have to go to Tehran. He should be able to mislead him long enough for that. Bolt could prove useful. Perhaps he might be tricked into introducing the virus into Iran's military system himself.

At Vandenberg Air Force Base in California, the early morning sea crashed relentlessly against the high rocky palisades.

Along the top of the palisades stretched a large, pristine strip of real estate that made developers salivate. The ocean here was hazardous for navigation, but the grassy rolling land displayed stunning sea and sky views that took the breath away. Instead of multimillion-dollar estates, this grand acreage held a series of well-spaced concrete launching pads with tall housings, and the low, tidy cluster of administrative buildings of one of the United States's most important air force bases.

This morning the ocean fog hid the rocket's fiery liftoff from the view of the nearby town's residents. But the deepthroated roar echoed across the valley for about five minutes, alerting them another payload had gone into space.

This launch was not for spying, photo reconnaissance, or ocean surveillance. Sent aloft by a quasi-governmental consortium called Galactic Players, the new satellite would relay phone calls, video images, and data around the world. It was in perfect operating condition.

It had been tested, checked, retested, and rechecked.

A security officer was assigned to call Clifton Olds at Langley to inform him of the successful launch.

The communications satellite had a vital mission. Once it or any of its cousins entered orbit, it could link any point on the globe below with any other point. All that was needed was a dish at both of those two spots. Then hotels could receive reservation information from headquarters, convenience stores could send in sales reports, paging companies could track people nationally rather than in just one city, and bankers could transfer funds, pay bills, and make loans. Another advantage the satellites offered was that more than one point could receive a single signal, which made the orbiting machinery ideal for distributing television programming.

The role of this just-launched satellite was simple. It and all its components were sanitary, healthy, uncompromised. Because of that, the satellite was expected to end U.S. communications troubles in the areas it covered.

If it did not, then the United States would have conclusive evidence that someone or something was interfering with communications from the ground.

In the Gulf Hotel, Sally Mather, aka Sarah Maizlish, poured rum and Coke into a tall hotel glass. Her back to General Akbar Salehi, she opened the tiny white packet and dropped in the powder. She whisked the drink with a plastic stirrer. She laid the stirrer on the bar and carried two glasses toward the general, who sprawled across the gaudy floral pattern of the suite's sofa.

The curtains were closed against the Dubai night, but muffled street sounds floated up. Horns, engines, an occasional siren. Sally liked the sounds. They were normal, reassuring.

"You are really blond?" he asked her, his words slurred. In Tehran it was against his religion to drink alcohol. In Dubai he didn't worry about what was against his religion in Iran. This was his sixth drink that evening. Sally had waited to drop in the knockout powder until he was back in the suite and already drunk.

"Really," she said, smiled, and sat beside him.

She ran her fingers down his cheek, felt the stubbled texture of his skin. Unlike most Iranians in government service, he had no beard. In a coarse way, he was handsome with his broad features and large moist eyes. She reminded herself of that, looked for things in him that might appeal to her, in case she had to go to bed with him.

She sipped from her glass. She'd tried everything that evening, all her usual tricks, hints, flatterings, and carefully couched questions. But she'd learned nothing about Daniel Lambert or Iran's new nuclear facility. She was frightened for the physicist. The longer the Iranians had him, the shorter his life expectancy.

If she had to, she would go to bed with the general. It was trite but accurate: sex loosened a man's tongue. But all she had to do with this subhuman creature was get through tonight. This one night.

Smiling at her, the general drank deeply, set his glass on the low coffee table before them. He grasped her fingers, crushed them to his heart as if he were a mooning schoolboy.

"Blond all over?" he said, his eyes large and hopeful. *"Everywhere?"*

"Why, general," she said primly, "that's a personal question!" She reached to the coffee table, ferried his glass back into his hand.

"I know, Sally," he said, enunciating carefully. "I intend to get quite personal with you."

She ran her fingers down his other cheek, smiled at him.

"If you finish your drink," she suggested shyly, "we can go into your bedroom and discuss it."

His dark eyes glowed. His narrow lips smiled. He lifted the glass, threw back his head, and drank.

"Now!" He set the empty glass on the table, took her hand, stood, and walked unsteadily to the bedroom.

"Let me help you," she said softly, guiding him to the bed.

His eyelids closed, snapped open again.

"That's what I'm here for," she told him. "To help you." She pressed him down on the cotton coverlet. "You are a great man. Your country is very fortunate to have you." She took off his shoes.

He was listening. She hoped he would remember this part, the words of admiration, the caressing, her undressing him. Early tomorrow they would awake in bed together, naked. She would tell him what an exceptional lover he was.

"I want to know about you," she said. "Everything. What you like. What you do. Your work. Iran is such an exciting country . . . "

By the time she started on the buttons of his shirt, he was snoring.

The night lengthened, and Bolt continued his faithful watch over the hotel. After Sarah, the general, and the Falcon retinue had returned, Bolt found the three white limos locked into the hotel's garage two blocks away. The three chauffeurs had vanished into the night, eager for their own good time.

Which was what the general had had. He'd staggered from his limo toward the hotel, Sarah supporting him on one side while on the other, holding him up under the shoulder, was a little colonel in a Falcon's uniform. The colonel shot outraged looks at Sarah, but she ignored him. On the hotel's doorstep, General Salehi stopped abruptly to give Sarah a lingering kiss.

And then the whole group had trooped inside.

Bolt refused to feel jealousy. This was business. Sarah's chosen business, and his.

He stayed in his window alcove and waited until the lights on the seventh floor went on. Then he reconnoitered the area, found the three garaged limos, checked the hotel's quiet back exit where a beat-up old Honda was either parked or deserted.

He returned to the nearly silent street and climbed three steps to the front door of a closed investment business. Here were double recessed wood doors and a view that included, to the right, the hotel's front door and, to the left, the mouth of the alley that anyone leaving or entering the hotel's rear door would have to use.

Bolt sat down on the chill marble landing and leaned back against the doors. Not as comfortable accommodations as Krenchell had acquired for the night, Bolt was sure, but he was accustomed to it.

He half closed his eyes and drifted into a semiawake trance. The hours passed slowly. Bolt dozed and awakened dozens of times. Faint in the distance he could hear ships chugging into port. The stars were dim, clouded by the city's lights. Occasionally he stood and shook out his muscles, then returned to his trance on the hard marble.

It was during the long dead hour before dawn that he first heard—or perhaps sensed—the footsteps. They were quiet, padding steps, trained. It was far more than a wakeful citizen taking a restful stroll.

Bolt recognized the rhythm of trained surveillance and avoidance. If he was right, the surveillance was of ,the Gulf Hotel, and the avoidance was of him. He'd been spotted by someone he hadn't known was out there.

Eyes slitted, he waited as the steps echoed from the right—the hotel's front—in a quick, quiet run. Then a pause. More running, almost in front of him.

He saw the figure, a man in a black jumpsuit. The guy skirted a pool of streetlight. For a moment his back was to Bolt.

Bolt got silently to his feet, ran toward him.

CHAPTER
17

Bolt slowed, crept forward. The man was all intensity and alertness. He was slender, shoulders rounded in a crouch as he hid in the dark shadow beneath a date palm. He had a small black plastic walkie-talkie in his hand, and a revolver holstered beneath his armpit. His face was averted, watching the Gulf Hotel. A trained recon expert.

Bolt was almost there, ready to take him, when he sensed a sudden change in the man. A stiffness, a higher level of awareness perhaps. The man rotated slightly to face faint sounds—the smooth purrings of well-tuned engines in the distance.

As if released from an enclosure, the engines suddenly grew louder.

Now they were coming down the street toward them.

The man took an unconscious, eager step forward. He raised his walkie-talkie to speak. But as he raised it, he turned more. Instantly he froze, grabbed his revolver. He'd caught Bolt in his peripheral vision.

Bolt ran the last six steps, kicked high. The revolver slapped from the man's hand.

"Yakob Bolt!" the man whispered, astonished, as he stared at his attacker. His arms and feet were wide apart, ready to lunge.

"I know you?" Bolt stopped, too. And the man's face fell into place in his memory. An Israeli soldier. "You're from the Dimona installation."

The man spun on his heel and raced away down the street in the opposite direction from the hotel, from the powerful-sounding cars that were approaching through the silence.

Bolt turned to look at what the Israeli had been waiting for.

The general's white limos were crawling up the empty street to the hotel's curb, a ghostly caravan in the predawn.

Bolt checked his watch; forty-five minutes until the sun rose. He ducked into the date palm's shadow to watch.

Amazed, he saw the contingent from the night before repeat its actions. It swept out of the old hotel and into the waiting limos. In the street's lamplight, the general's face was drawn and pasty. He wore sunglasses and held Sarah close beside him. She was still—or again—in her red business suit. The general seemed miserable with a hangover, but refused to let it slow him down.

Once loaded, the limos made U turns and regally moved away down the street in the direction from which they'd come. Slowly they increased speed. As soon as they were out of sight, Bolt bounded down the steps toward the hotel.

A new registration clerk was at the desk.

"I have an appointment with General Salehi," Bolt told him.

"You've just missed him."

"Yeah, I'm late. I'm supposed to interview him for a feature story." He pulled out his credentials, showed them. "I'm a reporter with *The Sydney Times.*"

"A reporter," the clerk repeated, nodded. The clerk was of medium build with a broad nose and teeth that clicked as he talked. He seemed to enjoy the clicking. It gave him individuality in a dead-end job in a dead-end world. That could be useful to Bolt.

"How about this?" Bolt put the credentials away and pulled out the fat yakuza roll of U.S. currency. "I'll plug the hotel in my article if you'll rent me a car to catch up with the general."

The clerk watched the roll. Bolt peeled off a fifty. The clerk looked away, silent. It would cost Bolt more.

"Where's the general going?" Bolt continued, laid down another fifty. "The foreign editor'll can me if I don't get this story. You can tell your boss you're the one who got the free publicity for the hotel!"

The clerk clicked his teeth. Not yet enough.

Bolt peeled off another fifty, and another, and another. The clerk was silent so long, and so much money was piling up on the countertop, that Bolt finally reached across, grabbed his collar front, and yanked him up, nose to nose. Even at this early hour the guy's breath stank of garlic.

"I didn't expect to have to *buy* the car," Bolt said. "This is a rental."

"Yes, s-sir."

With one hand, Bolt halved the pile and stuck it inside the clerk's jacket pocket. He returned the rest to his own.

"Where's the car?" Bolt demanded.

"Behind me, s-sir."

"Show me."

The clerk led Bolt around the registration desk

and down a hall. At the end he opened a door onto the dark alley. There stood the ancient Honda Civic that Bolt had noticed during his recon. The body was rusted, and big gashes afflicted the doors and fenders. It looked like a war casualty.

"I paid two hundred bucks for this?" Bolt said, incredulous. It was worse than he'd imagined. "Does it run?"

"I drive it every day." The clerk's teeth clicked at the insult. He handed Bolt the key. "The general is going to the camel races near Adh Dhayd. There's a map in the glove compartment." He hurried back into the hotel, still a loser. He couldn't get the highest price even when he had a monopoly.

Bolt slid behind the Honda's dirty wheel. A layer of grease and dust covered everything. He inserted the key, turned, and the motor choked, coughed, and finally sputtered to life.

He got out the map to Adh Dhayd. Sarah, the Mossad, and the Israeli Defense Force had a plan. It looked as if it were scheduled for Adh Dhayd. One way or another Bolt would be there.

Israeli Major Ed Cohen took the call at his desk on the carrier cruising the Arabian Sea off Oman. He was going over one last time the plan for the raid. The map was spread flat on his desk. As he listened to the recon report, his gaze focused on the terrain surrounding Adh Dhayd. It was flat desert, with protective hills in the distance to which the helicopters would fly as soon as they had their cargo.

"Jacob Bolt?" he repeated the name. "You're sure?" The voice at the other end of the line was dim from a poor connection, but the answer was clear: "I saw him with my own eyes. He attacked me!"

The major sighed. They should have held Bolt at Dimona. There would have been problems later with the CIA, but it would have been only two days, and the CIA would have forgotten the incident once Dr. Lambert was safely retrieved. Success was good for all of them. It kept morale high, and support money flowing.

Major Cohen ordered the recon man to return to base and hung up. At least all else seemed ready.

Not an easy mission, but very possible. Thinking of the difficulties of Entebbe, Major Cohen decided it was more than possible. It was relatively simple. He would remember to tell his wife that when he returned. She worried too much. He looked at the photo on the desk: Deborah and his son Josh. Two years old now. The kid loved his toy jets and helicopters. He had the biggest collection of any boy in the kibbutz.

The first hesitant rays of pink dawn rose through the ebony night, spreading slowly, high over the desert racecourse.

Camels bawled. Long Mercedes sedans, chauffeur-driven Rolls Royces, sturdy Chevrolet pickups, and jaunty Range Rovers rolled to stops facing the course. Behind them waited more than two hundred stomping, snorting, impatient race camels. The animals' earthy stink mixed in the clean dry air with the odors of diesel fuel and oil.

Sally Mather and General Salehi sat in camp chairs that the ever-prepared Falcons had had stored in one of the limos' trunks. Sally's purse was on her lap, and at the bottom of it was her small Colt. She and the general sat alone like the tourists they were and drank harsh steaming coffee from delicate china cups while a Falcon armed with an AK47 stood behind them with a shiny silver thermos, waiting to serve them. Many men at this event carried weapons, and they hoisted them around with great casualness. This was still the frontier, no matter how many luxurious vehicles, radios, and portable television sets.

The land stretched off in an ocean of sand toward the twin coastal emirates of Dubai and Sharjah. The racecourse was a simple pounded track that ran in a straight line to the horizon. As the sun rose, the bleak desert landscape turned from brown to beige to glittering lemon yellow.

"The Arabs call their camels ships of the desert," the general instructed Sally. He was Persian, not Arabian, but he and his ancestors shared millenia of history with the Arabs. His eyes were hidden behind the dark glasses and he drank his coffee in gulps. "The camel was their warrior's mount, cargo carrier, standard of wealth. It was the source of almost all their necessities—milk, hides, wool."

"And now it's no longer needed."

"That's right." He looked at her with appreciation. A woman who could comprehend the importance of a camel was worthwhile. "The camel is obsolete. The days of nomad Bedouin are finished. In one generation we in the Middle East have built highways to connect our oases, and bought Jeeps and pickups to patrol our dunes."

Thirty camels lined up. Bedouin trainers hoisted up Pakistani and Bangladeshi boys to jockey them.

The barefoot boys wore walkie-talkies slung from their necks.

"They're so young!" she said.

"Six to ten is prime. They wear Velcro on the seats of their pants, and the saddles are covered with Velcro. You see, all of us appreciate Western progress."

"The boys stick to the saddles," she said, understanding.

A Bedouin in a long white robe and the traditional white *khaffiya* covering his head raised a pistol and shot into the sky. A roar of excitement rose from the crowd.

The camels raised their heads, complaining. With sticks the jockeys beat the animals' bony flanks. Reluctantly the ungainly bodies responded. The beasts and boys took off in a straight line down the course. A fleet of cars and trucks drove along with them. Enthusiastic drivers and passengers shouted encouragement at the camels from their open windows.

"*Ya Allah! Ya Allah!*" Bedouin trainers yelled into their walkie-talkies. "For God's sake, hurry!"

General Salehi drained his coffee cup, held it over his shoulder for his Falcon to refill. Ahead of them the camels and vehicles disappeared in a cloud of desert dust.

"They will go six miles, then come back," the general told Sally. "Ah, camel racing. A magnificent sport. And a good investment." He was feeling better, expansive as he instructed this young blond innocent. "A top thoroughbred can bring two million dirhams."

"About six hundred thousand dollars," Sally said, genuinely impressed.

He patted her knee, sipped his coffee, a contented man. "Almost as worthwhile as a good woman," he told her.

"Even an American woman?" she teased. "Americans are still not welcomed in Iran, I'm told."

"Ah, yes. You Americans are *shaitans*, devils." The tone of his voice convinced her that he felt otherwise.

"Aren't you disturbed being with me . . . especially after . . . last night?" she said. "Our . . . intimacy . . ."

"It makes it better, my dear." He handed his empty coffee cup to his Falcon aide and waved him away. Hung over, still a little drugged from the knockout powder, but as always full of his own importance, he willingly accepted the night of passion she had so graphically described. He peered at her over the tops of his sunglasses. "The forbidden is always sweeter. And you are so very blond. Most gratifyingly blond."

"I wish I could go to Iran with you."

"It can be arranged. I sometimes invite foreign guests to stay at my home."

"But I can't leave my job."

"The one barbarism of the Western world is that beautiful women think they must work."

She smiled at the general, finished her coffee, and looked over her shoulder until she saw a Falcon who wasn't staring off at the horizon, waiting for the camels and accompanying horde to gallop back. She gestured and he came, without ever looking at her face, to retrieve the cup.

"It's too bad," she continued to the general. "Iran is a fascinating country. And you're a fascinating man. I really did think you were a king. You exude . . . such power."

"Thank you, my dear."

"Iran under the shah always seemed to be a powerful nation. You had a huge military, and of course all the weapons we gave you. But now . . ."

"The war with Iraq drained us," he said curtly.

"It's too bad," she said soothingly. She put her hand on his knee. She drew little circles on the smooth Egyptian cotton of his trousers. "Wouldn't it be nice if we were allies? I mean, then we could still be giving you our state-of-the-art technology, help you raise your standard of living. We'd computerize everything! Maybe even start up a nuclear power plant for you!"

He chuckled, picked up her hand, kissed the fingers. "So beautiful. Why do you worry your beautiful self with such things? We have plenty of computers. What we don't have is enough blond women. Now watch ahead, the camels will be coming back. Then you will see excitement! But I warn you, don't get in front of a Bedouin's rifle. If he wins, he'll be sure to shoot it off. If he loses, he might shoot the owner of the winning camel!"

"These people carry guns like people in my country carry briefcases."

He laughed. "Charming! You are charming!"

Billowing dust and the herd of noisy, stomping camels told Bolt he'd found the racetrack. It was isolated, unmarked, and located in a vast desert wilderness. Without a map he'd never have found it.

He climbed out of the Honda. The old car had

stopped dead three times on the road here. Each time it had sputted back to life and bounced along fine until the next abrupt halt. He parked between a big pickup and a low-slung BMW, hoping their presence would protect it. There was no public transportation back to Dubai.

He moved among the parked vehicles, keeping his distance from the camels. The animals were born with bad tempers, and were notorious for kicking and trampling when crossed. He avoided looking at the Bedouin with their rifles and pistols. They drank coffee, traded stories, and watched the dust cloud in the distance.

He continued moving, working his way toward the front of the cars. Handlers were preparing the next set of reluctant camels, urging, pulling, and prodding them closer to the start line.

And then he saw them. Sarah Maizlish and General Salehi, sitting alone together like best friends . . . or lovers.

Bolt stayed back, watching. Sarah and the general were drinking coffee and talking. Bolt's gaze swept the area looking for signs of the Mossad or of Israeli commandos. But all appeared normal, or as normal as an outsider could perceive at an event so exotic to the Western mind.

He heard an odd sound. Almost a crackling. Again his eyes surveyed the racecourse and its surroundings. He couldn't quite figure out what the sound was. Yet it was familiar.

The noise grew louder, a buzzing.

Then more distinct.

Even though he shouldn't have been able to, it seemed to him he could hear the rotors beat.

There were helicopters. Two big ones. And they were headed here.

CHAPTER
18

"There's the racecourse," Lieutenant Greber said loudly over the roar of the helicopter's rotors. "Directly ahead." High-powered binoculars to his eyes, he gazed out at the early morning desert.

"Yeah, I think I see it," Major Ed Cohen said. Beneath his hands the SA 365M Panther's controls vibrated. The second Panther was positioned to the side and slightly behind. It was a comforting feel, the helicopter's familiar sound and sensation. Also there was the knowledge of being in control. That was important to Cohen. He could have ordered someone else to pilot the bird, but he ran his missions from the front.

"The camels have just taken off," the lieutenant said. "There go the cars and trucks after them."

"Good. Just as we'd hoped. We'll increase speed, get there while the race is at its most distant point."

Cohen radioed instructions to the other pilot. With most of the spectators riding alongside the racing camels, General Salehi would be left back at the starting line with his own soldiers and a few Bedouin. It was a manageable number for the two attack helicopters. But it would leave them only minutes to complete their work and get out of there.

They were silent as the racecourse grew more distinct, a butterscotch blot dotted with vehicles and a miniature herd of camels on the pale morning sand.

"It's going to be a hot one," the lieutenant observed. "Water mirages all over the place."

The major didn't respond. He watched the racecourse and listened to the Turbomeca motors and felt the nearly forty-foot blades spin overhead. He thought about his son, Josh, who had a cold. And his wife, Deborah, who worried too much. And his father, a pilot who had died in the Six Day War of 1967. He wondered whether Josh would grow up to be a pilot, too. For a moment he felt a tremendous surge of pride. And then, as was his ritual, he wiped everything from his thoughts.

Everything but the mission.

Slowly, bit by meticulous bit, he reviewed their carefully conceived plan. Today's work would surprise the world and cause outrage in parts of it. But it would send out a warning to terrorists and the governments that supported them that their immoral warfare against Israel must end, for if it did not, the retaliation would be rapid, extensive, and, when necessary, as brutal as the acts of the terrorists themselves.

Bolt watched the two camouflage-painted helicopters approach. They were big birds, close to fifty feet long, he estimated. He studied them as their features grew clearer. There were no nation's markings painted on the skins. Suspicious but explainable as emirate helicopters on maneuvers. And then he saw what he had already begun to think. It was the only way it could happen out here where speed and accessibility were vital. The helicopters were armed with rockets and machine guns. Again explainable as local maneuvers, but Bolt didn't believe it.

Not after the way Sarah had taken off from the Dimona facility; she'd left because she had something important to do. And then she'd gone after General Salehi, spent the night with him—a top leader of a nation that considered Israel its enemy, a general whose prize soldiers were the Falcon commandos who had kidnapped Israel's top nuclear administrator. It was too much of a coincidence that two armed helicopters should be on a straight course now toward the race track where the general sat exposed, relatively vulnerable, with only a dozen men to guard him. Were they planning to execute him?

Suddenly General Salehi jumped up. He'd spotted the helicopters. He shouted and pointed at them. Bolt moved in closer.

General Akbar Salehi's heart pounded. Absently he pressed a hand to his chest. The helicopters could be anyone's. Perhaps Dubai's ruler had sent a courtesy greeting. Maybe they carried a vital message from Tehran. Or it could be a simple coincidence that two helicopters happened to be passing overhead. Yes, it could be any of those possibilities.

Except that the helicopters wore camouflage paint. They had no markings. And they were armed. *Heavily armed*.

The general jumped to his feet, knocked his

camp chair over. "Colonel Rizvi!" he bellowed. "Rizvi! We're being attacked!"

A deep thrill vibrated through him. His heart thundered as if it would break his ribcage. It was erotic, almost orgasmic, this excitement. He *knew* those helicopters were after him, knew it with an animal instinct that he'd first noticed in the jungles of Vietnam and later honed to a trusted intuition in the sadistic border skirmishes between his country and Iraq. It had been years since then, but he hadn't forgotten. How else had he survived Khomeini and his purges? How else had he managed to be Khomeini's victor?

"Rizvi! Get the weapons!"

Sally Mather held her purse to her chest as if it were a talisman. She watched Falcons run to the limo trunks, flip them open, and pull out AK-47 ammo and two antitank Armbrusts with shells. Highly dangerous, easily portable, the Armbrusts fired from the shoulder and cut through armored vehicles at three hundred meters like a knife through warm butter. With a maximum range of fifteen hundred meters, the weapons shot 67mm shells that weighed about a pound each. Enthusiasts called the lethal weapons Armbusters.

The general and his men carried more firepower than the Mossad had estimated. But it still wouldn't be enough, Sally thought grimly.

"General?" she said, touched his sleeve. The helicopters were coming within range of the Armbrusts. They wouldn't fire on the group yet. They wanted the general alive. Soon she would take him. It was her call.

General Salehi turned, his eyes glowing. Not crazed, but overfull of himself and his strength.

"Don't believe anyone who tells you struggle is noble," he said. He gestured back at the helicopters, faced them with his radiant eyes. "Winning is!" His manner added *at any cost.*

He stood there arrogantly, in his own mind a giant among weak men. Sally watched the helicopters and thought about Daniel Lambert, wondered where he was, what the general's men were doing to him this very moment. Was he even alive? Images of pain and torture filled her mind. She'd seen the shaking, twitching shells of survivors after questioning by jihad forces.

She looked at the general. Loathing swept through her. She took the little Colt Cobra Model E3 from her purse. A .38 Special, it shot six bullets and weighed less than half a kilogram. It was in the bush leagues of big-time armaments, but correctly applied, it was just as persuasive as the Armbrusts.

She jammed the Colt into the general's back, a little harder than necessary. He jerked with instant recognition.

"Tell your men to drop their weapons," she told him. "Now!"

The general hesitated. Then he seemed to swell with determination. No one would—*could*—intimidate him!

"Fight for Allah!" he roared to his men. He waved his arms, summoning them to their aggressive peaks, infusing them with his own commitment. "Kill for Allah!"

"Stop it, general!" Sally said, twisted the Colt into his back.

He jerked again, sullen, silent.

"*Ay! Ay! Ay!*" the Falcons shouted to their leader. They ran to positions. Two Falcons wrestled with the Armbrusts. The rest of the commandos divided and zeroed in on the incoming helicopters, aiming their AK-47s.

Around them the white-robed Bedouin began to understand the extent of what was happening. They called warnings to one another and scattered away, pulling favored camels with them. In the distance the tan cloud that signaled the progress of the race had reversed directions and was now returning.

"I will die a happy man!" the general suddenly shouted to his troops. "For the Falcons. For Iran. For Allah!" He stiffened, prepared to martyr himself to Sarah's bullets.

Ay! Ay! Ay!

"Don't be a damn fool," she snarled at his back. "You'll die all right. A failure *and* a fool!"

He shrugged, his gaze intent on the sky.

The helicopters swooped low. The Falcons' AK-47s barked. The bullets streaked upward.

The helicopters separated, passing through the rifle fire. Metal erupted on their sides like rows of small volcanos from the Falcons' bullets.

As the helicopters flew over, their machine guns strafed the desert floor. Sand spun up in thin, stinging clouds. Four Falcons flew back, bloodied. One screamed in pain and terror.

The general had a sudden revelation. "I'm the fool!?" he crowed triumphant to her. "You are! You aren't allowed to kill me. Otherwise you would have done so by now!"

She sped the muzzle of the Colt down his spine to his tail bone and down over his buttocks. She rammed it in high between his legs.

He froze.

"I'll shoot off your balls, you bastard," she told him in a deadly voice. "It won't kill you, but after the surgery you'll live in your own private hell. A eunuch!"

"Who are you?" he gasped.

"Walk!" she said, lifted the muzzle hard into his testicles. "To the closest helicopter! And order your men back. Now!"

He moved forward tentatively, stepping high, almost on his toes. "Hold your fire!" he yelled through the landing helicopters' noise.

Bolt watched as the helicopters swayed gently and settled down like enormous metal birds. Sand sprayed up in tornadoes, whipped by the spinning blades. The Falcons shielded their eyes. Bolt closed his briefly, then squinted. The helicopters' machine gun fire raked across the Falcons. Another eight went down.

Sarah and the general neared one of the choppers. Sarah had everything under control. She had her pistol stuck high up between the general's legs, on his balls. And her face was suffused with cold fury. Whatever the general had said—or done—was coming back full circle to him now.

Sarah was forcing the Iranian leader to the helicopters. It must be a kidnapping, what the Mossad and Israeli commandos had planned all along. Perfectly executed. Why?

And the answer came instantly to Bolt: logically, it was the first move to a prisoner exchange. The general for Dr. Lambert. Bolt smiled. Damn clever. The international community would be

indignant, furious at first, but in the end, who
could blame the Israelis for getting back their own?
Even Israel's worst enemies held grudging respect
for the outnumbered, resourceful nation.

As Sarah and the general passed, the Falcons
near them looked up. The general was talking to
them. They dropped their AK-47s, fell to the
ground to protect themselves from stray machine
gun bullets. The Falcons who were farther away
strained to hear over the constant roar of the
beating chopper blades.

Bolt moved in. Might as well hitch a ride back
to Jerusalem. The car he'd rented was worth less
than the two hundred dollars he'd paid, and he
would drop a note with a couple hundred more to
the clerk with the clicking teeth in the Gulf Hotel,
just to ease his conscience.

Soon the incident with Dr. Lambert would be
turned over to the diplomats and negotiators to ar-
range. Bolt continued to smile until it occurred to
him that he still hadn't resolved his initial mission: Who had killed Bushi Nakamura, and why?

And suddenly he had something else to think
about, to assess. He felt the disquieting sensation
of stealthy movement behind him. From the
corners of his eyes he saw a long morning shadow
flit and stop.

Swiftly he turned, caught the AK-47 as it slashed
down toward his head. There were three Falcons,
and he was trapped between them and the helicopters. They must have circled around when he'd
closed his eyes against the stinging sand. One
Falcon was the little colonel, the leader of this
breakout from the main group. The second aimed
an Armbrust antitank gun at the closest helicopter.

The third attacked Bolt. The colonel had a plan, and it included the elimination of Bolt, who was physically in the way—quietly so Sarah wouldn't hear, wouldn't reflexively blow the general's testicles off.

Bolt twisted the AK-47, crashed it back into the Falcon's belly. The man doubled over, vomited.

And the smokeless, flashless Armbrust exploded. It had no more sound than a pistol shot.

Its shell connected with the gas tank of the first helicopter. Instantly the chopper erupted in a searing orange-red fireball. Sarah and the general dove apart, dropped for safety to the sand.

Machine gun bullets from the remaining helicopter beat the sand, closing in on the Armbrust.

Bolt hurtled across the three meters toward the Falcon with the big gun. But the commando had already reloaded. He aimed the Armbrust again. Fired.

The lead helicopter's machine guns ripped across the desert floor, going for the weapon that had hit the other bird. Outside Major Ed Cohen's window the helicopter blazed in a solid ball of flames. Everyone on board had to be dead, Cohen knew. But he ignored it: the heat, the stench, the loss of his friends. The growing fear in his gut. Steadily he directed the bullets. Soon he would eliminate the Falcon's weapon. Save his bird and the mission. Almost there.

Two men had been fighting. One dressed in the Falcon uniform, the other as a tourist. The Falcon was on the ground, and the tourist was lunging toward the Falcon who held the weapon that had got the other bird's gas tank.

And suddenly the major saw the Falcon spasm. The weapon had gone off again.

Metal screeched as the shell ripped through his bird's gas tank. He broke a cardinal rule. He thought about Deborah and Josh, pictured them clearly in his mind. Would Josh grow up to be a pilot? He would never know. The lieutenant next to him screamed. The inferno swallowed them.

CHAPTER
19

Too late, Bolt rammed the Falcon back into the ground. The Armbrust flew out of the man's hands and landed with a dull thud.

The other chopper's gas tank burst in a thunderous explosion. Thick flames encircled the helicopter and licked up to the sky. A man's voice cried out in agony. Someone called for help in Hebrew. The odors of diesel and incinerated flesh stank in the air. Heat from the two firestorms swept across the desert.

A mighty shout of triumph arose from the surviving Falcon commandos.

Sarah scrambled to her feet, aimed the Colt at General Salehi who lay on the ground, shaking his head with confusion. It looked as if he'd been knocked unconscious by the helicopters' blasts. The murderous look on Sarah's face told Bolt that this time she would kill him. The original plan had failed, so General Salehi must die. At least she would have that. Revenge.

Bolt raced across the desolate sand. He tackled Sarah. Not only the general would die, but she would, too. The Falcons would mow her down.

Bolt crushed her into the sand beneath him. She struggled, slammed a fist up toward his face.

He ducked. The fist skidded ineffective across his skull.

"Stop it, Sarah!" he whispered rapidly. "They'll kill you!"

She rained blows at his head, neck, shoulders.

"I've got an idea," he insisted, trying to hold her down. "Play along with me."

She struggled to get her hands free.

"A tigress!" commented a voice over him. The owner of the voice leaned down. It was General Salehi, his cruel mouth thin with anger. He touched the muzzle of an AK-47 to the center of Sarah's forehead. "A blond tigress."

Sarah was suddenly very still. "Monster!" she breathed.

"A tigress in ewe's clothing," he went on. "Are you really a true-blue American, my dear? Or perhaps you live in Israel and belong to that inferior race we call the Jews?"

Furious she opened her mouth to speak again, and Bolt slugged her. The sequence of events that would have followed were unacceptable to Bolt: She would have told Salehi what she thought of him and Iran, and he would have put a bullet through her forehead. So instead of speaking, her beautiful blue eyes burned deep anger and betrayal at Bolt. She would never forgive him for this. And then she closed the lids, unconscious.

The general grabbed his shoulder, pulled him up. Bolt stared into the man's liquid eyes, felt the force of the hungry ambition that ruled him. Around them the remaining Falcons gathered—the colonel and five soldiers.

"Who are you?" the general demanded.

"He tried to stop us!" said the short colonel at

his elbow. "When we were firing the Armbrust at the helicopters!"

."You interfered?" the general said, ready to kill Bolt—kill anyone—who stood between him and his destiny.

"I'm a journalist," Bolt said. "It's stupid for anyone to get killed." He shrugged. "Sure I tried to stop your friend. A lot of men burned to death in those helicopters. I also stopped her." He gestured down at Sarah. He looked directly into the general's eyes. "From killing *you*."

"You are a pacifist?"

"Not exactly. I despise waste."

"Ah. You think people can settle their differences amicably. Negotiate. Compromise. Use diplomacy." There was a sneer to his tones.

"Something like that."

"You may have saved my life, Mr. Journalist, but you are still a fool!"

"Perhaps," Bolt said and smiled. "But it looks to me like I've got a hell of a story."

The general laughed. The colonel laughed, and the five remaining soldiers laughed.

"Ah," the general said, flung an arm across Bolt's shoulders, "then your newspaper will be pleased. Is it a large newspaper? Important?"

"Very large," Bolt assured him, "and important. You will receive a lot of publicity."

The general led Bolt back to the two canvas camp chairs. One of the Falcons set up the general's chair, which he'd knocked over earlier. They sat, Bolt in Sarah's chair. Behind and to the side the two helicopters still blazed in scorching fireballs. Black smoke rose from the destruction and trailed off into the blue sky.

"They're coming back," the general said, looked eagerly ahead.

The earth vibrated from the pounding of the camels' hooves. The animals from the first race were closing in on the start line. The Bedouin trainers trotted back from where they'd scattered, their white robes flapping around their ankles as they shouted last-minute orders into their walkie-talkies. Other trainers coaxed and ordered the second group of camels into a skittish line, readying them for the second race.

Meanwhile two Falcons dragged Sarah to the front of the first white limo, propped her in a sitting position against the bumper, and tied her chest and arms to it spreadeagled. Her head dangled forward limply. Then the Falcons picked up their dead and wounded, loaded the wounded into two limos, and piled the corpses into a third. The fourth white limo was kept empty, reserved for the general.

"I can't believe my good luck," Bolt told him. "I thought you looked familiar, then I saw the Falcon patches and I was sure. You really *are* General Akbar Salehi, commander-in-chief of Iran's military."

"Should I know you?" The general gestured for coffee.

"Only if you can look through a British news machine and see the reporter on the other side. I researched the Middle East heavily before I left Sydney. Your photo's all over. There are a lot of rumors, too."

"Ah, rumors. Such as?"

Two china cups of coffee arrived on a silver tray. The Falcon offered a cup to the general, then to Bolt. As the general drank, Bolt held his coffee and talked.

"That you are the most fit ruler for Iran."

"Ah, yes," General Salehi said, pleased. The camels thundered across the line. Jubilant cheers erupted from the crowd. There were three gunshots in celebration. A group of admirers tried to surround the sweating camel that had won, but the beast kicked high, twisted, and broke away. Its owner and its trainer shouted accusations at each other and jumped into a Jeep to chase after as it loped across the desert to freedom.

"You are from Sydney. The *Times!*"

"Just been assigned to the Middle East," Bolt said.

"You may not like it here," the general told him. "But you will never be bored. I promise you."

A Range Rover skidded to a stop in front of the general. A middle-aged man in a bristly black mustache and short beard sat in the back seat, wore a Bedouin's white *khaffiya* and robe. He looked out at the general.

"You have had a problem, General Salehi?" the man asked politely in Arabic, gestured at the flaming helicopters.

The general stood and walked toward the vehicle. Whoever the bearded man was, he was important. The general's stride was casual, but nothing else about the encounter was. General Salehi interrupted himself for no ordinary personage.

"It's over now," the general said. "I hope we did not disturb you. May I offer you a cup of coffee? Good, strong coffee."

"No thank you, general. Some other time. Pleasure to have you join us." He studied the general's cleanup operations and nodded approval.

If there were official questions, he would say he had not been here and knew nothing. "Come to Sharjah for a visit. But for now, the next race begins!"

With his riding crop the bearded man gave his driver's shoulder a smart tap. He, too, wore white Bedouin robes. The Range Rover took off, dust spewing from its wheels. The sporty vehicle skidded to a halt, engine idling, beside the next group of race camels.

"Sharjah's deputy ruler?" Bolt asked, drank his coffee.

"You *have* done your homework," the general said with approval. Next to obedience, the general found thoroughness the most desirable trait in those around him. "Sheikh Abdul Mohammed el-Agib," he confirmed.

A pistol shot exploded, and the second line of camels lumbered away toward the horizon, slowly, reluctantly picking up speed. Drivers and passengers leaped into their vehicles. The cars and pickups sped after the animals, soon caught up. And the race continued on, trailed by a dense billowing sand cloud. Back at the starting point, the left-behind herd of camels bawled, the helicopter fires crackled and snapped, and the Falcons turned over shovelfuls of sand, hiding the blood of their fallen.

"Tell me why that woman wanted to kill you," Bolt said. His gaze surveyed the vast desert landscape, ancient grounds that absorbed violence and love with equal neutrality. How many bones had been hidden here, buried with guilt or treachery or solemn, honorable ceremony? It gave Bolt a sense of timelessness, and of despair. Looking at the wasteland, this could be the age of Solomon or the later era of treacherous gulf pirates just as easily as it was space-age Earth approaching the twenty-first century.

"She is insane," General Salehi said.

He sighed and shrugged as if he were accustomed to the attacks of scorned, enraged women. He drained his cup, handed it to the Falcon behind him. Bolt finished his, also handed it to the Falcon.

"I no longer found her interesting," the general explained. "She did not want the affair to end."

"You have this problem often?" Bolt asked, amused.

The general's eyebrows raised. "For a man who adores women, once is too often," he chided Bolt.

"Is she really Israeli?"

"Mossad, of course. Obviously the relationship between us was impossible. But I will take her back to Tehran, try again."

"Take her back tied up?"

"I hope not," the general said fervently. "But she is a stubborn, difficult woman, as you saw. That is why I lose interest. Then she does something like this, and I am intrigued again." The general threw up his hands in frustration. "Women, particularly blond women, are my downfall."

Bolt watched Sarah. She was moving, coming back to consciousness. Her jaw would hurt for a while, but at least she was alive.

"I hope you will not be insulted if I ask to see your credentials," the general said. "I am sure you are who you say, but today there are so many charlatans . . ."

"I understand," Bolt said, handed his passport and the newspaper's plastic-coated I.D. with his color photo to the general, followed by credit cards and a Sydney driver's license. "Enough?"

The general examined each carefully, at last nodded, satisfied. "Enough." He handed them back to Bolt.

"Tell me, general, what was this fight all about? Who were in the helicopters?"

"Difficult to say," the general said cheerfully, drank his coffee, looked out at the dusty sand cloud that was growing smaller. "I have enemies, and my country has enemies. Since none of those in the helicopters survived, perhaps we will never know. But you did see that they attacked first?"

"It looked simultaneous to me."

"That's because I saw that they were coming in to attack," the general explained patiently. "Did you expect us to sit here and let them strafe us?"

"Maybe they weren't planning to. Maybe they expected to shoot warning shots around you, then talk."

"Naive, Mr. Bolt. Very naive. If you are correct, then one stray bullet could have killed one of my men. I could not allow that to happen, could I?"

"A difficult situation," Bolt agreed. "How did you manage to attract such violence?"

"It is only my responsibility?" the general asked, growing angry. "What about those in the helicopters? I refer you to an ancient Chinese curse: May you live in interesting times. Think about it, Mr. Bolt. There is nothing boring about humanity's existence today. No one in his right mind wants violence, yet we are inundated by it. We call ourselves civilized, yet we stockpile weapons to keep our enemies afraid so that they will not attack. I am a realist. These are the interesting times the Chinese referred to, and we are cursed."

Bolt studied the general, his well-padded barrel

chest, thin cruel mouth, blazing liquid eyes. "You are a man of your time."

"Exactly."

"Tell me about Tehran."

"It has returned to normalcy." The general smiled. "And it is particularly lovely and peaceful since Iraq no longer bombs it."

"But I hear there are shortages. That incomes are down. That the economy struggles. You have young men crippled from the war who have to beg because they can't find work. And commerce is so weak that families can't support the war widows, and they end up prostitutes in Jamshid, the red-light district. Are these problems part of the 'interesting' times?"

"Exaggerations and misunderstandings," the general said with equanimity. "Tehran flourishes. As long as the world wants our oil, Iran will be a rich nation. I can't see an end to the need for oil, can you?"

"What about nuclear power?" Bolt asked.

"Nuclear power?" the general said, repeating carefully.

"Iran has a long, colorful history. Don't you think it's time it entered the Nuclear Age?"

The general was silent. "All you know of Iran is what you read and hear. You have no real knowledge of our struggle, of our fight for Islamic independence. The sacrifices our people willingly make."

"Like the *basij*, the boys your mullahs talked into volunteering to be martyrs in the war. Please. That's no sacrifice. That's murder."

The general nodded. "Some believe so." He watched Bolt carefully, as if he were evaluating

him. As if he was deciding whether he could use
Bolt.

"I'd like to go to Tehran with you," Bolt said,
"see your struggles for myself. Report on them."

"Surely you must have an itinerary?" the general wondered casually.

"No itinerary," Bolt assured him. He knew the
general wanted no embarrassing questions if Bolt
should suddenly disappear. "I can leave with you
whenever you like." And a newspaper reporter
whose stories could be picked up internationally
could be useful to the general, build his image, if
handled right.

"Very well," General Salehi decided. "We will
stay until the end of this race. Then we will go to
the airport and fly home. I have much work to do,
a big day of appointments, but a man must relax,
too."

"That's why you enjoy camel races."

"And other pleasures."

The general looked over at Sarah. She lifted her
head.

"Animal!" she yelled.

He laughed. "Move the Mossad woman to one
of the cars," he told a Falcon in Arabic. "Not mine.
The one where our dead lie. She must learn
humility, obedience. We will take her to Tehran."
To Bolt he said in English, "I promise that you will
grow to love my country. It is a nation of endless
possibilities."

The camels and vehicles pounded back to the
starting line. The morning sun shone brightly
down on them, illuminating the surrounding dust
cloud into sparkling billows. Without the evidence of automobiles and walkie-talkies, the race

could be straight out of *The Arabian Nights*.

"Yes," Bolt told the general. "I look forward to investigating those possibilities."

CHAPTER
20

The kindest description Jake Bolt had ever heard of Tehran was that on a good day it resembled Ankara, but without the ambience. As Bolt rode through the city streets in the back seat of General Salehi's freshly washed white Mercedes limousine, he found that the metropolis of some six million had become, if anything, more shabby, dusty, and listless.

Trash littered the streets. Buildings, signs, and sidewalks needed scrubbing. There was little laughter or gaiety as people made their way to markets and stores. The dominant sound was the endless roar of traffic. Vendors hawked food beneath half-finished skyscrapers begun while the shah was in power. Billboards and oversized posters of the severe visage of the Ayatollah Ruhollah Khomeini and the softer countenance of his successor, the Ayatollah Mohammed Masumian, stared down at the subdued citizens as they quietly went about their business, glowering reminders of retribution against sinners.

And then came musical sounds across the rooftops, an event that happened five times a day. From the tall, graceful minarets pealed the calls to prayer: "Come to salvation. Pray. Come to salvation. Pray."

"Your new leader, Mohammed Masumian, is popular?" Bolt asked as the sounds died down at last.

"Popular enough," General Salehi said. "We are a nation imbued with Islam. The ayatollah leads in promoting virtues and discouraging vices as stipulated by the Holy Sharia."

"The Muslim commandments."

"That is right. According to current practice, this means imitating Western life-styles, no matter the reason, is a sin, an offense, a liability. Also criticism of the ruling Islamic party, using alcohol or drugs, and the exposure of women. Mohammed Masumian continues Iran's orderly progress toward eliminating these vices."

"Do you support him and his ideas?" Bolt asked bluntly.

Women moved along the sidewalks like anonymous shadows in their full-length black chadors. Males seemed to wear whatever they pleased. There were mullahs in their traditional turbans, school-boys in cotton jackets and trousers, and businessmen in three-piece suits. Revolutionary Guards hopped out of a car to lecture a chador-dressed woman who wore a forbidden rainbow-colored scarf and had an exposed curl of hair on her forehead. If she was a first-time offender, she would be sent home or to religious classes. If a repeater, she might be whipped or jailed.

General Salehi answered carefully. "I am a Muslim, first and last. Whatever differences I have with the way our leadership views the details of everyday Shiite life are simply differences. Remember, I grew up under the shah's very Western regime. I have that background, that training, so it is perhaps more understandable that I tend to be more . . . broad-minded."

"And yet you survived Khomeini's fundamentalist purges. Many, particularly in the military, did not."

The general smiled a cold smile. "I am easy to work with," he said.

They drove past a martyrs' fountain with red-dyed water that looked like fresh-spilt crimson blood. As the line of white limousines entered central Tehran, Bolt saw a billboard that declared in Farsi, "We are neither East nor West, but Islam." Photographs of young men—martyrs—killed in the Iran-Iraq war decorated the windows of shops and homes.

"There's a sense the war's not over yet," Bolt observed.

"It will never be over," the general explained, "Islam's original precepts are no idols, no saints, no one between man and Allah. The Ayatollah Khomeini resurrected militancy, exporting Iran's revolution to the more moderate gulf states. But that has been a failure. Thus far. Who knows what the future holds? Shiites are patient. As long as Iran is still an undeveloped nation, it cannot live without the rest of the world. It cannot survive in complete isolation. And so we must do business while we continue to fight, but now we fight for prestige, recognition, and to have our view of the world accepted."

"And your personal view is Shiite Muslim."

"That is right. Opposition from the outside world simply causes the people to rally. We unite internally."

"You personally want to export the revolution?"

"I am a realist. A patient realist. The revolution will spread. With time."

"What do you want for Iran?" Bolt asked.

The general was quiet. On the curb a four- or five-year-old girl modestly draped by a black veil to her shoulders stepped from a mosque to a chauffeur-driven Mercedes. Her father, a mullah, an Islamic religious leader, climbed in after her. In all nations, even in those that officially abhorred privilege, privilege still existed—and it had its prerogatives. In fact, Bolt remembered that during the Iraq-Iran war, the speaker of Iran's parliament called for young men to volunteer for military service while his own son lived safely far away in Geneva.

"Independence," the general said at last. "For Iran I want independence, respect. We can be a giant among nations. Yet we squander our resources fighting with our gulf neighbors."

"Over religion."

"Yes, over religion. And land. And history. This is hard for Westerners to understand, but Islam is more than religion, it is a way of life. For some of us simply not following all Islam's guidelines does not make us any less religious. Some of us believe those who turn guidelines into laws are fools. Others believe the Koran is open to various interpretations. Whatever, a man is a man. Weak, fallible. A man must have his fun. A man makes mistakes." He shrugged. "Life must go on. I want Iran to go on."

"With you leading."

The general bowed his head modestly. "If Allah so desires."

They drove past once-grand hotels and public

buildings whose sidewalks were painted with the flags of Israel, the United States, and the Soviet Union. Pedestrians trod busily over the Star of David, the Stars and Stripes, and the Hammer and Sickle, wearing the paint thin, leaving dirt.

"You see," the general said, gesturing at the dingy painted banners on the concrete, "they have been there years. We call it walking on our enemies."

The line of limos drove up a tree-studded slope, past palatial homes set back from the quiet street behind solid walls. Overhead the sky was darkening with rolling black cumulonimbus clouds. There would be a storm.

"No isolationism," the general said. "But no appeasement either. Iran can no longer be bought as the United States once bought us. I, personally, am interested in good deals for Iran—in commerce and defense."

"But the current government is not."

The general shrugged. "They have an Islamic fundamentalist view." He looked up the street where elaborate wrought-iron gates were slowly, automatically opening to admit the first limo. "We are here. My villa."

There were no houses in sight. "You must have a large estate," Bolt said.

"Large enough," the general said.

"Your father's?"

"First it was my father's. Now it is mine."

The general's limo stopped at the top of the curved drive outside massive rosewood entry doors. Behind them the wrought-iron gates swung closed. Falcons carrying rifles patrolled the inside perimeter of the white-walled grounds. More Falcons ran from behind the house to open the doors to the limos where the wounded lay. The short, angry colonel disembarked and took charge of the unloading.

Bolt and General Salehi walked up the tiled stairs to the house. It was a gracious Mediterranean-style villa with blue tiled roof and a wide tiled veranda extending the length of the front.

"Very impressive," Bolt said.

"Thank you. I hope our interview was helpful," the general said.

"It's a beginning."

The double entry doors opened and four Falcons stepped out, snapped to attention, welcoming the general home. The general returned their salutes. Two held open the heavy doors as he passed through. Bolt followed into the elegant two-story foyer. Behind them thunder cracked across the dark heavens. Rain pelted down.

The doors closed behind Bolt, and he followed the general across the marble floor.

Suddenly the lead Falcon nodded. In unison the Falcons dropped their AK-47s and pointed them at Bolt's gut and back. Bolt's chest contracted at the sight of so much firepower directed at him. At this range, one itchy trigger finger and he was dead.

"General," he said calmly.

Bolt took another step. Instantly a Falcon moved in front of him, his muzzle pointed at Bolt's navel. The message was clear: if Bolt kept walking, he was dead.

Unconcerned the general moved on up the wide, painting-hung staircase that curved to a second floor. He had known this would happen, had probably ordered it.

"Do not worry yourself, Mr. Bolt," the general said. His voice echoed across the cavernous foyer where Bolt stood frozen in place. "Just simple security. Be courteous to my men, and they will be gentle with you."

"Thanks," Bolt said. "I appreciate the warning."

The general disappeared onto the second floor.

In the villa's basement Dr. Daniel Lambert lay stiff with pain, tied naked to a metal hospital table. Cigarette burns covered his belly and thighs. The air was hot, and the heat and pain caused sweat to pour into his wounds.

"You will help us, Dr. Lambert," the small muscular man with the scar on his left cheek insisted. A cigarette dangled from the corner of his mouth. Smoke curled like an evil tendril upwards. He had a low, monotonous voice that grated like a slowly dripping faucet.

Lambert said nothing. It was too much effort. All he could think about was the pain. It was becoming too familiar, an enemy whose face he knew so well.

"Speak!" the scarred man demanded.

He took the cigarette from his mouth. Pleasure thickened his slashed face. He lowered the cigarette toward Lambert's belly, an inch above the skin, and traced a path downwards.

The scientist shuddered, flinched.

"No," Lambert whispered. It was more a groan than a word. "No."

"Wrong answer!"

The Falcon torturer jabbed the cigarette into

the white tender flesh of the man's inner thigh next to his testicles. The scientist screamed.

Sally Mather stood at the barred window and looked out at the magical Elburz Mountains north of Tehran. Black storm clouds clustered and roiled, occasionally opening so that chunks of blue sky and bright sunshine could spill through onto the ragged peaks and valleys.

Gingerly she touched her jaw and turned back into the room. She felt slightly sick, both from Bolt's blow and from a feeling of enraged helplessness. She glared at the room, opulent with Old Persian carpets, thick drapes, and oil paintings. There were two doors. Both were locked. One led into the hall. The other was on the adjacent wall. She didn't know what it opened onto.

She had been able to find no obvious way out of this sumptuous hellhole.

She returned to the barred window.

Her room was at the back of the villa. Below her spread glistening green lawns, a flower garden, and a football-sized dirt-packed training area that extended into a woods. Near the villa was a four-seat armed helicopter parked on a concrete landing pad. A half-dozen Falcons struggled to put a tarp over it before the next siege of rain struck.

Damn. She pushed up the window glass, grabbed the bars, shook them. Damn, damn, damn!

The door opened. She turned, ran to it, prepared to attack. A chador-clothed woman stepped in, AK-47 carried easily in her big arms. Her long black skirts trembled around her legs as she paused just inside the door.

"Stay back!" the woman warned in broken English. "I been told about you. You too close, I shoot!"

Sally Mather froze.

The woman gestured to someone in the hall. A tall Falcon entered carrying towels and clothing. The woman spoke to him in Farsi. He dropped the load on the bed and left.

"My name Monireh," the Iranian woman said. "Monireh. Say, please."

Sally repeated the name.

"Good. Now take bath. Dress. In there."

"No."

"You stink. Need bath. Now." Monireh hefted the AK-47. "I shoot. Okay with me."

Sally studied the woman. Short and heavy, she had a broad, determined face. The smoothness with which she handled the weapon told Sally she knew what she was doing.

Sally walked into the marble bath. There was a large square sunken tub that filled the end of the room. All the fixtures on the sink, toilet, and tub were gold. The mirror was framed in gold and ivory.

"Turn on water," Monireh ordered.

Sally turned it on.

"Take clothes off. Get in."

Sally stripped off the filthy red business suit, climbed into the tub.

Monireh approached. "Get back," she told Sally.

Sally moved to the far side of the tub. Monireh poured perfumed crystals into the frothing water. A sweet aroma arose—heavy, spicy.

"What's that for?" Sally asked.

Monireh favored her with an enormous, broken-toothed smile. "The general. He like good-smelling woman!"

Sally knelt in the water. It was warm, relaxing. She sighed. Now she knew the reason for her excellent accommodations. Perhaps the general found her even more exciting, now that she'd threatened to shoot his balls off.

"Monireh," she said. "We should talk. Tell me about yourself."

But Monireh shook her head. "I been told about you," she repeated stubbornly. She put down the toilet seat lid and sat, the AK-47 trained on her charge. "Wash."

Sally washed. She thought about the general's hands upon her and washed harder. She had to find a way out!

CHAPTER
21

In London, Sir John Sutton looked across his broad desk at his old friend and MI6 colleague Hugh Willoughby. Willoughby was in his late fifties with twinkling blue eyes, dashing silver mustache, silver hair, and a slightly florid face.

He's getting a little long in the tooth, Sir John decided, then, remembering his own age, corrected himself: *We're both getting old*. But not so old that we can't rout the bloody criminals. Look how well Willoughby and his Yank chum Jake Bolt did in Tokyo. Now that was a nasty job—cleaning up the pink coke. Very nasty. Although something was still amiss with the whole Tokyo business, a very obvious problem since Iwa Matsumoto was murdered. And then there were the damn worrisome computer and communications troubles . . .

"So, John," Hugh Willoughby said nervously. "What do you have for me this time?" He lit a Players cigarette, inhaled.

"I can tell you're worried again, Hugh. I'm not putting you out to pasture any more than I'd put myself out to pasture."

Willoughby smiled. "Plenty of steam left in the old engine, eh, John?" Willoughby said, pleased.

"Plenty," Sir John agreed. "And now it'll come

in handy. We've just received a sad piece of news about one of your old friends, a Dr. Daniel Lambert. I believe you went to school together?"

"King's College," Willoughby answered automatically. "What's happened to Dan?"

"Kidnapped by the bloody Iranians. You knew Lambert was head of the Israeli nuclear facility? Yes, well, seems the Iranians may be building and staffing their own plant, and naturally they want a top scientist and administrator. So they kidnapped Lambert."

"Oh dear god."

"Yes, you see the point. Iran with nuclear capability is a dangerous idea to begin with. Madmen run the country. Then kidnapping Dr. Lambert has brought to our attention that some of our missing scientists might also have ended up in Iran. Over the past year three have disappeared."

Willoughby smoked. "I'm on my way, I hope?"

"Indeed so, Hugh. To Tehran. Please stay away from the embassy. We do like to keep the channels open in case the government were to take a more humane change of heart. All this bloody fundamentalism is a dreadful bother."

"I'm on my own? No back-up?"

"'Fraid not, Hugh. Know you'll do a jolly good job. Just like Tokyo."

"Tokyo is still unresolved," Willoughby reminded his chief.

"Quite so. Quite so." Sir John shuffled the papers on his desk. "Leave as soon as you can. Fly first class. MI6 will bounce for it. Happy to."

"What am I looking for?" Willoughby said in a bewildered tone. "Tehran is a large city, John."

"Of course, dear boy." Sir John felt properly

humbled. He'd forgotten to give Willoughby the most vital piece of information. Maybe he was getting older than he thought! "There is a quasi-terrorist commando group called the Desert Falcons that the Israelis tell us handled the kidnapping. They're under the direct control of—"

"General Akbar Salehi," Willoughby said. "Jesus. You don't make this easy. Salehi is a wolf. Unprincipled, unpredictable, and bloody smart."

Sir John stood, extended his hand. Willoughby stood, switched his cigarette from his right to his left, and shook Sir John's hand.

"I know," Sir John said. "Thought you might enjoy the match."

"Match?" Willoughby said. "It could be a bloody massacre!"

In Moscow, KGB agent Yuri Fyodorov drove his Volga toward Sheremetyevo International Airport on the city's outskirts. The traffic was light, but then in Moscow it usually was, except during rush hours. The cost of an automobile was still far beyond most workers' paychecks.

After a long, cold, dreary spring, today was warm and sparkling with Moscow's bright northern sunshine. The improved weather also improved Fyodorov's disposition. Although he was on his way to Iran, he minded less. Perhaps by the time he returned, the possibility of summer would be real.

A fireplug of a man, Fyodorov was in his forties, a little less than five foot ten, with a blond crewcut. When he caught sight of himself in the Volga's rearview mirror, he tried to recall what he'd looked like twenty years ago, even ten years ago. He couldn't remember.

His wife Olga claimed he'd always looked this way, that he'd been middle-aged since birth. But, he was separated from Olga now. His son, a ballet student, only occasionally managed to fit him into his schedule, and likely had no opinion at all about his father's age and aging. His teenage daughter was much like her father, probably middle-aged herself. For a man who'd always done what was right, Fyodorov thought, how could so much of life have gone so wrong?

Once he'd believed completely in the ideology of the Communist party. Once he'd been to-the-marrow proud of being a top KGB agent. Now he was simply grateful for Mikhail Gorbachev. Maybe with Gorbachev the Soviet would become the nation he'd thought it was. Yes, Gorbachev offered hope, and so Fyodorov didn't need to leave the KGB. Not yet at least.

He turned his mind toward the coming mission. That's where he needed to concentrate his energies. The mission was difficult, and he was a little rusty. He'd spent the last few years riding his desk, not out in the field. He'd been solving bureaucratic snafus, handling boring negotiations, making quick trips to various embassies to put out brushfires. Fundamentalist Shiites were not part of his everyday expertise. And the whole scenario stank with potential disaster.

First he'd discovered that Iran was putting together a nuclear facility. Next he'd found that the KGB's special computer expert, Viktor Markov, was on his way undercover to Iran.

After the disturbing communication problems

the Soviet Union had been experiencing the past few weeks at home and around the globe, Viktor Markov might have gone out on his own in search of the trouble. That would be like Markov, arrogant, self-assured. Or perhaps Markov had been kidnapped by the Iranians, who surely could use a computer man of his brilliance. Whatever the reason, Viktor Markov was too important to the KGB to lose.

Fyodorov sighed. The embassy in Tehran did not want a bonafide KGB man showing up on its doorstep, not with diplomacy—such as it was—offering possibilities there these days. So he would have to use other means to get close to General Akbar Salehi, the contact the clerk believed Markov had made. If it hadn't been for the clerk, Fyodorov might never have discovered Markov's whereabouts. But the clerk was angry at Markov for some slight. Since Markov never disappeared during a crisis, Fyodorov had believed the clerk, and then found corroborating evidence in the papers pulled on one of Markov's old covers—Horst Renssauer.

And so now Yuri Fyodorov, tired KGB agent, was on his way to Tehran, Iran's misbegotten capital city.

As he drove he filled his memory with the sights that characterized his beloved Moscow—the elegant onion domes, the gracious wide boulevards, the thick swaying birches. He hoped like hell this mission wouldn't take long, but the more he thought about it, the more convinced he was that it would.

Or perhaps it would simply be short and violent, which was equally worrisome.

Deliberately he thought instead about Viktor

Markov, wondered what he was doing, where he was, whether he was all right.

But that didn't work either. Fyodorov suddenly realized he was short of breath. It was far better to fight than to wait. Fyodorov told himself to calm down, relax. But his stomach knotted in the familiar response. This was an unusually dangerous situation, and he didn't like it one damn bit.

In his villa office General Akbar Salehi listened carefully to Colonel Ahmed Rizvi's report.

"I cannot promise to deliver the Majlis," Colonel Rizvi was saying in Farsi. He sat in his usual chair across from the general's rosewood desk. "The legislators are uncertain. They think, by and large, after Khomeini's excesses, that Masumian is a much better leader. They will ride with him unless he does something stupid."

"He's not likely to do something stupid," the general observed.

"Agreed. To our advantage is that the Majlis are not Masumian's backers totally. They believe you would maintain the fundamentalist view at least at home, but they need evidence that you have the strength, the vision, the ability to orchestrate Iran's reemergence as a world power."

"The nuclear plant is our evidence. And the mullahs?"

"Again, they feel you've proved your allegiance to the Holy Koran and to the Shiite ways. But as our religious leaders, the mullahs want to know you will have the power to spread our revolution to other Middle East nations."

"Of course." The general was pleased. "I will

deliver all that and more! What about our competitors—the groups led by the old shah's son and the Marxist Islamic Peoples' Mujahedeen?"

"Mostly talk, little action," the colonel reported. "If they sense a weakening of this government or a potential change in leadership, they will come like vultures. But when we step in quickly and show our strength, they will disappear back to their chest-beating and haranguing. Your only problem will come with being named shah."

"The people still hate the old shah."

"With reason," the colonel agreed. "He made a terrible mistake with the oil-price revolution. Instead of channeling the new wealth into Iran's development, he allowed U.S. arms merchants to persuade him to waste it on huge arsenals of inappropriate and utterly useless weapons."

"I remember," General Salehi said, his keen military mind still offended by the squandered money. What materiel could have been bought! "The flood of petro-dollars filled the pockets of government officials outside the military."

"And galloping inflation made the majority of the nation worse off than before," the colonel reminded him.

"First I take over the government," the general said. "Being named shah can come later. I commend you, Rizvi. You've done a remarkable job!"

General Salehi stood up, excited. He strode to the window. Out there where the spring rain beat gray and bleak on the horizon stood the craggy Elburz Mountains, the site of his nuclear installation, protected and hidden at the back of a valley and dug into a stable mountainside. He had the facility and the staff. With Daniel Lambert, he would have the proved administrator.

"Is Lambert ready to cooperate?" the general asked.

"He's stubborn," Rizvi said. "A stubborn old Jew. He trembles and cries, but he won't yield."

"Rest him now. Start the chemicals tomorrow," the general ordered. "We will strip his personality, his individuality, leave nothing but the intellectual ability. He will cooperate. Everyone else has. Everyone *must*."

"Some have died."

"You are forbidden to let him die!" the general snapped. He paced behind his desk. "Is everything prepared for tomorrow night? We must move rapidly. Now that the installation is finished, it's even more likely that word of it will get out. And there might be questions about the disappearance of our Jewish guest." With luck, Lambert's disappearance could be kept secret until he was no longer needed.

"Everything is ready," Rizvi assured him. "Everyone is invited and has accepted, and the chef's are preparing an elaborate dinner."

The general stopped, stared at his old comrade. There was something wrong about Rizvi's tone. Something that had been slowly building. When had he first noticed it? Three months ago? Six months? But it had been indefinite then. Now it was certain. He looked hard at Rizvi, and Rizvi looked back, unflinchingly.

"You are well?" the general asked.

"Very healthy," Rizvi answered.

"Something troubles you?"

"Only the usual."

"Ah." The general sat at his desk, folded his hands, leaned forward. "We had to do it. It was necessary. You must remind yourself of that. Allah will understand. It is all to his glory."

Rizvi bowed his head. "I hope so."

The general stared a moment longer. When a man started questioning, it was always wise to give him work to do. "Check into this Australian journalist, Jake Bolt. See if he is who he says he is."

Rizvi brightened, even smiled slightly. "Yes. And the woman, too?"

The general hesitated. "I am sure she is Mossad. You heard the commando scream in Hebrew. Oh, very well. If it will please you. The woman, too."

In the villa Jake Bolt sat in a first-floor office and answered questions about himself and his life in Australia. The Falcons were deadly serious about their job, checking his credentials. Finding the SIG-Sauer under his sports jacket instantly skyrocketed their suspicions.

"A journalist carries a serious gun like this?" asked the one Falcon who spoke English.

"The Middle East is a violent place," Bolt said.

"You say you flew here on commercial airlines. There is no way you could have smuggled this weapon into Dubai."

Bolt smiled. "There are ways."

"How?"

"The mail, if done correctly." Bolt was sweating. This was to be expected. After all, they had the weapons; all he had was his wits. "The military. Diplomatic courier."

Restless, suspicious, the Falcon circled the small windowless room. The room was barren, with only a metal table and folding chairs, and it seemed airtight and soundproof. Which again worried Bolt. What went on in this room?

First the four Falcons had politely searched Bolt, and immediately found his gun. The English-speaking Falcon questioned him while the three others stood against the walls with their AK-47s always visible, easy insurance that Bolt remained where he was and a graphic reminder that they were in charge. Respectful, menacing, the Falcons had been well-trained.

Since Akbar Salehi was a military man, Bolt decided, he must have assumed the world and the international press would respect his toughness, not mind if he hazed a reporter a bit. If that was all this was. Hazing. Making a point. Or was there more? Had the general discovered he was connected to Sarah Maizlish? Was the general playing with him, planning to squeeze whatever he could out of Bolt and then kill him?

"How did you get the gun into Dubai?" the Falcon demanded.

"I sent it with my newspaper's courier," Bolt lied. If they checked, he was dead for sure.

"A newspaper courier must use regular airline channels."

"Yeah, but we send so many documents and supplies, and everything's packed so tight that it's too much of a hassle for the airlines to check. Unless they get a tip."

The Falcon stalked around the room, thinking about Bolt's answer. Bolt sweated more. At last the inquisitor barked, "What about all the American money?" He stabbed a finger at the roll of yakuza bills.

"A convenience. Every Middle East nation likes U.S. dollars. Remember, I was going to Dubai, not Iran."

Again the Falcon stalked around the room. "Where do you live in Australia?"

"It says on my driver's license," Bolt said. "832 Mathilda, apartment B."

"You have no accent. Why is that?"

"No *Australian* accent," Bolt corrected him. "I have a California-U.S.A. accent, if there is such a thing. I was raised in California. I moved to Sydney with my parents when I was a teenager."

"Education?"

"University of Sydney."

"Overseas work?"

"None. This is my first assignment."

"What was the weather like when you left?"

Bolt almost answered, then stopped. Although it was spring in Tehran, it was autumn in Sydney.

"Nippy," Bolt told him. "Soon the leaves will turn colors." The Falcon showed no response to the correctness of the answer to the trick question. He continued hammering at Bolt another two hours, trying to wear Bolt down, make him make a mistake. At last he stalked around the room one more time, nodded brusquely, and left. The three guards stayed at their posts, lazily watching Bolt, fingers curled confidently around their weapons. He hoped everything he'd told the Falcon was accurate, but Christ, he could be wrong. He'd never set foot in Sydney!

The door swung open and the Falcon stepped back into the room. There was no change in the commando's expression. Bolt couldn't tell whether he'd passed or whether they were going to kill him.

"You will come with me," the stoned-faced Falcon said.

Bolt followed him out into the first-floor corridor, the three guards close behind. One of them carried Bolt's SIG-Sauer.

"Where to?" Bolt asked.

The lead Falcon was silent. He turned left, strode along the corridor, Bolt and the guards following. Ahead was a door beneath a staircase. Perhaps it was a closet of some kind. Or maybe it went down to a basement. A basement did not sound good to Bolt. Was that where they were taking him? Would he find Sarah there?

"Where's the blond lady?" Bolt asked. "What have you done with her?"

"Silence!" the Falcon said and kept walking.

CHAPTER
22

Jake Bolt showed no sign of his relief as the lead Falcon passed the door and turned up the tiled stairs. Below them a woman in a black chador scurried down the hall. A door opened and quickly closed, but in time for Bolt to hear both men's and women's voices.

The little group continued along the upstairs corridor past arched window alcoves that looked out at the dark angry sky. Lightning ripped startling silver from rolling black cloud to rolling black cloud. Thunder rumbled and split the heavens. The rain pelted down harder onto the cobbled courtyard below. The two-story villa was built in a square, completely surrounding the inner courtyard.

The Falcon opened an ornately carved door, announced Bolt's name, and stepped back to hold the door open as Bolt passed through into the plush office of General Akbar Salehi.

"Ah, yes," the general said, rising. He extended a hand. "Mr. Bolt, good to see you again."

"An interesting way you have for welcoming visitors to your home," Bolt remarked.

The general laughed. "Surely you did not mind? Think of the news potential: *"Journalist*

Interrogated by Middle East Commandos!" Please sit, Mr. Bolt. Join us. You remember Colonel Rizvi, my most valuable assistant?"

One of the Falcon guards laid Bolt's SIG-Sauer on the large polished desk. The colonel leaned forward, examined the weapon, seemed to ignore the general's words. The Falcons stood around the walls, weapons ready. Bolt was on probation.

"Of course," Bolt said crisply, studying the profile of the small, narrow colonel as he set the gun back down, satisfied. "I remember Colonel Rizvi. We met over an Armbrust."

The general laughed again. "Testy, Mr. Bolt. If you stay in the Middle East, you must learn equanimity. Patience. The patience of an eternal land. We have fought so long that suspicion flows through our veins like blood. It's inherited from our ancestors, who were great survivors. Like suspicion, our patience too is inherited."

"The patience of the desert falcon?" Bolt said.

"Exactly. How intelligent of you to see that. Now I must go into my capitol office for meetings, but Colonel Rizvi will show you around the villa." He locked Bolt's gun into his middle desk drawer and stood.

"What about the woman?" Bolt said.

"Sally? Ah, my inamorata. She is nearby, of course. I have decided to take her back."

The general chuckled and walked around his desk toward the door. Bolt and the colonel followed.

"She is a spirited one. Forgiving her will be a delight."

"I'd like interview her."

"Perhaps later." The general paused, and a

Falcon quickly opened the door. "She is resting now."

They walked out into the hallway. In the distance lightning streaked ragged across the stormy gray-black sky.

"After her nap then," Bolt said.

An edge of steel entered the general's voice. "You may interview her when I say. Please remember, Mr. Bolt, you are a guest in my home. Unlike the West, the Middle East understands the sanctity of privacy, even from the press."

"I'll keep that in mind," Bolt said.

The general shot him a surprised look. He was unaccustomed to irreverence, to men who made light of his orders.

They turned and walked in the direction opposite from which Bolt had arrived. They passed more windows set into alcoves. At last they descended stairs that led to the cavernous foyer.

"As you tour my villa," the general resumed in his gracious-host voice, "you will find that it also doubles as our Falcon headquarters. You will see for yourself the progressive way in which we conduct ourselves. We command everything from state-of-the-art weapons to the finest computers. Islam rules our hearts and minds, and technology improves our ability to honor Allah."

The sentries at the massive front doors opened them, and the general stepped out. Instantly another Falcon snapped open an umbrella over his head, and he strode dry to the back door of his limousine.

"This way, Mr. Bolt," Colonel Rizvi said. His narrow face was tired, bored. This was not his idea of important work. "I'll show you the public rooms first."

They crossed the marble-floored foyer and entered a corridor to the left.

"This is the receiving room," the colonel said and slid open tall double wood doors. "The general meets visitors here, officials from other nations, our own Islamic leaders, even neighbors." Decorated in various hues of blue, the room was filled with heavy furniture standing on beautiful Old Persian rugs. The drapes were brocaded, and a grand marble fireplace filled the far wall.

"Looks as if it dates from his father's time."

"Yes, I saw it first when I was a student at Tehran University," the colonel said. They walked along the corridor again.

"Didn't General Salehi go to the university?"

"We met there."

"And you've been together ever since?"

"Almost. Occasionally I was transferred to work with other officers. The shah believed in providing broad experience to certain of his people."

"Certain of his *privileged* people?"

The narrow-faced colonel glanced at Bolt. "That's right." His tone told Bolt he had no regrets. "But I was an early supporter of the Ayatollah Khomeini, since the mid 1970s."

"Even before General Salehi?"

"Long before the general. The general was in Washington, and I was sent to the embassy in Paris. The ayatollah was in exile in Paris. I met him there." The colonel slid open another set of double doors. "This is the banquet room. The table was built from mahogany brought from the Sudan."

"Also from the general's father's time?" The table looked as if it seated forty-eight.

"Yes."

It was a magnificent room, and the magnificent long carved dining table was its centerpiece. Overhead hung a sparkling cutglass chandelier. Black-robed women were laying out silver- and gold-decorated place settings of fine china, flatware, and crystal.

"A party?" Bolt asked.

"Tomorrow night," the colonel said. "Unfortunately, you will not be able to attend. You are scheduled to leave in the morning. If anything newsworthy occurs, I am sure the general will notify you."

"Too bad. I'd like to meet his friends. Or is this business?"

"A bit of both."

They returned to the hall.

"And will Mrs. Salehi be there?" Bolt asked.

"The general's wife died a number of years ago, an automobile accident in the Alps."

"I'm sorry. Children?"

"Three sons. Two died fighting the war against Iraq. The youngest boy is in Switzerland at boarding school."

"Must have been hard for the general to lose his sons."

"It was an honor. A holy war. I also lost two. My only two." The colonel's voice softened. "Martyrs for Islam."

Then he strode ahead of Bolt, showing him the book-lined library, the television room with wet bar and pool table, the large kitchen staffed by the cloaked women, a barracks that would sleep fifty Falcons, and a motor pool with polished armored trucks and Jeeps, transport trucks, and one tank. There was also an armory, but the colonel declined to unlock it, and a security room, which the colonel told Bolt he wouldn't understand. As they left the motor pool, the colonel waved vaguely out at the downpour and described a helicopter pad and training area.

"Impressive," Bolt said. "You're a small city here, a fortress."

"Almost," the colonel agreed as they returned to the front of the villa. "Upstairs, of course, are the guest bedrooms, as well as the general's office, which you saw. Along here are the offices for secretaries and support staff."

"And the computers?" Bolt asked.

"You know computers?"

"The general mentioned they were state-of-the-art," Bolt said. "Does he mean it?"

"The general always means what he says," the colonel said. He turned down a first-floor corridor opposite the public rooms. "The general is brilliant, of course," he continued.

"You're sure?" Bolt said. "Sounds to me as if you have doubts."

"Look at this and tell me I'm wrong."

The two sentries standing outside the metal-doored computer room snapped to attention. The colonel told them in Farsi that Bolt was a newspaper reporter to whom the general had given permission to see the computers. His last words were impatient, as if *his* word should be enough, never mind the general.

The Falcons stepped aside.

The colonel pressed a fist-sized padded button on the door, and it opened with a slow, quiet pneumatic whoosh. Inside was an enormous, brightly lighted windowless room filled with sophisticated computer equipment. Computer scientists in white jump suits worked at rows of consoles. In the center was a sleek, elegant supercomputer.

"You have a Cray-2," Bolt said, impressed.

"You know this machine?"

"I'm familiar with it. One of the finest super-computers in the world. Released to the market in 1985." The C-shaped machine accounted for sixty percent of all supercomputers sold. "It's hand-wired to minimize the distance signals have to travel," Bolt explained, touching the smooth me-tallic gray case. "And it has four processors. The next generation will have sixteen processors and use chips made of gallium arsenide as well as the usual silicon. Electrons can travel ten times faster through gallium arsenide, so the new supercom-puters will have more raw power, more blazing speed. But this one, the Cray-2, is a revolutionary machine, and it will hold its own for a long time to come."

"You do know computers," Colonel Rizvi said.

"You can run a lot off this machine," Bolt went on, scanning the monitors around the room. "Looks like you have your military system on it."

"As a matter of fact," Colonel Rizvi said, sur-prised that Bolt could tell just by looking at the screens, "we do."

"Hooked up to command central?" Bolt asked. "Wait a minute. He stared at the configurations on the monitors around the room. "This *is* command central! I'll be damned. The commander-in-chief does like to work at home, doesn't he!"

"He does not have to make explanations to anyone here. And he has a duplicate operation at his downtown office."

"Did he put this together?"

"He found the staff, gave them the orders, oversaw the work, and channeled the government money to it."

"Amazing," Bolt said, walking around the room where military codes, missile trajectories, weapons locations, and a host of other pertinent data and graphics showed in glowing color on the screens. The Cray-2 was on the U.S. government's list of equipment forbidden to be exported to certain nations, including Iran. "He *is* brilliant." And devious to have accomplished the Cray's import.

Rizvi nodded. "We must go now. Come."

They walked toward the door.

"Why," Bolt went on, "I'll bet he's savvy enough to do just about anything."

Rizvi said nothing. He punched the pneumatic button and the door slowly reopened. Rizvi headed out toward the hall.

"I'll bet he could even put together a nuclear plant," Bolt said.

Rizvi's back stiffened. He hesitated, then resumed his usual stride.

"This way," Rizvi said, leading Bolt up the back stairs Bolt had taken after the Falcons had questioned him. "We go to your room."

On the second floor, they turned down the corridor away from General Salehi's office. Outdoors through the arched windows the storm had finished. The sky had paled to a pearl gray and the wind moved gently through the trees, sprinkling leaf-caught rainwater to the wet, glistening ground.

Rizvi nodded at the sentry guarding a door at the end of the hall. He unlocked the door, went inside. Bolt followed.

"Your room and bath," Rizvi said unnecessarily. He went to a second door and peered inside. "Towels and washcloths all in place. You came without luggage, so the general ordered a clean shirt for you." He opened a closet door. Inside hung a plain white shirt. "It belonged to one of our Falcons who seemed to be about your size."

"Please thank the general for his generosity and graciousness," Bolt said politely. He passed the double bed, easy chair, lamp, desk, and went to the window. In the distance stood the tall, purple Elburz Mountains, showing pristine from the rains. He checked his watch. Almost five o'clock.

"Rest, relax," the colonel suggested as he returned to the door. "The general will be home in two hours. Dinner at eight. You will please stay in your room until someone comes for you. This is, after all, a place of government business, and much of it is classified. No one is allowed to wander around."

Bolt showered, shaved, and changed into the clean shirt. It was a good fit, although snug in the shoulders. He paced the room, thinking about General Salehi, Sarah Maizlish, Dr. Lambert, all he had seen this day, and the alleged nuclear plant that certainly seemed to exist, if Colonel Rizvi's shocked but silent reaction was to be believed.

There was a lot wrong about the villa. It was more than its being an armed camp with Falcons and their AK-47s and G-3s everywhere. It was also more than its being an unofficial government office where the military's central computing system was located. The oddness had to do with the general and the ambience of the villa. It was almost as if the place was in waiting, like a bride with a date and no groom.

The general was waiting for something, something so critical that it would change his life, and perhaps Iran.

Bolt listened at the door. He heard nothing, which meant the sentry was there, but not moving and not snoring. Bolt needed to investigate the villa alone, no tour guide. If he were right in interpreting what the general was saying about Sarah, she might be up here on the bedroom floor, awaiting the general's attentions. Bolt figured he ought to be able to stop that from happening.

He went to the window, pushed up the glass. There was a narrow ledge just below his window. It extended the length of this building. With luck it went around the building, too. He looked down at the green lawns. He was lucky. The rain had stopped, but no one was out yet to enjoy the sunshine.

Bolt stepped out onto the ledge, slowly stood erect, pressing his back to the stucco building. He inched toward the window of the next bedroom.

CHAPTER
23

General Akbar Salehi lowered his head with respect and took the chair offered him. The Ayatollah Mohammed Masumian, successor to the fanatic Khomeini, was looking unfortunately well today, he thought. The ayatollah had a long white beard, gray fringe over his ears, a bulbous nose, and steel-rimmed eyeglasses that gave him a scholarly look that was not quite earned.

"Allah willing," the Ayatollah Masumian told the general, "the warrior Iranian people will maintain the revolutionary and sacred rancor and anger in their hearts. They will use their oppressor-burning flames against the criminal Soviet Union and the world-devouring United States and their surrogates."

"Allah willing," the general agreed.

"As long as I live I will follow the teachings of our beloved Ayatollah Khomeini," the Ayatollah Masumian continued. He sat in a soft leather chair next to the window. Outside lightning flashed and thunder rolled over the dreary city. "I will not allow the real direction of our policies to change. We must always adhere to the ayatollah's tenet of 'neither East nor West.' We must rebuild without the help of any satanic nations."

"We have made great strides rebuilding the military," the general reminded him.

"The military is one of our fundamental and primary objectives in reconstruction," the ayatollah said with approval. "You have fulfilled your assignment well."

"We will talk more tomorrow night," the general said. "Remember, you have agreed to join us for dinner at my villa."

The ayatollah inclined his head graciously, the teacher to the student. "With pleasure."

President Hojitolislam Sayed Eghbal laid down the daily *Kayhan* newspaper and sighed. He was a tall, slender man with overlarge hands and feet and an intense demeanor that constituents found attractive at election time.

"Shush is alive again," he told General Salehi. "We close down one red-light district, and another is reborn. Sin and excess." He lifted the newspaper to read. "Listen to this: 'Notorious women entertain undisciplined customers, while the extent of drug abuse and peddling is so pervasive that passersby can see hundreds of addicts roaming in the Shush quarter.'"

"An evil tragedy," General Salehi said of the small South Tehran area. He'd been there himself, enjoyed it many times.

"There's more," the hojatolislam said, glowering. He read, "'All the wrongdoers in the neighborhood were arrested in a sudden raid. They included thirteen hundred women, a large number of men, and seven hundred children and adolescents. There were some people with vices and criminal record who will certainly be executed.'"

"The Majlis must pass a bill for harsher punishment for drug-related offenses," the general advised. "The death penalty must be mandatory for those found guilty of possessing one ounce of heroin or eleven pounds of opium."

The Hojatolislam Eghbal listened carefully. "You are a thoughtful, pious man," he told the general approvingly. "You have excellent ideas. If you were not commander-in-chief, I would suggest you put yourself up for the Majlis."

The general smiled, pleased. "We will talk more. Remember, you will come to dinner tomorrow night at my villa. Eight o'clock."

"I remember. I look forward to the occasion with pleasure."

At the posh, striking hall built by the shah, the Majlis gathered. The Majlis, Iran's national assembly, was made up of legislators elected to four-year terms. General Salehi stood in the balcony, a commanding figure as he surveyed the semicircle of desks facing in row after row the high raised seats of the presiding officers at the back of the room. There were so many turbaned mullahs that the Majlis looked like a religious service. Top government officials sat in the front row while members walked around the arcs of desks, conferring with one another as was the custom in any parliament during tiresome speeches.

General Salehi shook hands, asked about sons, offered advice, and exchanged gossip, all in his own private, secret campaign for shah. Afterwards he went downstairs to the carpeted corridor outside the meeting hall. There legislators sat on the floor listening to concerned constituents. An old Middle East custom.

The general repeated his questions and his jovial comments, again received the approval and acceptance of these men who had the ability to elect him shah. Some of the legislators were neither clerics nor members of the majority party, some were conservative mullahs and some were liberal mullahs, but all were—or said they were— loyal to Khomeini's revolution. All knew the rhetoric of militant Shiite rule. Every action was justified by religion: "in the name of Allah." The general had learned the lesson well; he had ac- quired power and would acquire even more power here.

While in the corridor, Horst Renssauer found him, asked for the introduction to the Ayatollah Mohammed Masumian. But the general had a better idea. Much better to have the Swiss banker come to his villa tomorrow night before dinner. That way the ayatollah could sign the papers for the secret bank account in the general's presence, the general could hide the papers for safekeeping, and after dinner . . . well, the papers, the five million U.S. dollars, and everything else would be his. And if Horst Renssauer were to be lost during any sudden violence in Tehran, he would at least have executed his duties, and his employers would be grateful. They would send the check to Akbar Salehi, lifetime president of Iran. And not question the money's ultimate destination.

The general was delighted at how easily the Swiss banker agreed to this change of plans, and the general said goodbye to him with genuine enthusiasm.

At last General Salehi left the Majlis hall. He would stop by his office to do some desk work, and then he would return home—with luck, earlier than expected. He'd have dinner with the odd Australian journalist, whom he hoped would do him some good in the international media, and then later, there would be the blond woman. He looked forward to the blond woman. He would not admit it to her, but he hardly remembered bedding her in Dubai. Strange for him, a man whose memory was as legendary as his sexual appetite. But then he'd been drinking. It wasn't like the days of the shah when he was permitted to drink half the night and fuck the other half. A man functioned better that way.

He sighed with nostalgia and strode toward the hall's main entrance. Those days would come again. But meanwhile, this had been worthwhile—the visits with the ayatollah, the hojatolislam, and then the Majlis. It reaffirmed that he had support, and that if the Majlis and the mullahs would not give him what he wanted, then he could take it by force. The less powerful leaders would come along, and so would the people. They would crown him both shah and hero, the man who made Iran a nuclear power.

Daniel Lambert stared up through pain-slitted eyes at his captor, the man with the knife-slashed left cheek. There was happiness in the animal eyes. If there was such a thing as evil, this was it, the joy of one human torturing another.

Suddenly Lambert heard sounds, frightening sounds, a hoarse voice wailing and begging for the pain to stop. There was uncontrolled horror and desperate suffering in the voice. And then he realized the awful truth. The voice was his.

Jake Bolt stepped quickly along the ledge. He peered in the first window, saw another bedroom almost identical to his own. There was no way he could escape through that door; he would be too close to the sentry who guarded his own bedroom door.

Carefully hugging the wall, he moved on. He passed two more bedrooms and came to a window through which he could dimly see shelves. It was a linen closet. That could be useful. He looked all around, saw no one, then worked the window up and open. He slipped inside.

There were rows of shelves with towels, washcloths, sheets, soaps, detergents, and scrub brushes. He pulled off the top piece of black cloth, held it up. It was a chador, one of the anonymous floor-length robes and shawls that Muslim women were required to wear in Iran. He thought a moment, tucked it under his arm.

He cracked open the door, peered out into the long corridor. At the end most distant from his own bedroom stood another sentry. Sarah's? He counted the doors—six. It was worth the gamble. He closed the door, returned to the window, and climbed out. He again moved along the ledge.

And then he froze, held his breath. A group of Falcons passed beneath him, heading around the villa. One glance up and he would be discovered. It was stupid to hold his breath, he told himself. He made himself inhale, exhale, slowly. The solemn

Falcons moved briskly, not speaking, as if in prayer or ordered to be silent.

He watched warily as they at last disappeared into the arched passageway that led to the barracks. He needed to move quickly now. More Falcons could appear at any moment.

He felt his way across the narrow shelf, counting windows, until he neared the one that should go with the sixth door. But it was barred! And then came a welcome sound. Across the city from the highest minarets pealed the calls to prayer. The sentries would be distracted, turning to face Mecca as they praised Allah.

Bolt looked in the barred window, saw exactly what he'd hoped. He stared, savoring the sight of tall, slender Sarah as she gracefully circled the room like a caged tigress, all restless energy and passionate resentment. She was healthy . . . and angry. How in hell could he get into the room, or more to the point, get her out?

He loosened the window, began to pull it open. Before he could finish, Sarah was there, glaring at him.

"Jacob, what are you doing!?" she whispered.

"Saving you," he said, annoyed. "Ever hear the words *thank you* ?" She could be the most irritating . . .

"Go away," she said. Her blue eyes blazed.

"You're nuts. You know that?" He looked around her room, saw the side door.

"Go away, Jacob! You're going to make a mess of everything!"

"No, you are," he told her, "if you don't keep your voice quiet. Is that door locked?"

"And if it is?"

"Fuck off, Sarah."

He moved across the ledge to the next window, opened it, and dropped to the floor inside. It was a man's bedroom, decorated in leather with military battle paintings on the walls and a man's comb set on the dresser. There was an envelope on the dresser, too. Bolt picked it up. It was addressed to General Akbar Salehi.

Bolt smiled grimly and surveyed the room, the room of the general himself, conveniently next door to Sarah's. He should have guessed.

He opened the envelope. It was a social invitation to a dinner next week. Of no importance at all. Quickly he searched through the drawers, then the desk, then the wastebasket, and at last the medicine cabinet in the adjoining bathroom. It was as if this were a motel room, not a private bedroom. Nothing of the man was here, just the mementoes of a general—photos, plaques, medals, a colored sash.

Bolt went to a photograph on the wall, studied a picture of the general with the Ayatollah Khomeini. They stood close, looking like father and son. It was dated a week before the ayatollah's death, but there was no evidence of the coming end in the cleric's eyes. He had the same gaunt, severe expression as always. The cancer that had supposedly killed him had changed him little, if at all.

There was a quiet tap on the door that adjoined Sarah's room.

"Jacob?"

He unlocked the door, opened it. She was standing there, waiting. He looked her up and down.

"Going to a party?" he asked.

She wore a long filmy white gown that showed her splendid naked shoulders. It was translucent and he found his physical reaction instant and demanding. Christ, she was frustrating. If he looked at her long enough he'd yank her down to the floor, to hell with the guard outside the door.

"Yes," she told him, lifted her chin. "Later. A little private party . . . with the general."

"Great." He threw the black chador at her. "Put it on. You're getting out of here."

"After I have what I want."

"From the general? You know that's his room?" Bolt gestured over his shoulder.

"It's hardly a surprise." She saw him watching her, opened the chador, held it up in front to shield her body from his gaze.

"It's a little late for modesty," he told her.

"How'd you find me?" she countered. She stalked back into the room, started to sit on the big bed, then changed her mind. She opted for a small chair next to the fireplace.

He stood in front of the fireplace, crossed his arms, remembered the events at the Israeli nuclear installation outside Dimona.

"You erased the intel about the Desert Falcons from your central computer system," he told her.

"Just stored it in another place," she said.

"How'd you know the computers were up again?"

"You mean," she said carefully, "why did I leave our cottage without waking you up?"

"Sneak out, is more accurate. All right. We'll start there."

"I don't owe you any explanations."

"Sure you do. I'm here. You need me. If I hadn't

been at the camel races, you'd be dead."

"But so would the general," she said grimly.

"Great, just great. You'd kill him, his men would kill you, and finding Doctor Lambert would take even longer. Not to mention confirmation on whether Iran is going nuclear."

She looked up at him a long moment. Then she said, "I'm sorry about all this, Jacob. Really. But I left the cottage because I couldn't sleep. Overtired, I guess. So I went over to security. It was a coincidence that the system was up and the stuff had just arrived. Everything was there: the identity of the Desert Falcons, the history of them, and then more information about General Salehi. I did a quick check and found out through a contact that he was flying to Dubai."

"And you went after him."

"Orders." She paused. "And I wanted to."

He looked at her and nodded slowly. Determination and justification had settled like stone on her sculptured face. His desire for her ebbed. She was a competitor. A beautiful, sexy competitor. But that was all.

"Jake." She seemed to sense a change in him. She stood up. The dark chador slid to the floor. She walked to him feline and nearly nude in the flimsy gown. "Please."

She touched his cheek, ran her fingertips down to his chin. Desire hit him again, hot and insistent. He grabbed the fingers, pulled her to him. She lifted her mouth, soft and yielding. The perfume of her surrounded him, filled his head. He held her tight against him and kissed her. She melted warm in his arms.

"I want you to get out of here," he whispered in

her hair. "Put on the chador and slip out. Go to the British embassy."

She leaned back, looked up into his eyes. The face was setting again into the stone mask. "Can't. I have a job to do."

He studied her. He could tell her she'd just be in the way, that he might think of her instead of the work he had to do here, that she posed a terrible danger to him—that through her General Salehi might find out his real identity. But he knew it made no difference. She would not go.

He dropped his hands, stepped back.

"Take care of yourself," he said and walked to the door.

"Jacob!"

He closed the door quietly and sprinted to the window.

CHAPTER
24

Daniel Lambert lay in a sea of pain. He'd passed out again. He could tell because of the jolt upon reawakening. Like a million knives the pain swept over him, worse than before. Sweat burned his eyes and wounds. Feebly he pulled against the wrist restraints.

"*Ab*," the animal torturer told someone behind him. "Water."

Lambert opened his puffed eyes to narrow slits. Every movement hurt. His arms ached and throbbed, but he couldn't stop his reflexive jerking against the restraints. The arms, his body, the whole universe was out of control.

And then suddenly cool water splashed on his mouth. Eagerly he opened his lips. The water poured over his face and he swallowed greedily, choked, coughed, and swallowed more. Then the water stopped. Lambert shuddered with a sigh and stiffened, waiting for more burns, cuts, beatings . . . His mind reeled, shut off. Too impossible to comprehend what might happen next.

The two men talked in Farsi, seemed to be arguing, but Lambert couldn't understand what they were saying. Hands untied him, picked him up, and hoisted him to his feet. He cried out. Pains

like electrical shocks shot through his body from
the rough handling. The men laughed and hauled
him toward the door. Their sick laughter echoed in
his mind as unconsciousness took him mercifully
back into a black, thought-free world.

Sarah Maizlish paced her bedroom, worrying
about Jacob, wondering what to do next. What
could she do? And then her gaze settled on
the chador on the floor. Not for escape . . . but for
search . . .

She slipped on the billowing robe, tied the
black laces, fastened the shawl around her face so
none of the blond hair showed.

In the bathroom she scrubbed off her ruby
lipstick and blue eye shadow and applied tan foundation to darken her skin. She studied her face—
still too young. With an eyebrow pencil she lined
her forehead and drew two long arcs around her
mouth. She smoothed the marks, blended them
into the foundation, then applied a light coating of
brown and blue shadow beneath her eyes in two
semicircular disks. She smiled at the worn woman
she saw in the mirror. Plain and tired, the perfect
Shiite vassal, indistinguishable from the millions
of other females in Tehran.

She took a stack of towels from her bathroom,
tried the door to the other bedroom. Jacob had left
it unlocked, as she'd expected him to. He would
still hope she would escape.

She glanced at the general's tidy room, swept
into his bath for more towels, and then went to the
hall door. No window ledge for her. She took a
deep breath, lowered her head submissively, and
opened the door.

Like a black anonymous shadow she rustled away from the sentry who guarded her door. She headed down the long corridor. Her heart beat into her ears as she waited for him to shout for her to stop, to identify herself. What was she doing in the general's bedroom!? Rifle shots would ring over her head . . .

But there was only the shuffling of feet behind her as the sentry adjusted his position. Perhaps he was accustomed to seeing women leaving the general's bedroom. Perhaps? She smiled at her naiveté. Of course he was accustomed. The general's promiscuity had been detailed in the Mossad report. Even if Iran had shut down, the general hadn't, and as long as he was discreet, he would be able to continue his affairs.

When she was beyond the guard's view, she slowed and began her investigation. She searched around the second-floor perimeter, saw empty bedrooms and a linen closet, and passed by one door where two sentries stood guard—maybe the general's office? There was no way she'd get past them into the office; she couldn't speak Farsi.

Downstairs on the first floor she found the public rooms, clerical offices, and the computer complex. Unspeaking, her eyes downcast modestly, she walked through all but the computer area. She would need to speak Farsi to enter there, too. She successfully, silently passed Falcons, male servants, and chador-clothed female servants.

This was a silent house, almost a mausoleum, she decided. Occasionally a door would open somewhere and she would hear men's and women's voices chattering, even laughing. But she never found those rooms. Perhaps when she passed through, everyone turned quiet, waiting for her to smile or talk or somehow signal that she would not report normal human emotions as against Allah's revolution.

Then as she was shuffling through a back corridor she noticed a door beneath a staircase. A Falcon came out of it and she heard a sound, something human but muffled. It sent chills down her spine. Was it a scream?

She continued past. She needed to go in there, but where would it lead? She pushed away the beginning tendrils of fear and envisioned the house's shape and the location of the door. There couldn't be a room behind. And then she had the answer. Downstairs. The door would open onto a stairwell that descended to a basement of some kind.

Basements were not usually places where a stack of towels would gain entry. She slowed, thinking. Then moved to a door she'd opened earlier. Inside was a supply closet. There she exchanged her towels for a bucket. She poured in soap and water and lugged the bucket and a mop toward the nondescript door beneath the elegant tiled staircase.

She opened the door and a stench of mildew, dampness, and . . . human decay swept up to her. Again there were the sounds. Now she was sure. They were human cries of pain. What was going on down there? She bit her lip, closed the door, and dragged the bucket to the wood stairs. She knelt and began scrubbing.

Falcons climbed up and down the stairs, walking over and around her as she cleaned the planks. She worked quickly, nervously, going down step by step. Wails and cries for help occasionally echoed beneath her, sending fear straight into her heart. Was Dr. Lambert here? If he was, she didn't want to think of his condition. Whether he was even alive . . .

She worked harder, the hot soapy water on her hands soothing in the cold, moldy, oppressive atmosphere that rose from the stone corridor below. As she neared the bottom step she saw a long metal desk with a Falcon sitting behind it, studying monitors that showed stone cells occupied by huddled men.

This was a prison. The conclusion hit her hard, even though she'd already guessed. A secret prison where torture and god knew what else could take place with complete impunity. To be kept here was to be lost.

The Falcon peered over his desk at her, said words in Farsi. She kept her gaze lowered, grunted something unintelligible, and scrubbed harder, cleaning a path across the stone floor away from his desk. Through her lowered lashes she watched with relief as he returned to studying his monitors. A large key ring full of keys hung from his belt, the metal clinking as he moved.

There were two corridors here. One that ran left and right parallel to the hall above from where she'd just come, and another that intersected where the Falcon guard sat. Falcons strolled along the passageways, their lethal AK-47s and G-3s carried at their sides like simple toys. Many wore partially full key rings dangling from their belts. Their casualness told her they weren't worried about escapes, and the sparse key rings indicated that the only one with a full set might be the guard at the desk.

She noted that the Falcons disappeared from sight at the ends of the corridors, and from the way they walked, that they were simply turning corners. If so, then this underground prison was built in a square, running beneath the four wings of the villa above, with a central corridor directly under the courtyard. Metal doors with big rings lined the corridors.

She worked her way toward the central passageway. The wash water was growing filthy. Too many boots walked these stone floors. A rancid stink of urine and sweat burned her nose.

And then she heard a voice talking. A quiet, tired voice speaking *English*. With a British accent! Cultured, educated.

"We must never give up," the voice said. "Tell them as little as necessary. Make mistakes. Work slowly."

"That won't stop them," said a voice with an American accent. "They take what we do and learn from it. Remember, nearly a million of their scientists and leaders abandoned Iran after Khomeini came to power. And then there were Khomeini's purges after that."

"They lost most of their intelligentsia," said the Englishman. "Escaped or dead. That is why we are so vital to them."

Maizlish slowly scrubbed, listening as the voices rose and fell in conversation. And then she heard footsteps behind her. She turned slightly so she could see, and backed away against the wall.

There were two Falcons, and between them they dragged the limp body of an older man, perhaps in his sixties, perhaps even older. She tried not to stare, but her gaze fixed on the unconscious man whose bruised, misshapen face looked familiar beneath the purple swellings. Suddenly he seemed to jerk awake. His eyes opened and he gazed straight into Maizlish's eyes.

Recognition passed between them. Dr. Lambert! Maizlish felt her heart rise to her throat. Bruised face, burned and bruised arms, blood-stained pajamas that must hide a terribly damaged body.

She opened her mouth to speak, then remembered where she was. She ducked her head.

"Ma—— Ma——." The scientist tried to talk. His feet struggled to gain balance on the floor.

The Falcons who supported him dragged him toward the cell door next to Maizlish. It was the cell from which she'd heard the voices. She scuttled back. But just then his body contorted, legs swinging wildly.

She felt the blow, never even saw it coming. In an instant her ears rang. Her black shawl fell askew. A rush of cold dank air surrounded her head. Lambert had kicked her!

The Falcons bellowed in Farsi and dropped Lambert in a heap on the floor. They yanked Maizlish up between them. The one with an evil scarred face grabbed a fist full of her pale hair and held it up to her face. She stared at it wide-eyed, her scalp stinging with pain, and then at him as he yelled over her shoulder to the guard back at the desk. She couldn't understand the words, but she knew what he was saying. They'd found the general's blond woman!

Instantly she leaned back, snapped a karate kick straight to the scarred-face's groin. But he nimbly stepped aside, pushed the muzzle of his AK-47 into her belly. He smiled with deep ugly pleasure, showing rotted brown teeth. She was his. All his. He gestured, and his companion unlocked the cell door. With a quick, sharp gesture, he shoved her back. She stumbled and fell into a dim cesspool of stink. Daniel Lambert landed on top of her. The metal door closed with a harsh clang.

Jake Bolt was sweating. He moved across the ledge, stopping instantly each time a Falcon passed below him. If he was right, the general's office was around the corner and near the center of the next wing. He worked his way toward it, feeling the rough walls under his hands, the narrow ledge beneath his feet. It was at least an inch shorter than his shoes. The wind whistled past him, whining over the tiled rooftop.

At last he reached the window, checked inside. Not that one. He tried the next. No. And the next. Yes! He studied the empty room, the big rosewood desk, the leather chairs in perfect order. No one was there. He pulled up the window, dropped lightly inside, and went instantly to the desk.

The top center drawer was locked. He found a polished brass letter opener, popped open the lock. There sat his SIG-Sauer. He picked it up, savored its comforting weight. He checked it. It was loaded, ready to go. He slipped it back into his belt holster beneath his sports jacket and suddenly felt dressed. He'd been naked before.

For a moment he thought about Sarah . . . how she'd looked in the general's gown . . . but he pushed the image from his mind. Damn Sarah. Anytime he thought about her, he could see her perfectly in his memory. Perfectly.

He searched through the general's drawers. Besides the usual assortment of pencils, pens, and papers, he found a two-year daybook. He flipped through it, noting the social engagements and notations of appointments with government officials, military leaders, and maneuvers with the Falcons. All seemed ordinary. Then he had an odd idea. He flipped back to the date of the Ayatollah Khomeini's death. Three pages were torn out—three full days. Quickly he checked the rest of the book. Nothing else was missing. Only those three days.

He looked earlier in that week, saw the usual appointments. Then noted that Colonel Rizvi's name appeared constantly throughout the book. But that was to be expected; Colonel Rizvi was the general's Number Two. Thoughtfully he returned the book to its place in the desk.

He popped open the lock to the file drawer. There were only a half-dozen files; the bulk of the general's records were probably kept by his clerical staff at the villa and downtown at his other office. He looked through, saw files on battle strategy, nuclear warheads, lists of important mullahs and members of the Majlis, and Colonel Ahmed Rizvi. Bolt pulled out the colonel's thin file. There was only one piece of paper in it. It was a letter in Farsi from the colonel to the general and dated a month ago.

The letter began with a paragraph of the usual greetings, then it said:

Allah willing, I will martyr myself in the sacred fields of battle, for if I do not, I must forever live with the soul-shaking guilt of

*what we have done. Our leader is gone,
and now you will be our new leader, some-
day our shah. Allah will forgive for it is all
to his glory. But I cannot forget.*

Bolt read the paragraph again. So General
Salehi wanted to be shah. Bolt was hardly surprised. That would explain the buildup of his own
private troops, the Falcons, and the secret development of the nuclear facility. But what else was
Rizvi saying? Something about "guilt" and "our
leader." Our leader? Khomeini probably. But what
did Rizvi feel guilty about? That he backed the
general in taking over the Iranian government?
That could be it. Or was there more . . . ?

The letter's last paragraph was a simple closing
in which the colonel again swore his allegiance to
General Salehi.

Bolt slid the sheet back into its folder and put
the folder back in its place in the file drawer. He
relocked the drawers. It was time to get out of here.
He returned to the window, thinking. Why had the
general kept the letter? Probably because it somehow incriminated the colonel. But of what? What
had they done?

Bolt looked down, saw the lawns were empty.
He stepped out on the ledge and moved toward the
corner where thick ivy grew up the wall. His next
stop was the first floor, the computer room.

CHAPTER
25

Jake Bolt climbed down the trellis and slipped into an arched doorway. He paused, allowed his senses to take in the surroundings. Somewhere in the distance he heard telephones ringing and typewriters ratcheting. He padded to a window, looked in. It was the stiff, formal receiving room. Now he was oriented, knew where he was.

He slipped through French doors into the room and then out into the corridor, melting into rooms whenever he heard someone coming. As he continued, he thought about the big dinner party the general was giving tomorrow night. There was something suspicious about it, particularly the close timing to Dr. Lambert's kidnapping. Yes, first the general's nuclear facility was finished, or almost finished, and now he had Lambert as a top administrator. If he were going to mount a coup, he would probably move fast, before news of the nuclear installation and Dr. Lambert spread and his opposition could marshal support.

No wonder the general liked the idea of an international journalist interviewing him. That would give the world a colorful portrait—sympathetic but tough, the general beset by adversaries in the desert, the general peacefully at home surrounded by loyal Falcons, and the general's wisdom and revelations about the little-understood nation of Iran. And the journalist would be safely gone before the coup began.

At last Bolt neared the computer room. He straightened his jacket, smoothed back his dark hair, and plastered a naive smile on his face. The guards watched him as he approached.

"*Shalam*," Bolt greeted them in Farsi. "Remember me? I'm the Australian reporter. General Salehi said I could have a closer look at your computer system."

"You know computers?" one of the guards said, impressed.

"General Salehi gave you permission?" said the other, suspicious.

"I know a little," Bolt said modestly. "Yes, the general thought I could report to the world the great advances you've made here." He studied the two in their crisply pressed tan Falcon uniforms. "Especially the quality and courage of the Desert Falcons."

The first guard stepped out of the way, followed more slowly by the second.

"We will be watching you!" warned the second as the first opened the door.

"*Teshekoor*," Bolt said, walking through. "Thanks. I won't be long." And finished, he hoped, before the general returned to the villa.

Bolt stood at the back of the room, quietly studied the scientists and technicians as they went about their business. He saw a young one sign off, and he memorized the code and encryption numbers.

"You are the Australian?" an older Iranian said, approaching. "I am Reza Hojjati, director of our computer center." His skin was sallow from too much time indoors and he carried a clipboard. Ballpoint pens jutted from a plastic case in his breast pocket.

"I'm the journalist, *naleh*, yes," Bolt said, and introduced himself. "Quite a complex you have here." He looked around with admiration, then gestured at the silver-gray supercomputer. "Amazing that you've got a Cray-2. Not an easy machine to import from the United States."

The Iranian scientist gave a small, knowing smile. "There are ways. Especially if you are a man of the caliber and resourcefulness of General Salehi."

"You have a high opinion of the general?"

"An excellent man. Religious, intelligent, hardworking."

"A good leader?"

The Iranian bowed his head in agreement. "A superior leader."

"Good enough to lead Iran?"

"Perhaps." The Iranian stared curiously at Bolt. "Why do you ask?"

"Seems like a good man to me," Bolt said innocently. "And Iran is drifting, needs a strong hand to guide her into the future."

The scientist nodded solemnly.

"What do you think of Colonel Rizvi?" Bolt asked.

"A pious man. Second only to our general."

"Khomeini respected both?"

"The ayatollah respected the general, but he loved the colonel like a son."

"In all families there are fights," Bolt observed carefully. "Did the general or the colonel ever fight with the ayatollah?"

"Never!" the scientist said, moved restlessly on his feet. He wanted to return to his work. "In fact, both were with him when he died. They wept over the ayatollah's sanctified death bed. The newspapers carried the photograph of it, and when the general made a bid to lead, I think our people wanted him. But the mullahs and Majlis were against it. The general is too strong, too *big* for them. Like Khomeini he overshadows everyone."

"So they chose Mohammed Masumian instead."

"*Naleh*. Yes, he is one of them."

"Ah, I understand," Bolt said. "But I'm keeping you from your work."

"*Teshekoor*," the scientist said politely. He moved toward a computer console.

Bolt stepped toward the banks of computers. "Mind if I try my hand?" he asked.

The scientist waved his permission, already engrossed in the hypersonic plane on his computer screen. He had done his duty as host, now he wanted to work. The plane on the screen rotated in myriad colors, sky blue to tangerine.

Bolt sat, quickly keyboarded in the codeword and encryption number he'd memorized from the young scientist he'd observed earlier.

He worked rapidly, called up the nuclear installation, found it to be located north of Tehran in the Elburz Mountains. He talked with its computers, whose data showed it was completed, ready to pull rods. He memorized its location, latitude and longitude.

Then he searched until he made entry into the inventory of Iran's vast arsenal of missiles and rockets. When armed with nuclear warheads there was enough firepower, he discovered,.to hold the globe hostage and turn the Middle East into radioactive rubble. Bolt was shocked at the extent.

He had no time to dwell. He asked the computer about Daniel Lambert, found his complete biography and the cryptic notation *Under study in Tehran*. Bolt was surprised. He'd expected Lambert to be at the Elburz facility. Did that mean the doctor was here? In General Salehi's villa? But where? Bolt had had a complete tour, with the exception of the security rooms. What else had he not seen?

Immediately Bolt began to search. He called up the villa's security system and found an odd track. There was something going on in the basement. At last he was able to tie into the basement security monitors. On the screen before him appeared a cell of some kind with two prisoners sprawled ragged and listless on the stone floor. He switched to two other monitors, found similar scenes. The conclusion was inescapable: the general had a secret prison!

Some of the prisoners were hurt; wounds showed on faces and limbs. There were no beds, tables, or toilet facilities. Just the floor and a large pot. He looked at three more cells, each small and containing one or two prisoners. There were mostly male prisoners, none in soldiers' uniforms. Instead they wore an assortment of clothing, everything from pajamas to the remnants of business suits. No sign of Lambert.

He switched to the computer system itself, discovered that it not only controlled the villa's security, but that it tied into security at various installations; as well as providing intelligence and various informational bases.

He sat back, thought for a moment. Sometimes you had to take a gamble, rely on intuition. Do the opposite of what Vernon White in Honolulu wanted, *ordered*, you to do. Everything about General Salehi and his fortress villa warned Bolt that there was big trouble here. Too much power in one man's hands. Too much power derived from fanaticism, fear, religious fervor. Salehi's banquet tomorrow night loomed larger and larger in significance. Bolt didn't know what would happen then, but he sensed something vital would. Perhaps the coup.

He entered two small strings of code, planted them in the security software. His own private virus, harder than hell for someone else to find. At periodic intervals, the virus would make the computer system shut down. Then it would rise up again like a phoenix, working perfectly, reassuring everyone, until the next time it went down. And each time it went down, it would be for a longer period. Bolt gave a cold smile of satisfaction.

And immediately switched back to the basement cell monitors. Now he would make a thorough search for Lambert. He both hoped the physicist was there, and that he wasn't. He didn't like to think about what condition he'd be in.

Bolt studied three more cells, each more discouraging than the last, the number of those incarcerated in the primitive conditions weighing upon him like a mountain. He sensed these were not criminals. They were political prisoners ... or were they kidnapped scientists like Dr. Lambert? He knew that to be true when he found the monitor that showed the torture room. Such time and thought was seldom wasted on mere criminals.

There was a table with straps for ankles and wrists and chest, a cattle prod, a . . .

"There he is!"

Falcons swarmed suddenly around Bolt. He jumped up, grabbed for his SIG-Sauer, but he was too late. He'd been involved with the information on the computer screen, not attending to real business and watching his backside. Now there was nothing he could do. Twenty Falcons with their big AK-47s made an arc around him, pinioning him to the computer, each gun pointed at his heart. One snatched the SIG-Sauer from his hand.

General Salehi strode through their midst, a commanding, arrogant figure in his starched uniform and shiny black dress boots.

"Ah, Mr. Bolt," he said suavely in English. "My Falcon guards told me I'd find you here. We've just had a report from the Sydney newspaper you claim for your employer. I believe we have a misunderstanding. You are supposed to be a reporter." His voice turned to ice. "Not a spy!"

Bolt smiled. "And you're supposed to be a general, not a pretender to the throne!"

The general's eyes narrowed. "You are without understanding, typical of foreigners."

"And you're without conscience. How many people have you condemned to that inhuman secret prison of yours?"

The general's cruel mouth worked with fury. No one addressed him without respect. No one. His liquid eyes blazed.

"We seem also to have a misunderstanding about a certain Sarah Maizlish," he continued with controlled fury. "Your partner. She, of course, must die. As must you. I no longer can keep her safe in my upstairs haven. Until then, your punishment will be time—time for contemplation, time to remember the stupidity of misplaced heroism, time to worry what void lies on the other side of execution. You made a mistake saving the Maizlish woman's life." He waved a hand. "Take him. You know where!"

Two Falcons grabbed Bolt. He shook them off. Stalked alone toward the door.

"Very primitive, general," Bolt shot back at Salehi. "I thought you aspired to be a sophisticated international leader."

Salehi's face turned ashen. His hands knotted at his sides. As Bolt exited out the door, he called, "You will not live long enough to see my ultimate triumph!"

The Falcons took Bolt around the villa to the door he'd noticed earlier beneath the tiled back staircase, then down to an evil-smelling cellar where worn stone floors attested to the years of use this prison had seen. He observed the head Falcon guard who sat at a front desk, saw the screens that monitored each cell, noted the enormous key ring that rattled from his belt.

"Is Dr. Lambert here?" he asked.

The Falcons ignored him, pushed him toward the center aisle.

"Our general has a surprise for you," grinned the Falcon to his left. He unlocked a metal cell door, pushed it open. "Look who is waiting for you!"

And then he rammed his AK-47 into Bolt's back, slammed him into the dim cell. There Sarah knelt over the prone body of a older man. Lambert!

"Jacob," Sarah said sadly, "I'd hoped they wouldn't get you."

CHAPTER
26

Along the street outside General Salehi's villa strolled Hugh Willoughby. It was nearing dusk, and he'd had a tiring day, what with the flights, customs, and the time-zone changes. If he'd been in his right mind, he told himself, he'd have stayed at his nice hotel and left the footwork till tomorrow. But he wasn't in his right mind. As evidence for that he took his continued devotion to MI6. Gad. What a fool. Already his feet ached.

But he had a halfway decent lead, and here he was, back in harness. According to the British ambassador, whom he'd met on the sly when he first arrived in Tehran, there was a persistent rumor floating among the diplomatic upper crust that General Salehi was up to something rather large, maybe even momentous. Since Salehi had once been considered a personally ambitious man— until he'd signed up heart and bloody soul with the Ayatollah Khomeini—no one was particularly shocked when the rumors started. Now the question was, if true, what was the general up to? And how did a nuclear facility fit into his plans? Very troubling.

The ambassador had no information about Daniel Lambert, nor about missing British scientists. But he had mentioned that the general kept a healthy contingent of his Desert Falcons on hand at his villa. This put Willoughby to thinking.

Why keep so many commandos conveniently at hand? Admittedly Middle East leaders liked their little shows of power, harems if possible. But when harems weren't religiously correct, then at least bandoliered bodyguards in smart uniforms, long expensive foreign limousines, and trailing secretaries with stricken faces because the sheikh, or prince or mullah or general was too busy (too *important*) to make a reasonable schedule that a normal person could meet.

In other words, Willoughby smelled a rat. His finely honed sense of suspicion was alerted by an overabundance of personal commandos.

So he rented a car and drove off to the villa's address which the ambassador had slipped to him under the cafe table and Willoughby had later memorized and torn to shreds.

Now his rental car was parked five blocks away, and as the sun set over this dreadful hole called Tehran, Willoughby was doing recon.

Yuri Fyodorov stepped off the city bus and sauntered toward General Akbar Salehi's villa. The tree-lined avenue was wide, the traffic light, and the streets clean from the recent rainstorm. It was a pleasant twilight, not the smog-heavy, dry heat of Tehran's usual summer dusk that left your throat parched and your temper short. Spring, he decided, made the city better, but not much better. But then, no third-rate, dull gray Middle East metropolis could compare to beautiful Moscow.

Was he growing bitter, Fyodorov suddenly asked himself. All this carping about climate. No, it was simply too many years, too much experience at the old party line. Much better to look at the surface of things than to dig deep. Loyalty in disguise for ideology.

And ahead was General Akbar Salehi's villa, a monstrous monument to wealth and power, standing unashamed in a nation ruled by religion. He enjoyed the irony of how religion and so-called religious people seemed to couple so naturally with riches and power. But that realization simply confirmed his own prejudices —he was a Leninist socialist waiting for his nation to return to its heritage. With Gorbachev, there appeared to be hope. But he wouldn't hold his breath.

Meanwhile Fyodorov had a job to do, and he would do it well. Anything less would be a betrayal of himself. A man had to believe in something, and if it wasn't in his country, then it had to be in his individuality.

And so he'd located Horst Renssauer/Viktor Markov's hotel room but had not found Renssauer there. Renssauer had been seen at the Majlis, and then slipped out of sight. The logical place for Renssauer to go next would be the general's villa.

Fyodorov stood at the end of the block and analyzed the luxurious estate. There was a high white wall surrounding the grounds. He could see Desert Falcons patrolling the interior lawns, carrying rifles. AK-47s, they looked like. Made by the Soviet Union? Perhaps. Or China, Pakistan, or any number of other nations that had found the Soviet design reliable and useful for their particular needs.

The property swept down a gentle slope into a

stand of trees. It was a big estate, from what Fyodorov could see, plenty of room for a hundred Falcons to hide out, work out, practice, and relax.

He slipped among the trees that lined the side wall closest to him. The next-door neighbor's mansion was out of sight. He would move along here, circle the villa, see what he could pick up.

Jake Bolt quickly surveyed the cell. A group of six prisoners moved in from the walls where they had fled when the door had opened. There were five men and a woman, and they came to sit around Sarah and Dr. Lambert as if they were simply resuming their original places. Their clothes were tattered, and their faces told the story of what they had experienced here—hollow eyes, emaciated cheeks, and skin that looked stiff and gray, as if it had no resilience left. There were yellowing bruises on some of them. One man lay next to a wall, babbling to himself.

Bolt knelt beside Sarah, stared down at Lambert. "How is he?"

"He seems to be coming around," Sarah told him. "I can't tell yet whether there's any permanent damage."

"They know who you are."

She sighed. "I suppose you're going to remind me I should've left when I could."

"How'd you guess?" He smiled.

"Jake, anyone ever tell you you're a pain in the butt being right all the time?"

"Never anyone as beautiful as you."

She smiled and shook her head. "I look thirty years older in this stage makeup."

"Yeah. But I know what's underneath. All over."

"You've forgiven me for leaving you?"

"At Dimona? Sure. I would've gone, too. Just part of the business, like in India, remember? Besides, if we all die here, it's nice to go out with a clean record."

"Jacob!"

He chuckled. "Don't worry. I have a couple of ideas. Or maybe someone's already on the way to rescue us. Look at the good side. We came after Dr. Lambert. And we've found him."

"For all the good it will do you, young man," said a man's distinctly British voice.

"I'm sorry, Sir Carlton," Sarah said. "I haven't introduced you. Jake, this is a group of nuclear scientists and weapons experts that General Salehi's had kidnapped over the last year. Everyone, this is Jacob Bolt, CIA."

"Delighted!" said one.

"Pleased to meet you!" said another.

Sarah went around the group. "This is Sir Carlton Beers, England. Dr. Henri Le Petit, France. Dr. Joyce Mether, U.S. Dr. Donald Fritzen, U.S. Dr. Joachim Braun, West Germany. And there, lying down, is Dr. Bruce Coopersmith, England. Dr. Coopersmith has bad stomach cramps, probably a bacterial invasion."

"He hasn't been with us long, lucky him," Sir Carlton said. He was a tall, angular man with a lined face and bony fingers.

Bolt nodded at the little group. "Is there going to be a coup tomorrow night?" he asked immediately.

"We've heard rumblings," Sir Carlton said.

"I heard Salehi is lining up support," Dr. Braun said.

"He has the support of the military?" Bolt asked.

"He *is* the military," Sir Carlton said.

Sir Carlton sat on the floor cross-legged. He moved with surprising agility, considering his thinness and the bruises on his arms and face. The others sat beside him, a cluster of intellect that in different circumstances would have been the moving forces in vital departments in international scientific establishments.

"And he's a bloody smart boy," Sir Carlton continued. "He knows that if he succeeds at a coup simply through military force, he'll end up with a dictatorship. He doesn't want that. His ego is too big. He wants to be a popular leader, someone not only acceptable to, but admired by, even loved by the ordinary people and the majority of the legislators and mullahs."

"So that's where the nuclear plant fits in," Bolt said thoughtfully.

"He's making it as difficult as possible for them to say no," Dr. Mether agreed.   •

"And you will work there?" Bolt asked them.

"Some of us already have. Unfortunately," Dr. Fritzen said. "We did as little as possible, even built in a number of mistakes they'll be discovering for the next twenty years." He smiled grimly.

"Are all the foreign scientists here?" Bolt asked, thinking of the cells that filled this underground dungeon.

"Mostly now, yes," Sir Carlton said. "Perhaps forty of us. A few are still out at the installation, waiting for it to start up. Salehi's smart enough to realize he needs a man of Lambert's expertise to run it. I've heard that they're going to start chemicals on him tomorrow, force him to cooperate."

"Chemicals!" Sarah said, horrified. She stared down at Dr. Lambert, who was still unconscious.

"They've used chemicals on others?" Bolt said.

"On most of us," Dr. Mether confirmed. "They're monsters!"

"But it's not just us," Sir Carlton said. "I've heard the guards talking. Salehi has begun to use a combination of chemicals, brainwashing, and bribery to recruit foreign agents. Apparently he plans to develop a network."

Bolt was silent a long moment. Was it possible . . . "Did you see a young Japanese-Polynesian woman here? A yakuza who went by the name Tami Tanaka?"

"There was a Tami Konishi. About thirty, long black hair, very lovely. She wasn't here long. She must have broken rather easily."

"That explains the connection," Bolt said.

"The warehouse," Sarah remembered. "The slip of paper with the address."

"Yeah. Tami was working both sides of the street, for the yakuza and for the general. Buying or routing arms to supply the Falcons while keeping her Japanese connections as a cover."

"She sent the materiel through the Jerusalem warehouse and then on to the general, or wherever he'd direct."

The group listened quietly as the two agents finished their discussion. Dr. Lambert moaned. His eyes flickered open.

"Who are you?" he said in Hebrew, and his eyes closed again.

Sarah touched his throat. "His pulse is stronger," she said with relief.

Bolt looked around the group. "Were any of you here when Khomeini died?"

"I was," Sir Carlton said. His bony fingers moved up and down his tattered shirt front. "Why?"

"Was there anything odd about the death? Did General Salehi act peculiarly?"

"All I knew was what I overheard," Sir Carlton said slowly. "Khomeini was very ill five days, and cancer finally took him. He'd had the disease for years. Prostate, I believe."

"You think there was more to it?" Sarah asked, surprised.

"I'm wondering," Bolt said. "Say Khomeini learned that General Salehi was putting together a nuclear facility. He would've been furious. Khomeini insisted on control of everything. He'd look at General Salehi and see a commander-in-chief with not only his own private commandos but also growing nuclear capabilities. For Khomeini, that would be too much power in someone else's hands."

"Very speculative, I must say," Sir Carlton said dubiously.

"Why do you want to know, Jacob?" Sarah asked.

"Salehi's computer director told me about a photograph published in all the newspapers that showed the general and Colonel Rizvi crying over Khomeini's deathbed. The photograph was very popular among the people, attracted a lot of sympathy, which encouraged the general to make a move to be elected Iran's next leader. But the Majlis and mullahs blocked him—they wanted someone less powerful, Mohammed Masumian. But now the nuclear facility's complete, and I'll bet he's been politicking, lining up support."

The prisoners looked at one another and back at Bolt.

"What are you saying about Khomeini's death?" Sarah asked Bolt.

"I think there's a chance General Salehi killed him."

"Salehi killed Khomeini?" Dr. Mether echoed.

"It makes sense to me," Dr. Fritzen decided slowly. "Salehi is ruthless."

"And daring," added Le Petit. "He takes pride in making fast, important decisions."

"And he is a killer," concluded Braun in a thick German accent. "We have seen an abundance of evidence to prove that."

"But how did he do it?" Sarah began, then immediately answered herself: "Chemicals!"

"Exactly," Bolt said. "God knows what they're using here, but the drugs that make a man talk, or bend to the torturer's will, are also drugs that can kill. A small amount administered in a drink to begin with, then escalated more each day, probably injected toward the end when he's unconscious and the nurse's back is turned. In five days the victim is dead."

"Since Khomeini already had been diagnosed as having cancer," Sarah said, "the doctors would think it was simply the normal progression of his disease."

Again the group was silent. It was stunning to think about, somehow even more horrifying than Salehi's other evils. If a man can kill the religious leader he professes to love and follow, he is capable of anything.

"What can we do?" Le Petit said.

"Imagine the nuclear bomb in Salehi's hands!" Sarah said, her old-woman's face cold, determined. "We must stop him!"

"Easier said than done, my dear," Sir Carlton said.

Bolt nodded. "Yeah, but we've got to try. Tell me about this prison. When you get your food, guard changes, do they exercise you? Weaknesses of any kind. I want to know everything you know. Everything."

CHAPTER 27

Far behind the back of the elegant Mediterranean villa, Hugh Willoughby slipped around a dark, shadowy bush. Crickets, katydids, and other night creatures sang quietly. Above him gray clouds swept beneath the black sky like stately ships.

Willoughby was irritated, scratched from head to foot from a thicket he'd accidentally stumbled into. He hadn't observed anything of importance here, just the lights that glowed from the villa's multitude of windows, and the Falcon sentries that patrolled the grounds like hunting dogs on leashes. No sign of Dr. Lambert or of any missing British scientists. Willoughby was growing weary of the whole exercise and was contemplating a return to his hotel room, whose attractiveness increased by the minute. But there was one more thing he wanted to do.

He moved toward the forest that backed the property, curious about the extent of the training facilities he saw here. This General Salehi appeared to be an exceptionally thorough chap.

Ah, yes. This was a good place. Willoughby leaned back against a tree, took his pack of Players from his jacket, and looked out over the shadowy training yard. There was an obstacle course, ramming dummies, targets . .

"Like a light, Hugh?"

Willoughby almost dropped the cigarette. His heart thundered.

"Bloody Christ!" he whispered, pulled out his revolver. "Who's there?" He turned swiftly. It seemed to come from behind.

"An old acquaintance," the voice went on. It had a Russian accent.

"Show yourself," Willoughby demanded.

There was a hesitation, then a pistol and hand appeared from between the trees, then the arm, and at last the stubby, fireplug body of Yuri Fyodorov. Fyodorov's gun was aimed right at Willoughby's heart, which continued to pound as if Willoughby had just seen the beginning of World War III. Willoughby's faithful revolver returned the compliment, pointing at Fyodorov, although a little shakily.

"Well, Yuri," Willoughby said. "We seem to have a standoff. I trust you have a reason for bumping into me here?"

"Couldn't help it," Fyodorov said. "My god, man. Do you always make so much noise doing recon?"

"It was a blasted thicket," Willoughby said huffily.

"Ah, I see. Well. Sorry." Fyodorov seemed to repress a smile. "Do you suppose, Hugh, that we are here on similar missions?"

"Since we are equally hated by the Iranians, it's possible. Whom are you looking for?"

"One of our agents. And you?"

"Some missing scientists."

"Hmmm."

"Shall we put our weapons away?" Willoughby

said, noting the growing limpness of Fyodorov's hand.

"Together," Fyodorov agreed.

The two operatives watched each other's eyes for betrayal and slowly lowered their guns. They slipped them back into their holsters.

"Well, now." Fyodorov looked out over the training ground to the villa. "Have you heard any rumors about General Salehi? Any . . . world-shaking rumors?"

Willoughby thought about the phrase *world-shaking.* Fyodorov was obviously implying something he didn't want to say directly in case Willoughby had no knowledge of the information. No operative liked to give anything away. However, if they both shared the information, then a thorough discussion might lead to more knowledge for both of them.

"Actually," Willoughby said carefully, "I believe I have. In fact, the rumor has something to do with arms."

"Hmmm. Large arms?"

"Very large, very powerful."

"We are speaking about . . . nuclear?"

The two operatives stared at one another.

"A nuclear facility?" Fyodorov asked.

Willoughby nodded solemnly. "The KGB knows then. We believe Salehi has kidnapped some of our people to put the facility together."

It was Fyodorov's turn to nod. "Perhaps that is also the fate of my operative. A computer expert."

Then the sharp snap of a twig suddenly cut through the night noises. The two men melted back against the trees.

"Probably just the regular sentries," Willoughby said.

And the muzzle of a gun rammed into his back. Willoughby and Fyodorov stiffened at the same time.

"Not the regular sentries," corrected a voice in carefully enunciated English. "Walk toward the villa. Now!"

Jake Bolt and the prisoners were finishing their evening meal of bread and a thin, tasteless rice gruel when they heard an odd excitement in the corridor beyond their cell. Bolt and Sarah pressed their ears against the metal door.

"No, no!" Sir Carlton directed them. "There!"

He'd indicated a fine slit between two of the stones that formed the wall, carved out by persistent hands god knew how many years ago. Perhaps decades. The opening was low, where it would have less chance of discovery. Bolt and Sarah lay on their bellies next to it, trying to watch and hear.

"This one is empty," one Falcon said to another in Farsi. They had stopped at the next cell up the corridor. "We'll put them in here." There was a clinking of keys, and a door creaked open.

"Bloody Iranians and their damn Farsi," a very English voice complained from the corridor

Bolt gave a start.

"What is it?" Sarah whispered.

"Not *what*. *Who*! It's an old friend of mine—Hugh Willoughby, MI6!"

"Oh. Did he come to rescue us?"

"If he did, he's failing rapidly. Come on."

Bolt crawled across to the wall that separated the two cells. He looked low, searching for another crack. Sir Carlton pointed a silent finger, and Bolt and Sarah headed toward the narrow slit. Outside, the cell door slammed.

"Hugh!" Bolt called quietly through the crack.

Bolt watched as Hugh Willoughby rotated his head, looking all around the cell. "I must be losing my bloody mind," he told the other man in the cell. Bolt didn't know him.

"No you're not," Bolt said. "Over here, Hugh."

The other man gestured toward the wall, and he and Willoughby got down on hands and knees to approach.

"What're you doing here?" Bolt said staring into Willoughby's surprised eyes.

"Jake? My god, man. What are *you* doing here?"

Bolt briefly recapped the chain of events since Tokyo when he'd last seen the MI6 man and together they'd wiped out the Sakura coke operation. Then Willoughby told Jake about his superior's intel that British scientists had been kidnapped by General Salehi to create his nuclear installation. As they spoke, the rest of the prisoners crowded around.

"Your superior was right. We're from Britain," Sir Carlton said over Bolt's shoulder. He introduced himself and Coopersmith, whose stomach cramps had lessened enough that he was able to sit up and smile wanly.

"And who's this?" Bolt asked about Willoughby's silent companion.

"Yuri Fyodorov," Willoughby said. "A good man. KGB. I worked with him on a dicey prisoner exchange about ten years ago, and there have been other occasions. Ultra secret, don't you know," he added vaguely. "But now, seems one of his chaps is missing. Any of you know whether there are Soviet prisoners here?"

"None," Sir Carlton pronounced. The other prisoners nodded agreement.

"Did you talk to General Salehi?" Bolt asked Willoughby.

"No. Too busy to greet us, apparently," Willoughby said.

"Something big's happening tomorrow night," Fyodorov added. "From what we could tell, they've decided we'll keep until they have time to get around to us."

"Sounded as if they meant day after tomorrow, didn't you think?" Willoughby inquired.

"Believe so," Fyodorov responded politely. "I have a touch of Farsi," he explained to Bolt.

"Ah," Bolt said. "Around here, that helps."

"Look!" Sarah said suddenly. They turned. Lambert was struggling up to a sitting position. She hurried to him. "How are you feeling?" she asked in Hebrew.

"I thought I heard someone speaking to me," he told her dazedly. "I decided I must be dreaming."

Sarah smiled. "Not dreaming. You're awake, and very alive."

"Amazing," Lambert said. He ran his hands shakily over his belly. He grimaced.

"Can you walk?" Bolt said, squatting beside him.

"So you're here, too?" Lambert looked up. "I was the scientist the terrorists wanted to kidnap. And I didn't believe it. Strange."

"Remember, they plan to start him on the chemicals tomorrow," Sarah warned Bolt.

"Yeah, I know. But I have an idea of how to

handle that." He turned to Sir Carlton. "Do the guards always follow the same routine when they bring in food?"

"Yes. Why?"

Bolt addressed Sarah. "Did you notice how one guard carries in the tray and the other one stands in the door holding a rifle on us?"

"The other rifle must be out in the hall."

"Right," Bolt said. "They're leaving themselves open to attack."

"Yes, from someone who knows what to do." Sarah's blue eyes widened. "Of course. We can take them."

Bolt returned to the crack, explained to Willoughby and Fyodorov what he had in mind. The plan was dangerous, and it relied on the computer system malfunctioning to confuse the general and his Falcons. The system should be shutting down for the first time now. It would be for only a minute, hardly enough to worry anyone, but the next closure would be for five minutes, and the one after that for ten. Finally there would be a half-hour closure tomorrow evening just before the general's party. That should put a damper on his plans, but knowing the general, it wouldn't stop him.

That's what Bolt was counting on: the general's headlong rush to destiny. When he got there, Bolt would be waiting.

CHAPTER
28

The next morning General Akbar Salehi strolled the villa's corridors, enjoying the bustle and activity of his home being readied for the festivities. He was pleased. All seemed to be progressing nicely toward tonight's critical events. He thought not at all of the blond woman and her treachery. Instead he allowed himself the delight of remembering the ripe young girl, the daughter of one of his maids, he'd taken to bed last night. A virgin. Even an experienced man of his appetite relished the innocence and gratitude of a virgin.

He entered the public rooms, stopped to savor the Old Persian ambience and the antique relics. All the windows had been thrown open and the morning breeze freshened the air. Servants dusted the furniture and paintings, swept the carpets and floors, and made final adjustments to the gleaming china, silver, and crystal laid out on the great table in the dining room. The activity reminded Salehi of his father, and how proud—no, awed!—he would have been by his son's future.

The general stood in the kitchen doorway and watched the cooks over their pots. A wonderful aroma arose thick and fragrant, welcoming him. There was pungent *fesunjun*, duck marinated in pomegranate juice with walnuts, a real delicacy. There were spicy *kofte*, meatballs, *dolmeh*, stuffed vegetables, and fresh *nan sangak*, traditional bread cooked on a bed of small stones.

Yes, this would be a night for feasting and celebration. A great gala night that all who attended would never forget. After all, it was their future, too.

"Sir."

The general looked down at his torturer, the lieutenant with an ugly knife scar on his left cheek, who had just appeared at his side. He was a despicable little man, but very useful. The general controlled himself, never allowed the lieutenant to guess his contempt.

"About Dr. Lambert and the chemicals?" the lieutenant said.

"Yes?"

"Dr. Lambert is still unconscious. Do you want me to go ahead anyway?"

"Of course not! I want him alive, not dead!"

The torturer bowed and stepped back.

"Check him every few hours," the general ordered. "Let me know as soon as he's awake."

"As you command."

"What about the package?" the general reminded him.

"I have not forgotten."

The general glanced at the cooks, but they were occupied by their ovens and pots. He held out his hand, and the torturer dropped in it two small envelopes made from good bond stationery. Inside both was a slow-acting poison, a thallium compound, a different poison from the one he'd used on Khomeini. The general slipped them into his pocket.

"One in each of their cups of tea tonight," the lieutenant instructed. "More tomorrow and each day."

"Two weeks for it to be lethal?"

"About two weeks in this case," the lieutenant confirmed. He bowed again, turned, and exited the kitchen.

The general stayed longer in the clean stainless steel and porcelain room. He savored the warmth, the rich mixture of smells, the women intent over their cooking pots, and thought with deep burning pleasure about life, destiny, and Allah.

Jake Bolt slept through the night, Sarah Maizlish by his side. They knew it was morning only by the delivery of the breakfast gruel. There was no sunlight in any of these dungeon cells. Doctor Lambert returned to his prone position. The guard checked him, but the doctor's eyes remained steadfastly closed. Bolt asked for antibiotic ointment and bandages so they could care for the doctor's wounds. Surprisingly, it was delivered quickly. The general must have given orders to take care of his prize scientist.

Sarah treated the ugly wounds while the doctor said little, although sweat broke out on his bruised, puffy face from the pain. Soon a lieutenant with a slashed left cheek came to look at Dr. Lambert, who again pretended to be unconscious. Bolt recognized the lieutenant from somewhere! He stared, but couldn't quite place him. Recently . . . wait . . . yes!

Just as the scarred man was about to leave, Bolt told him in Farsi, "I saw you in Dubai with a friend of mine. In a bar, the Johannesburg. Two days ago."

"Jacob!" Sarah whispered a warning in Hebrew. "He's the torturer!"

The lieutenant acted as if he hadn't heard. He opened the door and exited. The lock made a noisy click.

"What was that all about?" Sarah asked.

"I saw him with one of our operatives, Marcus Krenchell. He could be a double agent. If so, that explains how Krenchell found out about this place."

"He enjoys his work," Lambert said, as he sat up, winced. "He is an animal. Look into his eyes sometime and you will see what I mean."

The day passed slowly. They had their noon-time meal, more bread and gruel, this time spiced with pepper. The pepper was exciting for those who had been imprisoned long, a relief from the continuously bland food that resembled cardboard more than any other flavor.

In the early afternoon Bolt sensed consternation, excitement out in the cell block. The Falcons were upset about something. He listened at the corridor crack, eventually heard comments about the computer being shut down, no one quite sure what was wrong.

Bolt smiled. His virus had worked!

"What is it?" Sarah asked.

"Psssst! Jake, my boy!" Willoughby called from the crack in their wall. "What's going on?"

Bolt told all of them about the virus he'd planted in the general's computer system.

"I wish it could put their military computers down for good," Sarah said.

"I have another idea that's better," Bolt said. "One that will eliminate their nuclear facility."

"How!?" Sarah asked.

Bolt grinned. "Oh," Sarah said, understanding that she wouldn't understand. "Computer mumbo jumbo."

"Best not to ask, my dear," Willoughby advised. "You won't know what he's talking about, and he'll get carried away and bore you to tears."

"Have you noticed," Fyodorov added, "that Americans are obsessed by computers?"

Sarah laughed. "How accurate you both are!"

The afternoon hours passed slowly. Tension in the dingy cell grew. People turned silent as the waiting became oppressive. Each had an assignment. Each knew exactly what to do. They'd rehearsed, repeated, questioned, and rehearsed again until all that was left was the horrible, boring, exciting, nerve-wracking wait.

When at last the guards fumbled at the lock, coming to deliver the evening meal, the prisoners stared at one another with mixtures of relief and horror.

Bolt and Sarah separated, Bolt to the side wall, and Sarah to the center of the room directly in front of where the tray was usually left.

The guards stepped in as before. One carried the tray of bowls. The other stood behind in the doorway, his AK-47 trained on the little group. The first guard set the tray on the floor.

Bolt kicked the rifle from the guard's arms. Sarah rushed straight at the kneeling guard's bent head.

Upstairs in General Salehi's office, Swiss banker Horst Renssauer sat in a leather chair across from the general and the ayatollah. The general was enthroned behind his long rosewood desk. In preparation for the party that evening, he wore his dress uniform, immaculate and perfectly pressed. Medals and ribbons decorated his chest in a gaudy display that testified to his heroic military experience.

Across from Renssauer in another leather chair sat the Ayatollah Mohammed Masumian, religious leader of Iran and successor to the Ayatollah Khomeini. His long white beard trailed to his gray-robed chest. He looked solemnly through his steel-rimmed glasses, past his bulbous nose, at Renssauer.

The Swiss banker wore a fine navy wool suit with thin black stripes. He had just finished telling the ayatollah the same story of the shah's bank account that he had related to General Salehi in Dubai. The ayatollah's hands eagerly reached for the papers that Renssauer held in his lap. Renssauer passed them over.

"This will go to our warrior people," the ayatollah told Renssauer as he leaned over the desk to sign. "The money will help keep the flame of our sacred rancor alive. We must fight forward, spread Allah's words, Allah's ways. We Shiites have lived too long in scorn and derision from the Sunni Muslims. Each time someone like you comes forth we realize again that Allah watches and provides. Allah is good. Allah is great. Allah is all-powerful."

"Yes, well," Renssauer said. "Thank you. The general's signature goes below yours, a witness."

The general smiled benevolently, his cruel mouth twisted into a grimace. Eagerly he signed, handed the bank's copies to Renssauer, and tapped the remaining into a neat rectangle.

"I'll put these away for security," the general told the ayatollah and the banker. He stood and walked to a painting. He swung it like a door away from the wall. Behind the painting was a safe. "We wouldn't want anything to happen to this."

The ayatollah nodded permission. He trusted his commander-in-chief. General Salehi put the papers inside, spun the lock. Renssauer slipped his copies into his briefcase and stood.

"It's been a pleasure, gentlemen," Renssauer said. "Now, general, I believe you mentioned a tour?" His source had told him the computer room was located on the first floor. Once inside, he would need only a few undisturbed minutes to plant Bushi's virus. Then he could leave this dreadful city in this misbegotten wasteland of a nation.

"Ah, but Mr. Renssauer must stay for dinner," the ayatollah said graciously. He stood also. "Seldom do we have such a banquet. Like his father, the general is renowned for his lavish feasts and stimulating discussions. You do think he should stay, don't you, general?"

If Renssauer read the general's expression correctly, the general had no such idea. In fact, the general looked as if he'd like to get rid of Renssauer as fast as possible.

"Actually, no—," the general began.

"Of course he must," the ayatollah continued, ignoring the general. "I insist." He took Renssauer's arm and led him to the door. "You will take us both on a tour, general. I haven't seen your beautiful home in its entirety for many years. And then Mr. Renssauer will talk to me about Swiss banks and Swiss banking laws. Although it is against our religion to charge interest, I would like to learn about your banks and the source of their great success."

"Delighted," Renssauer said and walked to the door with the ayatollah. This bought him extra time. If the general didn't give him an opportunity to plant the virus during the tour, then he could slip back to the computer facility during the dinner. And if the food was as good as the ayatollah promised, the stay would be additionally worthwhile.

"Very well. This way, then, gentlemen," the general sighed, acquiescing to the inevitable.

General Salehi led them out into the corridor and along the alcoved windows. The night air was soft and aromatic with the delicious smells of spiced meats and vegetables. The general was putting on a good front, Renssauer thought, behaving well despite his displeasure that the banker was staying to dinner. Renssauer wondered briefly why the general was perturbed, then decided it was probably some Muslim custom he didn't know about, and if he did, wouldn't understand.

As he contemplated how close he was to success in introducing the virus, he thought about Jake Bolt. At first he'd hoped to run into the CIA operative here, gain Bolt's unwitting help in his plan, but he'd seen nothing or heard nothing about Bolt. Perhaps he had not come to Tehran after all. Lucky Bolt.

Bolt rotated, slammed an arm back in a *ushiro hiji-ate* elbow strike into the guard's belly. The guard's rifle hit the floor. And Sarah rammed straight into the kneeling Falcon who had carried in the tray. She slammed him back into the wall before he could react. Bread and bowls of gruel flew into the air, splashed the floor and walls.

She snatched up the guard's AK-47, and Bolt reached out into the hallway for the food-carrier's rifle. He closed the cell door, and the two operatives stood with legs apart, rifles trained down menacingly at the two Falcons.

"Drop the keys, kick them over," Bolt ordered in Farsi.

The guard, face furious, let them fall to the floor. He kicked them toward Bolt. Staring at naked, glorious martyrdom doesn't look quite as desirable even to a Muslim fanatic.

"Stand up and turn around," Bolt said.

As the two Iranians sullenly did this, Bolt picked up the keys. He gestured, and Sir Carlton and Dr. Fritzen bound the two guards with their own belts and neckties. Before they were finished, Bolt and Sarah were racing down the corridor to the main guard station. It was only a matter of time until the Falcon guard noticed on his monitor the activity in the cell.

The man looked up just as Bolt reached the end of the corridor. The guy grabbed his rifle, lifted it, and Bolt hurled across the remaining distance, tackled the guard midchest. The man struggled, but Sarah shoved the muzzle of her AK-47 in his ear. Instantly he was quiet.

Bolt stepped back, dusted himself off. "Thanks," he said.

"My pleasure," she said.

Sarah was radiant. She loved action. Loved it perhaps more than anything, Bolt realized, seeing the parallel between them.

They took the not-so-fanatic-now guard back to the cell where Willoughby and Fyodorov waited.

"Take off your clothes," Bolt ordered in Farsi. The man was short and stout, and his clothes would fit Fyodorov.

"What?" the guard asked, incredulous.

"Off!" Bolt repeated. The man stripped, Fyodorov dressed in his clothes, and they tied him up. The four operatives slipped out into the stone corridor. Fyodorov went immediately to the front desk where he sat in the guard's chair and watched the monitors. The three others patrolled the halls, slowly picking off the rest of the unsuspecting Falcons. These Falcons, too, they put in Willoughby and Fyodorov's old cell.

At last all the guards were taken. Bolt sat at the computer console, located the prison schedule. They had another two hours until the guards were to change, a lucky break for them, perhaps enough time to complete their business.

"Let the prisoners out," Bolt told Sarah, Willoughby, and Fyodorov.

They took keys and ran along the passageways once more. As the cell doors opened, excited prisoners shouted, laughed, cheered. Great jubilation filled the dungeon.

And then the prisoners grew somber again, frightened. They weren't free yet. Above them in the villa waited General Salehi and the majority of the Falcons, armed, fierce, ruthless. The prisoners would have to fight their way out, and those who survived would have to steal cars and trucks, get themselves as best they could to friendly embassies.

But they were agreed. Even that uncertain fate was better than remaining here. Far better.

CHAPTER
29

Jake Bolt and Yuri Fyodorov climbed the stairs. An hour and a half had passed, and the banquet would be in full swing. Now was the time to strike.

Behind them came Sarah in her black chador. Willoughby waited below with the prisoners. Everyone was jumpy. The tension was electric. The prisoners had a few AK-47s and pistols, salvaged from the celled guards, but they needed more arms. They would have to pick them up during any fighting. But perhaps there would be no fighting, no violence. By now the computer system would be down again, and the general would be trying to hide the confusion and worry from his guests. Maybe the prisoners could slip out of the villa and into the street, find taxis, and drive safely away.

That's dreaming, Bolt told himself. This was a land where nothing was easy, everything was hard. It almost seemed that it had to be that way to prove that only Allah offered respite, and that a martyr got a good deal going to paradise because life on Earth was hell.

Fyodorov still wore the Falcon uniform and carried an AK-47. They hoped that with Fyodorov escorting him, Bolt would look like a prisoner and no one would stop them as they made their way toward the computer facility.

Bolt cracked open the door to the first-floor corridor, looked out. Falcons and servants were running up and down the hall. Fyodorov, Bolt, and Sarah entered the hall. Sarah headed toward a nearby linen closet to gather all the black chadors she could find, then she would go upstairs for more. She would deliver them to the prisoners to help disguise their escape.

Fyodorov and Bolt headed along the hall, ignored by the Falcons whose purposeful strides ate up the distance. As they passed the banquet room, Bolt stared in through one set of the open double doors. The long magnificent table was surrounded by nearly fifty guests who had pushed back their chairs and were leaning back, sated, happy. Servants had cleared the table, and fine tea, the staple Iranian drink, in tiny ornate glasses stood steaming in front of each visitor.

Bolt slowed, caught by the stentorian tones of General Akbar Salehi. He touched Fyodorov's sleeve, gestured that he wanted to stop for a moment.

"That is General Salehi?" Fyodorov whispered.

"The one and only," Bolt said.

They stood outside.

Inside the guests were watching a projection screen at the end of the table most distant from the general. There pictures appeared, one after another. It was the Elburz installation, in full living color. External shots of how the facility was built into the mountain, then internal shots of rooms, scientists, equipment. The general bragged about the top scientists, engineers, and technicians he had acquired, and of the great administrator who would get the facility off to a perfect start.

The guests wallowed in the grandiose descriptions. Then graphs appeared on the screen, showing the missiles that would be equipped with nuclear warheads. A giant wave of excitement and enthusiasm swept over the guests. The general saw it, and his voice took on a deep hypnotic quality. The listeners seemed to lean toward him while their gazes remained fixed to the screen, to the powerful future that was promised there.

"Who is not tired of East and West telling us what to do?" the general asked his guests.

"All of us are tired!" said one guest, and those around him clapped him on the back, agreeing.

"Who is not tired of our Middle East neighbors looking down on us Shiites as if we were a lower life-form?" the general said.

"All of us!" said a dozen guests.

"Isn't it time we arose together, we Iranians, and showed the Middle East, the West, the East, all the globe that we are Allah's people! That we work to His glory! That we expect respect for Him, and for ourselves!"

"It's time!"

"It's time!"

"Look to our common enemy," the general cajoled.

Beneath him the Ayatollah Mohammed Masumian, who sat on his right, and President Hojatolislam Sayed Eghbal, who sat on his left, stared around the general's neatly pressed trousers at one another, puzzled, not happy as they began to understand where the general was leading the willing crowd.

"Look to the Great Satans—the United States, Israel, and the Soviet Union!" the general exhorted. "Our common enemy! We walk on their flags. We hate them for what they have done to us!"

"Yes, yes!" the guests shouted from around the table.

"And what they will do to us tomorrow!" the general said.

"Yes! Kill them!"

"Yes! Kill them!"

"Now we *can* kill them if we must!" the general told them.

"Yes! Yes!"

"Kill them! Kill them!"

Again the ayatollah and the president looked at one another. Suspicious, uncertain, they looked down the long table at their followers who were so eagerly singing chorus to another leader's song.

The guests' intent faces were focused on the general, never wavered in allegiance to this exciting, visionary speaker.

"I have brought the great gift of nuclear strength to you, my brothers," he said in a soft, husky voice.

The quiet voice infused his statement with even more awe and drama just by the way he said the momentous words. The table was silent, listening, straining to hear. He had learned to work a crowd, Bolt thought with both admiration and disgust.

"And you *are* my brothers," the general said. His voice rose. "Aren't you?"

"Yes!"

"And I have given you nuclear power to rule the world!"

"Yes! Yes!"

"The ayatollah and the hojatolislam," he said

and gestured down at the religious and Majlis leaders, "have led you thus far well and good, but now it's time for *new* leadership! A new leader who can take you into the next century and create a world where Allah is honored by all!"

On cue a row of Falcons in crisp uniforms filed briskly into the room, encircling it. Some glanced at Bolt and Fyodorov in his uniform, but they passed by, intent on following their orders. Colonel Rizvi stopped just behind General Salehi's left shoulder. Soon the sleek, muscular commandos lined all the walls. Some of the guests shot them looks of admiration and respect.

"I would be your leader!" the general announced with pride. He opened his arms to encompass the room. "Allow me to guide Iran to global power in Allah's honor!"

The Falcons stomped their feet and shouted approval. The guests hesitated, then jumped up, picked up the chant. Behind the general, Colonel Rizvi applauded politely.

Again the ayatollah and hojatolislam stared at each other. Understanding passed between them. Their faces were hard, angry. They stood, raised their arms into the noisy air.

"Brothers!" they shouted.

"Brothers, please!"

Slowly the room quieted.

"You have elected *us*!" President Hojatolislam Eghbal shouted.

"*We* are your duly elected leaders!" the Ayatollah Masumian thundered. "It is against Allah's wishes to change until election time!"

"We changed when the Ayatollah Khomeini rode his righteous revolution back to Iran!" the general reminded the two leaders. *"We can change now!"*

The guests agreed, shouting and clapping.

Bolt watched grimly. The general was a worse threat to the West than the two less-powerful leaders, Masumian and Eghbal. And even if Bolt succeeded in destroying the nuclear plant, the general had the will and experience to build another.

Bolt strode into the banquet room.

The Falcons closest to him sprang forward, ready to take him.

"Iran is an old and honorable nation!" Bolt shouted in Farsi.

"Take him away!" the general bellowed.

"Who is this man?" demanded President Eghbal.

"Allow him to stay!" ordered the ayatollah. "I order it!"

The Falcons looked at General Salehi. He shrugged. He had plenty of time, and there was nothing Bolt could do now to stop him. Then Bolt looked down the table and found a surprise: Marcus Krenchell sitting between two turbaned mullahs. He was out of sight from the doorway where Bolt had stood. How had Krenchell managed to be included in this party? Ah, yes. Bolt remembered. Krenchell's cover as Swiss banker Horst Renssauer.

"Iran is an old and honorable nation," Bolt repeated as the room quieted.

Slowly the guests returned to their seats, and the Falcons to their walls. Except for four who clung close to Bolt, making certain he made no escape. Bolt glanced over his shoulder, saw Fyodorov in the background, waiting to see what

Bolt would do, whether he would need help.

"Why would you want an incompetent to lead you?" Bolt asked.

"What?" one guest asked, astonished.

"Turn on the computer!" Bolt said, gestured at a PC that had been rolled into the corner. "Why do you think that is here? To augment the slide show, that's why. To show you missile trajectories, payloads, rocket designs, and all the dramatic new ideas and improvements that make nuclear capability so flexible, so *usable*. Show them, General Salehi! Show them!"

"Yes, General Salehi!" President Eghbal said. "Show us!"

"Show *all* of us!" the Ayatollah Masumiam insisted.

The general stood very erect, his barrel chest jutting with indignation. "The computer system is down," he said curtly. "A temporary problem. My experts will have it up shortly."

"No they won't, general!" Bolt said. "I'm the one who put it down. Your system is infected by a virus. When it comes back up, it will be for only a few hours. Then it will go down again, for longer and longer periods until your whole system is gone forever. Unless you can find my virus!"

"The man is a fool!" General Salehi said, his voice full of scorn. "A charlatan! He doesn't know a thing!"

The guests muttered among themselves and shot hot looks of disbelief at Bolt. That argument wasn't going to do it. He needed something even more convincing. Bolt wasn't surprised. He'd saved the best for last.

"Why would you want a murderer to lead you?"

Bolt shouted over the undercurrent of discussion.

"What?" one guest said, shocked.

"Who are you speaking of?" said another.

"You must be mistaken!" said a third.

"General Akbar Salehi," Bolt told them. "*He is a murderer!*"

That statement got their complete attention. He looked at Colonel Rizvi, whose face had gone pasty, but there was relief there, too. Bolt remembered the stories he'd heard of the love between the colonel and Khomeini.

"No!" chorused the room.

"Liar!" the general yelled.

"He is an American spy! I should have executed him when I first caught him!"

"Ask Colonel Rizvi!" Bolt insisted. "The colonel knows!"

Suddenly the colonel's face turned as hard as the ayatollah's and the president's. Swiftly he reached inside the general's pocket, and before the general could grab the colonel's hand, he held on high two white packets.

"Poison!" the narrow-faced little colonel bellowed into the room. "Intended for our new ayatollah and president. General Salehi is a great general, but he is a sinful man! I confess!" Two tears rolled from his eyes. "I helped him to murder our beloved Ayatollah Khomeini! I have sinned equally! And now if you refuse to elect him, he will also murder our Ayatollah Masumian and President Eghbal!"

For a moment there was hushed silence.

Then pandemonium broke out in the banquet room. Falcons and guests shouted questions. One angry Falcon knotted a fist and belted another. The first didn't care that the general had killed the ayatollah, and the other found it an unforgivable sin. The Falcons' loyalties split. They fought. The other guests argued and fought. There was a gunshot. Then more gunshots in the corridors behind Bolt.

Bolt felt a tap on his shoulder. He ducked, melted back toward Fyodorov, leaving behind the chaotic room where one Falcon had already perished.

"Let's go," Fyodorov said, anxiously watching for an attack aimed at them.

"My idea exactly," Bolt said. They ran down the corridor toward the computer room. Bolt figured the computer system should be coming on-line in just a few minutes.

Dressed in their black chadors, the male and female prisoners swept up and out of the cold, stinking dungeon that had been their home for far too long. Some of them were armed, but most were not. Out in the first-floor corridor, two stopped and stared in silent appreciation of the paintings, the antique vase that stood on the hallway table, the hand-painted tiles that decorated the staircase that rose to the second floor. It was as if they'd never seen such beauty before.

"Come on," Hugh Willoughby said smartly. "Get the lead out!" He was dressed in the uniform of a Falcon sergeant.

"Hurry!" Sarah Maizlish urged. "This way!"

The two agents hustled the group along toward General Salehi's formal receiving room where French doors would open onto the grounds. They passed three servants. Each servant paused in turn, staring with surprise at the group of nearly forty in their long black robes, with the single Falcon escort. But the servants had been taught to obey, not to question,. and so they resumed their head-long rush back to the kitchen, balancing enormous trays filled with dirty china and silver.

Farther along the corridor Sarah Maizlish heard a commotion in a distant room. Shouting. Jacob's voice! More shouting. She wanted to go to him, but she couldn't. Dr. Lambert was with her. It was her job to get him to Israel safely. Damn!

She hustled the group toward the elegant re-ceiving room. She and Willoughby stood at the hall doorway while the prisoners crowded together, trying to file through. And then she saw the evil face of the torturer, the Falcon lieutenant, striding toward them down the corridor.

He seemed to recognize at once what was happening. He shouted something in Farsi, calling to someone behind him. He raised his rifle.

"Blast it!" Willoughby said. "I know that bugger!"

He and Maizlish snapped up their rifles.

A shot from the Falcon lieutenant's weapon burned past her ear. A prisoner to her left screamed. She and Willoughby squeezed their triggers, loosed a volley that ripped the torturer's gut.

He flew back from the blast, crimson blood spraying the air. His scarred face was astonished at his coming death, then a slow animal smile spread from his mouth to his eyes. He enjoyed the pain. Not only others' pain, but his own. Most especially his own.

"Oh, god," Lambert breathed. "Such sickness. Such evil!"

Two of the prisoners picked up the injured one and fled into the receiving room.

Now there was more noise in the corridor. Falcons poured out of somewhere. Willoughby humped down the hall, retrieved the lieutenant's rifle, and humped back to the door. Now about a dozen of the prisoners would be armed.

"We'd better bloody hurry!" he told Maizlish and the others. "They're coming down the hall!"

"No sentries!" Bolt told Fyodorov as they ran toward the computer facility's door. "Where in hell are they?!"

Bolt punched the button that opened the big pneumatic door. The sentries stood inside, helpless witnesses to the distraught scientists who huddled over their consoles, almost weeping as they tried to figure out what was wrong with their system. It had gone down every six hours since the first outage, and each down period had grown longer and longer.

Instantly Bolt and Fyodorov stuck the muzzles of their AK-47s into the midsections of the sentries. The sentries froze, weapons rising into place. Bolt and Fyodorov picked the guns from their hands.

"Let's get them out of here," Fyodorov decided. "Lock them up."

"Good," Bolt agreed. "I know a place."

The two operatives rounded up the scientists and the sentries and herded them to the windowless security room where Bolt had first been interrogated. As Fyodorov oversaw their entry, Bolt ran back to the facility. Fyodorov would return to guard the facility as soon as he'd finished.

Back at the computer room, Bolt found that the system was up again, and that Marcus Krenchell was working away.

Krenchell's stout form turned. "Bolt! Quite a speech back there. Seemed to stir them up. Stupid assholes! Fortunately, the dinner was good." His fingers soared over the keyboard.

"Find anything?" Bolt asked and sat at another console, quickly logged in code and encryption numbers.

"What?" Krenchell said. "Still checking. I'll let you know in a minute. What're you doing?"

"It'd take too long to explain," Bolt said, his fingers blazing away. "Tell me who the man in the Dubai bar was, the one with the scar on his left cheek."

"Why?"

"He's General Salehi's torturer."

"I know. He's also a damn good source."

"He informed on the general?" Bolt said.

"On the general, the Falcons, the Iranian government. Anything and everything. That's how I found out about the general's sophisticated computer setup. Made me think the source of the global communications problems might be here."

"I see."

Bolt grew silent, concentrating. He was working on a very simple principle, that speed caused friction, and friction—in the right situation—caused fire. Supercomputers achieved high processing speed by shrinking the distance electrons traveled within their wiring. Densely packed, they required a lavish array of supporting equipment to digest and transform astronomical amounts of raw numerical output. The wasted heat within the machinery was tremendous. For instance, the thermal output of the University of Minnesota's supercomputers was used to heat a garage. Many facilities—like General Salehi's in the Elburz Mountains—relied on industrial-sized cooling units to control the heat.

Bolt programmed in commands to turn off the cooling units within the mountain installation and to interfere with the scan controls of all the video monitors there.

"That's it," Krenchell said, standing. "No go here. Couldn't find a thing." He headed for the door.

"Wait a minute," Bolt said. "I'm almost finished."

"Can't. Got to try to get out of here. These people are lunatics."

"Hold it," Bolt said, remembering his colleague's inexperience in the field. "I need to pick up some other people. Then I'll go with you."

"Sorry." Krenchell was gone.

Idiot, Bolt told himself. He'll get himself killed. But Bolt couldn't stop his work. Too important. Now he entered an NP-complete mathematical problem and directed it to the Elburz facility's computers. NP-complete problems were exponentially obtuse, characterized by explosive growth. Even astronomy didn't have such big numbers. Bolt created a problem with so many branchings that there wouldn't be enough time in the history of the universe to use a supercomputer's brute-force approach to try all the possibilities.

Which should send the nuclear installation's computers smoking to their hot knees. Without refrigeration, the consoles would catch fire. And the interference with the scan controls would cause the video monitors to ignite, too. There would be time for anyone with brains to escape. Then according to the facility's layout, there was enough combustible material nearby that the whole complex, with luck, would go up in a blistering conflagration.

And that would be the end to Iran's nuclear threat.

If everything went according to plan.

"Put this on." Fyodorov stuck his bullet-shaped head in the door and threw a Falcon uniform at Bolt. "Hurry."

Fyodorov disappeared back into the corridor, and Bolt dressed. Now they had to figure out how in hell to get out of here.

Sarah Maizlish and Hugh Willoughby waited beside the French doors to the receiving room. They'd turned out the lights in the big room, and the group of prisoners crowded around. Beyond the glass panes Falcons were running across the moon-lighted lawns. It was almost as if they were mock skirmishing, involved in trial maneuvers, but the bullets were very real. There were three corpses just outside the French doors to prove it.

Now the band of forty needed a break in the fighting so they could run for it across the grounds.

"Who was he?" Maizlish asked Willoughby in the dim room as they waited.

The tension was thick in the room, almost palpable.

"Who?"

"The Falcon lieutenant. The torturer. You said you knew him."

"Knew *of* him," Willoughby corrected himself. "He's Jewish, a little secret he must have enjoyed keeping from General Salehi. His brother's an independent, works for any government with the money. I heard the brother was deep cover inside your nuclear installation near Dimona up till a month or so ago. They really are—or were—a slimy duo."

"Dimona!" Dr. Lambert said.

"The brother's the one who supplied the map, I'll bet," Maizlish said. Quickly she told Willoughby about the detailed map of the installation she and Bolt had found in the Jerusalem warehouse, a map only an insider could have drawn. When she got out of here—*if* she got out of here— she'd go looking for the brother!

Suddenly the hall doors to the receiving room slid open. General Salehi surrounded by fierce Falcons stood poised to fire from the light-filled doorway, AK-47s aiming at the tight group of prisoners. His moist eyes burned with fury. Hatred and revenge twisted his cruel mouth.

"Where is he?" General Salehi bellowed in Farsi, shook with rage. "Where is he?" he repeated in English. "Jake Bolt! I want him. My Falcons hunger for him!"

Bolt heard the general from the end of the corridor. He and Fyodorov ran past the grand banquet room where sporadic fighting was continuing. Two gunshots rang out from the room as they passed. Ahead stood a tight mass of Falcons, and Bolt guessed that at the center was General Salehi. The Iranian commandos were just outside the receiving room through which Sarah and Willoughby had planned to take the prisoners and escape.

Bolt could only hope they were still alive!

"Death to Bolt!" Salehi cried in Farsi.

"Kill him! Kill him!" echoed the Falcons.

"Death to Bolt!" Salehi shouted again.

"Kill him! Kill him!" they chanted.

The general was winning back his Falcons' allegiance by promoting the ancient tribal need of banding together against an outside threat. All nations used it at one time or another to infuse patriotism, blind or otherwise, and General Salehi had become a master at the savage rite. When Bolt had left the banquet room, he had thought General Salehi would soon be dead, probably killed by a former supporter, that the Iranian leaders and the Falcons would not tolerate the murder of Khomeini. But here General Salehi was again, rallying, exhorting, thrilling his followers.

"There he is!" a Falcon suddenly yelled, pointing down the hall to Bolt and Fyodorov.

The Falcons opened fire. Bullets bit into the wall and floor, sending shattered tile stinging through the air.

Bolt aimed the AK-47. Picked off the Falcon who had spotted them. The guy crashed back into the arms of his comrades. The Falcons scattered.

Fyodorov fired, another Falcon went down bloodied, and the two operatives dodged behind the tables and armoires that rimmed the wide corridor, firing and working their way toward the receiving room where Sarah, Willoughby, and the prisoners might be trapped.

But almost immediately new fire came from the receiving room. They were alive in there! It was a thunderous hail of bullets that decimated a half-dozen Falcons who had sought protective shelter from Bolt and Fyodorov, but not from the inhabitants of the receiving room.

Bolt and Fyodorov ran, taking advantage of the shocked lull.

Again fire splattered the hallway, raining around Bolt and Fyodorov as they scrambled for shelter. They fired at the hunched Falcons, some lying flat on the floor. More fire erupted from the receiving room.

Again there was a lull as the vulnerable Falcons scrambled back from the open receiving room door.

Bolt and Fyodorov pounded toward the room's back door, opened it, skidded into the dark interior.

Immediately bullets streaked past Bolt, singeing his flesh.

"Hold your fire!" Bolt called quietly. "It's Bolt and Fyodorov!"

"Hurry!" Sarah cried.

"They're escaping!" Fyodorov told Bolt, moving off at a quick pace toward the open French doors. Outdoors moonlight shone thin and silver on the lush lawn. A trail of black shadows moved in a silent, swift stream across the thick grass toward the distant bone-white wall that encircled the grounds.

Willoughby and Sarah knelt, firing back through the door at the Falcons who were at last growing few in number. Maybe they'd make it out of here yet.

And then came the sudden, terrifying shots

from outside. Shots probably aimed at the prisoners who were at last speeding toward freedom.

Bolt and Fyodorov slipped outside. There were shadows in the ornamental bushes that grew along the villa. The shots came from there. The two agents exchanged silent glances, nodded that they understood what the other had in mind, and circled quietly.

It was General Salehi and two Falcons, crouched, squeezing off rounds slow, unhurried, and deadly accurate.

The three looked up, swiftly turned their rifles onto the two operatives. The faces of the three were almost identical, the same mad fury, the same unreasoning drive that knew no sense or compassion or humanity.

But Bolt and Fyodorov were ready. Instantly they squeezed off rounds, and the two Falcon soldiers crashed back against the villa's wall. Their blood splattered inky black on the pale stucco.

And then there were more footsteps, running away.

"Jacob!" Sarah's voice called. "Yuri! Come! It's clear!"

But Bolt and Fyodorov were busy. They stared down at General's Salehi's gun. It was aimed at Bolt's heart, while both Bolt's and Fyodorov's were aimed at the general's.

"So, who goes first?" the general breathed. He was trapped, a cunning wild animal, and if he was going to die, it wouldn't be alone.

"You've lost, general," Bolt said. "Give up."

"Your run's over," Fyodorov said. "Quit, or I will kill you."

"I shall take Bolt with me," the general threatened. His liquid eyes shone in the moonlight as they darted from one captor to the other. "I shall take him straight to hell!" His cruel mouth worked over the unfairness of fate.

But then Bolt and Fyodorov saw Colonel Rizvi silently approach, a 9mm Beretta in his hand. A small figure, thin and narrow, with the stealth of a desert cat. He looked at them, shook his head, indicated he was after the general, not them.

"No, you won't kill Bolt," Fyodorov told him.

"Colonel Rizvi has other plans for you," Bolt said.

"You think I believe that? Next you will tell me he is just behind me. You must be mad!"

With the smooth, polished motion of a true professional, Colonel Rizvi with one hand pushed the general's rifle down so that it aimed at the ground, and with the other pressed his Beretta to the general's skull. A moment of astonishment clouded General Salehi's cruel face. He started to turn.

Rizvi fired. The general crumpled like a rag doll, a rag doll with no head and a twitching body that stole whatever dignity the human acquires in life.

"Go!" Colonel Rizvi told Bolt and Fyodorov. He looked down at General Salehi, the leader he had followed for so many years, loved for so many years. Tears poured from his eyes. Then he shouted. "Go! Go! Go! *Go!*"

Bolt and Fyodorov again glanced at each other. Yes, they must leave while they still had a chance to escape. They ran across the lawns, saw the last of the stragglers approaching the wall, some helping others who looked wounded.

The two operatives helped heft people over, and at last hauled themselves to the top. Bolt looked back at the elegant villa standing old and proud in the moonlight. There was still fighting going on in the rooms there, occasional struggles silhouetted against the windowpanes. A house of greed, dishonor, and great loss.

"Look!" Fyodorov said suddenly, pointing off toward the ragged mountains that were ebony black against the charcoal sky. "What's that?"

A tiny, bright yellow flame glowed suddenly to life. Joy and relief flowed through Bolt. The flame licked high, died down, then licked high again. Probably as new explosions rocked the facility, he thought. He watched for a long moment. He had done it! No longer would Iran be a nuclear threat!

"Come, my friend," Bolt said. "We'd better get out of here."

They jumped into the street, and ran after the prisoners who, like them, were on their way to freedom.

A chameleon with as many demeanors as necessary to acquire the power he sought, the heavyset man in the rich wool suit sat in his room on the twelfth floor of the most expensive hotel in downtown Tehran. He went by many aliases: Marcus Krenchell, Viktor Markov, Horst Renssauer, others. From his window he watched as a pinprick of golden glow erupted on the Elburz Mountains. It was an attractive sight, he thought. Such a small flame existing amidst such a great mountain range.

And then he stiffened. He looked harder, tried to decipher with certainty the exact location of the flame. The more he studied the area, the more agitated he became.

It must be the nuclear facility! Had that been what Jake Bolt was doing in General Salehi's computer facility, programming the installation to self-destruct? Fury rose like bile in his throat. All his work for nothing! He had successfully planted the virus, and now there would be no nuclear weapons to take over in Iran!

He sat back in his chair, staring at the bright flame.

Slowly he began to smile. He had many means to achieve his end. Remember, he told himself, the virus is already at work within the military systems of all the nuclear powers. He repeated that to himself and smiled wider. Soon he could take control. Yes. All was well with the world. *His* world.

CHAPTER 30

Jake Bolt sat in Sarah Maizlish's dusty, cluttered, charming apartment in En Karem just west of Jerusalem. His suitcase was here, his shower taken, and he was relaxing in the glow of exhaustion and satisfaction that came as a reward for a difficult mission. Even Clifton Olds seemed somewhat impressed. Wiping out Iran's nuclear facility accomplished that. But still the CIA chief had had a few hard words of criticism since Bolt had not solved Bushi Nakamora's murder, and had not found the contents and whereabouts of the mysterious package Bushi had sent to his Tokyo cousin.

Bolt sighed. That was life. Full of starts, stops, and incompletions. He'd head back to Langley tomorrow, not only to try to pick up a new lead, but also for some kind of conference Olds was calling with his top operatives about the global communication problems. It seemed there'd been a major incident—a missile had been launched somewhere out of Eastern Europe and successfully shot down a brand-new communications satellite recently sent aloft from Vandenberg Air Force Base in California. Very nasty situation.

Hugh Willoughby and Yuri Fyodorov had already left to return to their HQs to report to their relieved chiefs that General Akbar Salehi was no longer a problem. Actually it was interesting what was happening in Iran now. Colonel Ahmed Rizvi was going to stand trial for Khomeini's murder, but there was sympathy that he should be given a light sentence since Khomeini was widely hated and Rizvi had confessed with such soul wracked ardor.

It had been quite a mission, Bolt reflected. Willoughby had gone home with scratches and bruises, grumbling about the quality of assignments being dished out lately by Sir John, while Fyodorov had actually been jolly. The gloomy Soviet had told Bolt that beyond reading dry reports on stumped negotiations he hadn't seen any real action in years. Which was too bad, Bolt reflected, because Fyodorov was damn good in a tough situation.

Bolt fingered the strap of the camera Susan Sumono had passed on to him in Tokyo. It still had the photographs of his aborted vacation in Kauai. At first he planned to simply throw away the film, then he changed his mind. He'd intended it to be a real vacation, even though it hadn't turned out to be. In any case, it seemed like years ago now. So he'd take the camera back with him to Langley and give it to the CIA labs there to develop. It was free that way. And he'd donate the rest of the yakuza bankroll to the CIA's widows and orphans fund.

"Jacob," Sarah said, "come here, please."

He strolled back toward the bedroom, following the trail of lace and satin undergarments. Sarah Maizlish, the sexiest female agent on the face of the earth, was sitting up naked in bed. He smiled broadly and started stripping.

"What are you doing, Jacob?" she asked sweetly

"Taking off my clothes, of course."

"Ah, then we have a sexual relationship?"

"I hope so," he said fervently.

"No commitments. No obligations."

He stopped, his pants down to his knees. He realized what she was saying . . . asking . . . and he saw her answer in her eyes. It was the same as his.

"No commitments," he said, speedily pulling off the pants. He leaned over the bed, kissed her ear, her smooth cheek, her toothpaste-fresh mouth.

She ran her fingers through his hair. "Jacob, where *did* you get that scar on your ear?"

"Knife cut. Mindinao."

"Oh," she said, digesting. Then she smiled lazily, warm and pliable. "I think you told me a different story last time, but I don't care." The heady scent of roses filled his mind. "I'm glad you understand about not making a commitment," she continued. "I mean, I wouldn't want to ruin our relationship." Her blue eyes suddenly flashed.

"My idea exactly," he said. He pulled her down, rolled on top of her, and she rose up to meet him, all heat and power and passion. They kissed, and that was all that mattered now. Tomorrow they'd go back to work.